THE BEST OF AMAZING STORIES®

The 1927 Anthology

(with the original magazine illustrations)

Edited by
STEVE DAVIDSON
and
JEAN MARIE STINE

Amazing Stories Classics
Produced by Digital Parchment Services

AMAZING STORIES CLASSICS

ISBN 9781503307759

Copyright 2014 EXPERIMENTER PUBLICATIONS

Produced by Digital Parchment Services

Book and Cover Design: Frankie Hill

Contents

PUBLISHER'S NOTE	vii
INTRODUCTION	9
THE RETREAT TO MARS *Cecil B. White*	16
RADIO MATES *Benjamin Witwer*	44
THE MAN WITH THE STRANGE HEAD *Miles J. Breuer, M.D.*	60
THE PLAGUE OF THE LIVING DEAD *A. Hyatt Verrill*	74
ADVANCED CHEMISTRY *Jack G. Huekels*	120
THE FATE OF THE POSEIDONIA *Clare Winger Harris*	128
THE FOUR-DIMENSIONAL ROLLER-PRESS *Bob Olsen*	156
THE MACHINE MAN OF ARDATHIA *Francis Flagg*	172
THE TISSUE-CULTURE KING *Julian Huxley*	192
THE COLOUR OUT OF SPACE *H.P. Lovecraft*	220

PUBLISHER'S NOTE

One day I would like to see science fiction become a mandatory subject in public school curricula.

On the exceedingly remote chance that anything even vaguely resembling the foregoing should occur, I would insist that the entire archive of *Amazing Stories* be used for the primary text.

This could happen.

Like much of science fiction, it is possible though not highly probable.

The really cool thing about probabilities is that no matter how small a chance something has of occurring, it will eventually happen (though probably not in your lifetime and almost certainly not in your galaxy).

And the really cool thing about science fiction is that it operates in a probabilistic manner. What was once part science and part imagination has a good chance of eventually coming to pass in some form or another.

What you are holding in your hands right now is, in a way, proof of that concept.

Should the study of science fiction ever become mandatory, (one can hope) the texts have already been prepared in this and other volumes of the Amazing Stories Classics line of publications—anthologies, magazine reprints, "Best of"s, collections and novels.

Like many luminaries of the field—authors such as Asimov, Clarke, Bradbury, Heinlein, Williamson—I discovered *Amazing Stories* at a newsstand, albeit many decades after those wonderful authors made their own discoveries (I make no claim to luminosity).

I really fell in love with *Amazing Stories* when I learned that it was this very magazine that gave birth to not only the science fiction genre, but also to the worldwide community known as Fandom.

You not only hold in your hands a harbinger of the future, you also hold a genuine piece of history.

History, as Asimov and Hari Seldon taught us, is a key to the future. If this is so, then surely science fiction is the literature unlocked by that key.

History and Science Fiction.

Amazing Stories.

It's all here.

Read these tales and then go make some of your own.

—Steve Davidson, Publisher
Amazing Stories

INTRODUCTION

1927 was a banner year for *Amazing Stories*. It had to be, and it was. During the first year of the magazine's existence, Hugo Gernsback had relied almost entirely on reprints from Jules Verne, H. G. Wells, the Munsey Magazines, and fiction pieces he had previously run in his own science and technology magazines. For *Amazing's* second year, Gernsback knew that to survive he would have find new writers with up-to-date ideas—rather than Verne's 1860s retreads or Wells' fustian prognostications, written before the advent of motorcars, radios, the motion picture, the junior league, and jazz.

And in 1927, Gernsback didn't just succeed, he succeeded in spades. *Amazing Stories* introduced not only a bumper crop of new authors and fresh stories, but also introduced four brand spanking new tropes to the nascent world of science fiction; ideas that would grow and spread like shoots from seeds throughout the '30s, '40s, '50s, '60s, and '70s until they had become staples of genre fiction and films—and by the early 21st century had become, as pop culture tropes always do in their third generation, ubiquitous staples of mass entertainment and subjects of dinner table conversation everywhere. In fact, they have become so ubiquitous you may well even be sick of them. But in 1927, nobody was sick of them. Nobody had ever heard of them. They appeared in the pages of that year's *Amazing Stories* like an explosion in a fireworks factory and they were such good ideas more people have been using them each year ever since.

With shows like *The Walking Dead, Z Nation, iZombie, Dead Set, Zombie Apocalypse, Town of the Living Dead*, and *Helix* crowding the TV schedules, and a steady procession of same at the movie theaters, it's understandable if you feel a bit less than overwhelmed when you see the title "Plague of the Living

Dead," on the contents page. But A. Haytt Verrill's tale here isn't just another story of bloodthirsty zombies on the hunt, made more credible to post-industrial readers with a scientific rationale for their existence—it's the first such story ever! It's also one of the first stories of any kind to introduce zombie hordes to American readers at all. *Weird Tales*, then entering its fourth year, had probably printed one; one might have appeared in *Ghost Stories*, and perhaps as many as three, all told, had appeared somewhere in the tens of thousands of newspapers and magazines that were burgeoning across the U.S. But even that modest number may well be an overestimate. And even if any of these publications had contained a story featuring zombies, the explanation would have involved the supernatural, with their existence attributed to the magical powers of voodoo (which most people of the era did not find credible). Inventor/zoologist/archeologist/ explorer Verrill was the first to propose a scientific basis for the zombie phenomenon. His plague of unkillable, flesh-eating zombies returned from the dead is created by means of a chemical compound—and in fact, later 20th century investigations in Haiti proved Verrill's uncanny guess (if it was a guess, as a zoologist he had spent significant time in Haiti himself) to be correct, and the zombie-like symptoms observed there to have been induced by a rare chemical compound.

Pretty cool, huh? But Hugo Gernsback was just getting warmed up. The 1927 *Amazing Stories* was also the first publication to introduce the work of the now-legendary fantasist H. P. Lovecraft to a mass audience. (On the worst day of its existence, *Amazing* far outsold *Weird Tales*, then considered an arcane and somewhat unwholesome specialty publication, its circulation so abysmal it was constantly on the edge of bankruptcy .) Though often mistaken as a writer of supernatural fiction, Lovecraft was actually a science fiction author, whose famed evil gods—the

INTRODUCTION

Great Old Ones such as Cthulhu, Azathoth, Yog-Sothoth, and Nyarlathotep—were not gods at all, but highly advanced aliens from other worlds and dimensions possessed of extraordinary powers "indistinguishable from magic". They were inspired by Lovecraft's readings of the new discoveries of Eddington, Einstein, and other early 20th century scientists, which showed the universe to be of almost infinite size, filled by an almost infinite number of worlds, many of which were postulated to be the homes of other beings further evolved mentally and scientifically than our own; and even the universe we know of was not the be-all and end-all of existence, but merely one dimension among countless others. It was a chilling, daunting, in fact terrifying realization for a member of a species which had until recently conceived itself the center of its solar system and universe, and the single focus of that universe's God. And the story which Lovecraft gave *Amazing*, "The Colour Out of Space", was no less than the *first* of all his stories to strike that note of cosmic horror and make clear that behind the rites and ceremonies by which Cthulhu and the Great Old Ones were worshiped and summoned was science, not the supernatural. It was also the first printed piece of the truly great writing on which his reputation rests, containing a trope that struck literature like a lightning bolt, and one that other writers almost immediately began to emulate. It would be thirty-six years before the first film version of a Lovecraft tale appeared on the silver screen (*The Haunted Palace*, based on "The Case of Charles Dexter Ward") and fifty-eight years before *Re-Animator*, which established him firmly as a cinematic icon, was released.

Either of these stories, let alone both, would have been sufficient to make 1927 a standout year in *Amazing Stories'* fabled history. But Gernsback wasn't finished yet. He also introduced the work of a man whom the magazine's readers would consider one of the leading science fiction writers of its first decade:

Miles J. Breuer, M.D. Although physician Brewer would become famed for mind-bending stories of conceptual breakthrough, usually facing mortals with dimensional dilemmas—such as "The Gosstak and the Doshes" and "The Captured Cross-Section"—his debut in *Amazing*, "The Man with the Strange Head," took a different tack and its appearance would mark the birth of yet another trope that only now is becoming familiar. C. L. Moore's breakthrough novella, "No Woman Born" (1944), an uncanny mixture of hard science, penetrant psychological insight, and literary style, is considered a turning point in the history of science fiction. But, as editor and critic Groff Conklin noted in *The Big Book of Science Fiction*, Breuer's "The Man with the Strange Head" is considered "a precursor to 'No Woman Born,'" and there is every reason to believe that that Breuer's tale of a man who extended his life and strength through the creation of a mechanical body may also have served as a direct inspiration for Moore's novella—and through her, for Ironman's suit, and many other such stories along the way, as well.

Fourteen months after his inaugural issue and only six months after he began his push to fill *Amazing* with new writers and stories, Gernsback introduced the first woman author to appear in the pages of a science fiction magazine—and she introduced the first story in which the Earth is saved not by a hero but a heroine. The story, by new author Claire Winger Harris, was a pacesetter whose style, characterization and superior storytelling would only be equaled by the best of *Amazing's* male writers during its first decade. Recent scholarship has focused on Harris as a feminist author, and it is already evident here in "The Fate of the Poseidonia," her first published story. It is driven by the hostility of two men who are rivals for the love of the same woman and how (although he knows early on his rival is a bad guy) rather than saving the world, the hero's own

INTRODUCTION   13

jealous actions place the Earth in deadly peril (and, no, there is no mad scientist in this story.) It's a deadpan satire of males circa the 1920s, and one that is not without relevance today. But Harris doesn't spare women either; her heroine is so enraged at the hero's actions, which she takes as an attempt to control her, that she marries the villain—leading to tragic consequences for everyone. (And then there is the ecological aspect of the story, which may also be another *Amazing* first…)

But, trendsetters though they are, these four classics aren't the only first-rate stories Gernsback could boast of in 1927, and in this anthology you will find six more bests from that year, including "Retreat to Mars" by Cecil B. White– an "idea story" with a kicker at the end, much like the ones that poured from the pen of Don A. Stuart (John W. Campbell, Jr.) during F. Orlin Tremaine's tenure at *Astounding*—and Benjamin Witwer's "Radio Mates" which, unlike so many scientific-device-leads-our-hero-to-a-princess-in-need-of-rescue stories, offers a touch of romance between equally matched contemporaries. Then, with "Advanced Chemistry" by Jack G. Huekels, we see not only the first story about chemistry in an sf magazine—but a story which has achieved a fame of its own in scientific circles, and been reprinted in scientifically-themed anthologies as well as textbooks over the years. Bob Olsen's "The Four-Dimensional Roller-Press" is a dimensional romp, with a nod to Edwin Abbott's *Flatland*, that proved so popular with readers that four further "Four-Dimensional" sequels were demanded. "The Machine Man of Ardathia" was one of the youthful Forrest J Ackerman's favorite stories—and some years later he considered it a high honor to be allowed to collaborate with the author, Francis Flagg. Though bound to stir unease in many readers, "The Tissue Culture King" by biologist Julian Huxley (brother of Aldous), is an outlier among stories of its time, offering more than the era's usual degree of respect toward (and less than the usual degree of stereotyping of) the indigenous inhabitants of Africa—and easily one of the most gracefully written stories ever printed in a Gernsback publication.

It has been no easy task to choose the contents of this volume, given the many exceptional works published in *Amazing Stories* during 1927. But we believe that the classics reprinted here are truly representative of the best Hugo Gernsback published that year, and that post-millennial readers will find in each of them some of the same thought-provoking excitement that made these stories reader favorites at the time.

And, as a special treat for modern readers, we have paired each story with the original illustrations that accompanied their appearance in *Amazing*. Most are by the immortal Frank R. Paul, surely the first man to be paid to envision a new aspect of a new future every day. We believe these illustrations help recreate something of the atmosphere of that bygone era, and the pulp magazines in which they saw publication, in a way nothing else can.

—Jean Marie Stine, August 2015

DISCLAIMER

These works of pulp fiction have been adjudged a classic of both historical and literary value and, as such, are presented for the entertainment and education of contemporary audiences. The text, including the introduction to each story, is reproduced as originally published and written. It contains some material which, given our comparative cultural advances since 1927, may now be considered offensive to readers. While they can be read for entertainment, these stories can also be read as cultural text and as a window into the worldview of a previous era—along with that era's implicit presuppositions, for better and worse. The views and beliefs represented in these stories do not represent those of the current editors or publishers.

The RETREAT TO MARS
By Cecil B. White
Author of "The Lost Continent"

This second party succeeded in founding a colony on the high plateau region, where they built their gigantic monument to Mars. Their bodies were skilfully braced by a metal framework, which somewhat relieved the strain to which they were subjected; their average height was around nine feet; their lungs, which were deveoped to accommodate the rarer atmosphere of Mars, were enclosed by a barrel-like chest, but their limbs were pitifully thin.

Introduction

IF you are interested in Martian stories, here is one that will prove an eye-opener. The author of this story, himself a well-known astronomer and scientist, propounds an entirely new and interesting theory about the origin of mankind in this world, and sets forth excellent arguments for his contention. The idea is so unique and the story so well written that you are almost convinced that somehow or other the whole thing must be real. There are so many new ideas and new possible inventions contained in this story that we are certain it will secure a niche all by itself in your memory.

THE RETREAT TO MARS
By Cecil B. White

CHAPTER I

THE sun had dipped below the western hills, leaving a gorgeous mass of color in its wake. I stood there as the twilight arch swept up from the east, watching the shadows creep over land and sea while the faint evening clouds overhead turned blood-red under the last glancing rays of the sun.

Many times had I watched the setting of the sun and the evening shadows, while the mosquitohawks hovered overhead with their plaintive cries, or plunged whirring downward upon their prey. Never twice the same that picture held me, until the city lights sprang into being in the distance and the flashing lights of the sentinels of the coast pierced through the gloaming.

As I turned away to begin my night's work the crunch of footsteps on the gravel path broke the stillness of the evening. An elderly, bearded man approached. He had come up the trail and I had not noticed him until he was nearly upon me.

Visitors to my little observatory are not uncommon. A few, those who show interest more than curiosity, are allowed to look through the instrument, on the rare occasions when it is not engaged in photographic or spectrographic work.

"Mr. Arnold?" queried my visitor as he approached. "I hope that I am not intruding. I tried to get you on the 'phone today, but was unsuccessful, and having been told that I would find you here, I took the liberty of coming to see you."

"I am just about to open up for the night" said I, "and if you don't mind my carrying on with my work—"

"Not at all, not at all," he replied, "I can talk to you just as well — that is, if I will not be in your way?"

Having been assured that he would not trouble me, he followed me into the observatory and watched while I opened the shutters that covered the aperture of the dome.

This done and my right-ascension circle set I turned the telescope on the first star of my evening's program.

When I had started the exposure, and entered up the necessary data in the observing book, I turned to him.

"You must pardon me, my dear sir, if I appear to be rude or inhospitable, but I am anxious to obtain a spectrogram. (Ed. note: a photograph of the spectrum) of this star before it gets too far west for observing," I explained. "All I have to do now is to keep the star's image on the slit of the spectroscope—"

"I noticed that you were engaged in spectrographic work," he remarked. "How long will your exposure be?"

From his remark I gathered that he knew something of the work in hand, so I answered, "About forty-five minutes with this seeing. (Ed. Note: Seeing. The quality of the observing conditions. For first-class seeing the atmosphere must be very steady and the sky clear. Such seeing is, unfortunately, extremely rare.) It's a fifth magnitude star that I am working on. Would you care to take a look at it?"

He climbed up the observing ladder and stood beside me while I explained things to him. When I had finished he turned to me, half smilingly, and said:

"Is this seeing anything like it was last November when you made your remarkable observations of the planet Mars?"

"Apparently you have been reading my papers," I said. "No, conditions are not nearly as favorable now as they were at the time that other work was done. If I were to live a thousand years I doubt if I should ever see other nights to equal those four."

"Yes, I did read those papers of yours," he replied. "They are the cause of my presence here this evening. I am Hargraves, of the Smithsonian Institute."

I took his proffered hand. Hargraves was a well-known archaeologist, though I must confess that I should not have known of him except by chance. On glancing through "Science Abstracts" a few weeks previously, I happened on an abstract of a paper of his which aroused my curiosity, and I had looked up the original, which had proved highly interesting.

I admitted as much to him. He laughed. "We work in different spheres, as a rule" he said, "but this time I am stepping into yours. That was a great fight you had with Krussen and his associates over Schiaparelli's 'canali'."

"Wasn't it," said I. "The trouble with those chaps is that they do not know what good seeing is really like. They have, perhaps forty or fifty clear nights a year, none of which begin to compare with our good nights. Then, because they have a fifty-four inch refractor against my twenty-four inch, they think that they are much better able to see fine detail than I am. (Ed. note: The size of a telescope is denoted by the diameter of the lens, or, in the case of a reflector, of the mirror.) Let me tell you, Doctor Hargraves, those four nights were perfect, absolutely perfect. I was able to use my highest power of four thousand

and there was not the slightest tremor in the image. (Ed. Note: The powers usually used under good conditions for planetary work are from 300 to 800 times.) Had my driving-clock been perfect, I could have photographed everything I saw."

"I know," my companion replied. "Every detail of your drawings was correct. You may wonder how I — an archaeologist — know anything about the planet Mars, but I have a big surprise in store for you."

I looked at him in amazement.

"I don't wonder you are surprised,' he continued. "I have made some discoveries that I think no one ever dreamed of. As you are probably aware, I have only recently returned from Africa after a six years' absence."

I nodded, for in the paper I have already mentioned, Hargraves announced that he had made some startling discoveries in Africa as to the origin of mankind, . . . discoveries which overthrew previous theories about the origin of man, but the exact nature of his find was not to be made public until such time, when the records he had found hidden away in a remote corner of "Darkest Africa" were fully deciphered.

"Some years ago," he continued, "I became convinced that the rise of mankind took place, not in Asia where it is generally supposed to have occurred, but in Africa.

"This belief thrust itself upon me as I was writing a book which I never published; a book which was to have traced the migration of mankind from the place of its origin, over this globe of ours. I amassed a tremendous amount of data which led, when I came to piece it together, to Central Africa, and not to Asia as I had confidently expected.

"I searched again and again for an error which I thought must exist in my work, but the trail inevitably led to the same conclusion: Central Africa was the 'Garden of Eden' of mankind.

"As you are aware, this was contrary to all earlier evidence, so I did not care to propound my theories without further corroboration. On consulting with the heads of my department, laying the evidence before them, it was decided to organize an expedition to see if any fresh data was available on the ground itself.

"The expedition, a small one as such things go, was organized and led by myself. It was successful, but the results are not yet ready for publication. To you, however, I would like to show what we have found, the understanding being, of course, that it shall not be divulged until my work is finished. Could you come and see me at my hotel? I will probably be in town for a week, anyway."

"Why not come and spend tomorrow evening with me?" I asked.

So we arranged it.

Having finished the spectrogram, I showed my companion what I could of my equipment and turned the telescope upon a few of the show objects in the heavens, which delighted him immensely. After this I saw him safely started down the trail, equipped with a flashlight to light his way to the road, where his taxi awaited him.

Throughout the night I could not keep from wondering what Hargraves had found in Africa that could be connected with the planet Mars. The dawn found me without a conjecture and I turned in to dream wild dreams of Hargraves and Africa.

CHAPTER II

THE following evening found us comfortably settled in my den. I was eager to hear his story.

"I am not going to prolong my story with the details of the hardships of our journey" Hargraves began. "It is the usual stuff one reads in books of travel. Famine, thirst and fever played their usual roles, with the result that my two white companions were out of the game before two years had passed. One died, and the other had to be escorted back to the coast, where he subsequently recovered.

"With a handful of native bearers, I pressed on with the search, following every clue and rumor, only to be disappointed time and time again. We moved slowly and laboriously through unexplored Central Africa, ever seeking traces of man's handiwork other than that of the natives.

"I was laid up in camp with an attack of fever when another rumor was brought by a native who had heard of our quest. This time it was substantiated by evidence in the form of a curiously shaped piece of metal. This was, in form, somewhat like a shoehorn and pointed in two places with an ingenious form of ball-and-socket joint. On examining it closely I saw that there had been two other pieces attached to the central portion, which had evidently been snapped off. Where the metal showed its broken surface it was bright and crystalline in appearance, so that I judged the break was of recent date. At first I thought that the natives who had found it had cleaned it up, for the surface was bright and shiny.

"Lying there in my blankets, I questioned the messenger through my interpreter, but I was assured that it was just as it had been found some years before. The metal of which it was made was unknown to me. It looked like steel, with a lustrous surface, but it weighed no more than an equal amount of aluminum. Later tests showed that it had much greater strength than steel and that it was extremely hard; even a file would leave no mark upon it.

"From what I could gather it had been picked up in a valley lying some ten or eleven days' journey to the northwest of us, when several members of his tribe had ventured in on a hunting expedition.

"I say 'ventured in' because the whole of the area in question is looked upon by the local tribes as the abode of the dead, and it was only when starvation threatened, and hunger overcame their fears, that they dared to penetrate this forbidden valley.

"Impatiently I waited until I was well enough to travel, then we set out with the messenger as a guide. Gradually the character of the country changed until the swampy, fever infested jungle gave way to a rolling park-like country.

"Our way led steadily upwards until on the ninth day we were moving over a verdant plateau which was alive with small game. My little pocket aneroid barometer showed us that we were about four thousand five hundred feet above sea level. That evening we camped at the foot of a low range of hills and our guide assured me that on the morrow we should enter the forbidden valley.

"True to his promise, the following noon found us at the entrance to a little valley bounded, by low hills, through which flowed a considerable stream. The hills on either side were gloriously green, betokening a generous supply of moisture, the parklike character of the valley being enhanced by occasional groups of a species of oak tree, and here and there patches of a flowering shrub whose scent filled the valley with a delicious odor. The bark of this bush, I learned, was used by the natives in lieu of tobacco, and it was not half bad as a substitute, I can assure you, especially after one had been many months without the comfort of 'Lady Nicotine.'

"It was with the greatest difficulty that I persuaded our guide to remain with us, and then only after I had presented him with a charm in the shape of a ring, which I had to assure him would ward off all danger, did he consent to enter the valley with us.

"Late that afternoon, we arrived near the spot where our guide had found this metal object. We made camp at once and I set out to survey the valley.

"About a quarter of a mile from the camp the floor of the valley narrowed, bounded on the one side by a steep cliff and the other by a ridge which ran out at right angles from the southern slope. This formation immediately aroused my curiosity, for I thought that there must be some outcrop of rock here, which kept the flood-waters of the stream from removing it. Besides, I was anxious to learn something of the geological formations of this district.

"Attended by my guide, I walked down the valley towards this formation. Sure enough there was an outcrop of rock on the north side, a hard limestone formation whose foot was lapped by the waters of the stream. Wading through the shallow water, we crossed over to the south bank.

"Where the waters had removed the surface soil I saw what at first I took to be a rib of rock reaching into the stream. On closer inspection I saw that this was, not rock, but metal. It was worn and scored by the waters of ages, but on scraping away the soil above the flood level I exposed clean cut edges. A rib of the metal ran back into the hillside.

"WITH a sharp stake I probed the soft, loamy soil and was able to trace the direction of this rib up the hillside for a distance of perhaps thirty feet, where the covering became too deep for my probe to penetrate. Marking the spot where I could last feel it, I skirted the east and west sides of the mound with the hope of finding another clue, but I could see nothing.

"The tropical night shut down with its usual suddenness during my investigations, so we wended our way back to camp, where the light of a fire danced and flickered in the evening air. How I wished for a battery for my flashlight. The batteries, however, had perished long ago in the steaming jungle air, and I had to wait until morning with this discovery before me."

"I know how you felt," I interrupted. "I experienced the same feeling last night."

Hargraves smiled and continued.

"That evening I set the boys to work to construct rude digging implements from the scrub oak of the hillside. Crude they were, indeed, but they would serve my purpose in that light soil.

"Long before daylight, the camp was astir, and by the time the sun rose the morning meal was over and we were on our way to the mysterious mound. Setting the boys to work at intervals along a continuation of the line I had already traced out, the metal rib was soon located higher up the hillside, covered by some four feet of earth.

"I now saw that it might save time to have a couple of natives working directly on top of the mound, so transferring two of them, I directed them to clear away the top soil, while the others continued to trace the rib up the hillside.

"Two hours passed when a shout from the top told me they had made some discovery. When I arrived there they were clearing away the dry soil from what appeared to be a flat metal surface. Calling up the other boys we were soon at work removing the earth from the rounded top of the hillock.

"Little by little the metal surface was laid bare, showing it to be, not flat, but rounded with the exposed slope falling towards the stream. Late that afternoon we had come to the southern edge of the spherical surface. Here a smooth wall dropped away at an angle of sixty-five degrees with the vertical, as my clinometer showed. Something else was also revealed. We laid bare another metal rib which lay in a line with the first one.

"Again night cut short our work and tired out from exertions with my primitive shovel, I fell asleep directly after supper, to wake and find the eastern sky reddening under the rays of the rising sun.

"Working down the convex slope we gradually laid bare the surface until one of the boys revealed a crack in the hitherto unbroken surface. As the soil was rapidly removed we exposed a circular plate set flush in the metal. Near the periphery and diametrically opposite each other were two holes which we rapidly cleaned out, showing them to be let in the plate at an angle of perhaps thirty degrees.

"With the aid of the boys I tried to lift this cover, or whatever it might be, but it seemed to be as solid as the rest. A close scrutiny of the edge, which was a little ragged in one place made me think it might be threaded. With this in mind I placed two stout sticks in the holes and attempted to turn it, but with no success until it occurred to me to try the opposite direction. Throwing my weight on the lever with one of the boys doing the same on the other side I essayed to turn the plate once more. Suddenly we were both sprawling on our hands and knees. The plate had turned.

"Unmindful of my bruises, I jumped to the plate, and gradually we unscrewed it, the plate, with each turn, rising higher and higher from the surface in which it was set. When it stood fully eighteen inches high we came to the end of the screw and by our combined efforts swung the heavy disc of metal aside. Subsequent measures showed it to be twenty-eight inches in diameter and twenty thick.

"We had uncovered a hole some two feet deep, at the bottom of which was another plate. Arranged in the form of a square of twelve on a side were one hundred and forty-four equally spaced circular holes, each one about half-an-inch in diameter, and on the plate lay six metal objects. I picked these, up and examined them one by one.

They were similar in shape and size and were in the form of a rod of circular cross section, six inches long with a cross piece on top giving them the form of a capital letter T. Each of these

THE RETREAT TO MARS 27

were slotted across at various points, but no two in exactly the same manner, and on them were engraved strange characters. Here is a sketch of them."

Hargraves handed me a piece of paper on which was drawn the figures I reproduce here.

$$\Gamma \quad +\!\!\cdot \quad T\Gamma \quad \underline{\underline{11}} \quad T\!\!+ \quad \underline{\mathbb{I}\!\cdot}$$

"The thought struck me at once that these things might be keys to unlock whatever lay before me, so I tried one in a hole where it fitted snugly. Now, I asked myself, into which hole did each key fit. There were one-hundred and forty-four holes and six keys, so there were evidently 144!/138! (Author's Note: 144! 138! Factorial 144 divided by factorial 133 is 144 X 143 X 142 X 141 X 140 X 139=8,020,000,000,000 +. 3! = 3 X 2 X 1; 4! = 4 X 3 X 2 X 1; etc. Counting by twelves instead of tens as we are accustomed to do, hence the numbers ten and eleven will have separate symbols.) ways in which these six keys could be arranged, using all of them. Out of more than eight trillion ways of doing a thing with only one of them correct, the chances are somewhat against one's hitting the right combination by chance!"

"You might hit it once in a million years," I laughed, "if you could keep on trying that long."

"Well," he continued, "I saw that there must be some solution to my problem, so I looked for a clue and found it. One of the corner holes was marked

$$|$$

while the one diagonally opposite looked like this."

$$|\!\cdot\!\cdot$$

He drew these figures as he spoke.

"On the plate, above what I took to be the top of the square, were engraved twelve symbols, like this

·|᠌|ᒣ|-|-|+⊥⊥I⊥+⊣

"After copying these down in my note-book, I sat down to think it over. From the occurrence of twelves, both in the number of holes and the number of symbols, it might be possible, I thought, that the duodecimal* system was used by those who had made this thing. Following up this thought I saw that the symbols were, in order, zero to eleven according to our notation, hence the first of these keys was number two and the others 60, 38, 91, 42 and 108 respectively.

"Hurriedly I placed the keys in their corresponding holes and as I did so I felt the wards of the lock mechanism engage with the slots. Turning the keys as far as they would go I was now able to lift the plate with the aid of the boys, using the keys as handles.

"It was thinner than the former one, being about a foot or so thick, and as we lifted it I noticed that a number of radial bars on the underside had slid back into their sockets.

"YOU can imagine my feelings as I peered down and saw no other obstacle in my way. Sacrificing one of my few precious matches I leaned as far as I could over the hole. The match burned bright and clear; evidently the air inside was pure. Just below me I could see what appeared to be a platform. Taking a stout stick, long enough to reach it, I tested it carefully. It seemed quite strong and firm, so taking a chance, I lowered myself into the hole and my feet just touched as I hung from the edge with my hands.

"I could see by the light that filtered in from overhead that I was standing on a metal grating. It was not level, but tilted downwards to the north. As I had suspected, this construction, whatever it might be, had fallen over from the vertical and lay at an angle on the hillside.

"Ordering one of the natives to fetch torches, I stooped and peered around. I could dimly see that I stood on the top of a curved stairway leading down into the darkness. Grasping the heavy handrail with which it was protected I cautiously descended. I noticed that the steps were abnormally high as I went down. Later I was to know the reason. A few steps down and I came to another platform, which I could make out in the faint light as circular, surrounding a 'well.'

"Striking another match, I examined the wall behind me. In its surface I saw another set of holes similar to those in the plate we had removed. My match flickered out and, not wanting to waste any more of my precious store of them I climbed the steps and wriggled out into the daylight to await the arrival of the torches.

"Presently the boy I had sent arrived with a goodly load of dry, resinous sticks that would burn well and brightly. I lit one, and calling to him to follow me, I again lowered myself into the hole, remembering to take the keys with me. Stepping carefully for fear of falling on the sloping surface, I walked around the gallery examining the place. It was about twenty feet in diameter with a five-foot gallery from which led a second flight of steps. There were four sets of key holes in the wall about five feet above the floor.

"The second gallery was exactly like the first and I did not stop, but went on down the last flight of steps. This was evidently the bottom of the cylinder and, like the other two stories, its walls held the now familiar key plates.

"Going to the one on the lower side I examined it closely. Above the square of holes were twelve sets of symbols arranged in pairs, the first members of these pairs corresponding to the numbers on the keys. Evidently the keys did not correspond to the same holes as above, so, inserting them in their corresponding new numbers, I turned them as I had done before.

"Immediately, a section of the wall swung inward and there was a sudden rush of air which nearly extinguished the torch. The air pressure had been much less inside the chamber which now lay open before me, than outside, and the door was apparently airtight. No wonder I could see no sign of the joint in my first cursory examination of the walls.

"Before me, stacked around the sides, were a large number of box-shaped objects, held in place by bars reaching from floor to roof of the chamber, each box bearing a number. Removing one of the retaining bars, which fitted into sockets, I pulled down the top box of the tier.

"On the front of this box was a lever-like handle, this I turned, and as I did so there came the hissing sound of air entering a vacuum. Turning the handle further — it was quite stiff — the air rushed in with a final sigh and the lid of the box raised sufficiently for me to put my fingers under it and throw it back.

"The lever had operated an eccentric which had forced the lid up against the pressure of the outside air. The lid was tongued, and fitted into a corresponding groove in the upper edge of the box, and the groove was filled with a waxy substance which had made the joint air tight. I noticed afterwards that each box had a filled hole through which the air had evidently been exhausted.

"Carefully packed in a substance that looked like fine steel wool were a number of broad oblong cases, about the size of a standard volume of the *Encyclopedia Britannica*, the topmost of which I removed. It was of the same metallic substance that I had encountered all along, and on its edge was a little knob set in a recess. This I pressed and a cover flew back.

"It was a volume, and such a volume as the eyes of living man never saw before. There before me was the most startling illustration I had ever looked upon. Instead of the usual lifeless flat things we are used to, there lay a picture in three dimensions.

THE RETREAT TO MARS

The illustration depicted an animal or reptile — I don't know which it was — and it stood out there in the torch light like a live thing. I ran my fingers lightly over the surface to assure myself that it was not a model, or in relief, but it was as flat as a table top. The colors were marvelous; they had life and brightness in them which enhanced the natural look about the thing.

"At the foot of the case in which the picture lay was a tiny lever-like arrangement. I pressed this over and as I did so there was a tiny whirring sound followed by a click, and the picture flicked out of sight, and was replaced by another.

"One-half the page — if I may call them pages — was occupied by this new illustration, the other half being filled with characters, evidently writing of some kind. Page after page flicked by at my touch, the majority bearing those wonderfully executed illustrations in three dimensions.

"BOX after box was opened, and each was found filled with these strange volumes. I carefully replaced those I had removed and closed the lids of the boxes, replacing them in their tiers.

"Where was I going to start in this place? I felt like a child surrounded by novel toys, not knowing which to examine first. Then it occurred to me that everything was arranged in a methodical manner — the numbering of the cases and the volumes showed this. Looking on the door of this cell I saw something I had overlooked before. It was numbered ten, according to our notation. Number one must be on the first landing.

"The air was becoming thick and suffocating with the oily smoke of the torches, but I made my way to the first cell and opened it in its turn. Being warned this time, I had the boy stand back with the torch so that it would not be blown out. The pressure here was much lower than in the other cell. I was nearly overthrown by the sudden gust of air that drove in before me as the door swung back.

"This chamber was similar to the one below, and in the topmost row of boxes I saw number one in a corner. I removed this case and, as the air was becoming unbearable, I took it out into the sunlight to examine it.

"It contained what I may liken to a child's primer, profusely illustrated. The first volume was filled with pictures of common objects, each with a few symbols at the sides. Trees, rivers, lakes and mountains; birds, beasts and reptiles, the majority of which were unknown to me, were illustrated. The second volume contained composite pictures — simple actions of human-like creatures and so on. I saw at once that it would be quite easy for a man of average intelligence to learn this unknown language with the aid of this wonderful primer. To one who was accustomed to deciphering old writings, as I was, the task would be ridiculously easy.

"The setting of the sun drove me back to camp, but not before I had replaced and locked the place, taking the keys with me.

"By the light of the fire I studied my trophies that night. It might interest you to know just how the 'lessons' were arranged. Take for example the verb 'to walk.' In one set of pictures a being was shown in the foreground, approaching a hill. The second showed him, bent forward, walking up the hill, while a third showed him at the top. The characters were exactly the same in each case, but over the first was an inverted V; over the second, nothing; and over the third a V. The tenses were all indicated by a symbol above the verb. The degrees of adjectives were similarly indicated, hence it simplified the written language exceedingly.

"I sat and studied well into the night until weariness compelled me to cease, but at dawn I was awake and at it again. Throughout the day I worked, having given instructions to the boys to continue their work of removing the earth from around the cylinder.

"Every moment the system of writing became clearer, until late in the afternoon I came to a lone sentence set out in large characters. A rough translation of it would be:

"'WE GREET YOU. CONTINUE, WE HAVE MUCH IN STORE FOR YOU'

"Here was a direct message, and a message that made my heart leap. If I had worked hard up to this point, I worked feverishly now. Who, I wondered, were 'WE'?

"The following day another message was translated. It read:

"'THE PEOPLE OF ANOTHER WORLD GREET YOU.'

"I checked my translation again and again, but I had made no mistake. That was the meaning of the sentence.

"As the days slipped by I came across more of these interpolated sentences, all encouraging me to go on. This personal touch made me feel as though there were some beings anxious for my advancement so that they could communicate with me.

"The days grew into weeks before I had mastered the language sufficiently for the purpose of those who wrote it. In the meantime the natives had progressed with their task but slowly, due to the poor implements with which they had to work. They worked slowly but honestly, so I did not press them, for I could see I had months of work ahead of me before I even scratched the surface of the wonderful store of knowledge that lay before me.

"We were truly in a Garden of Eden, for game and fish abounded, while edible fruits and berries served to keep down sickness, which would surely have followed a meat diet. In this way I was able to conserve our none too plentiful supply of provisions. The head boy was an excellent shot, so our ammunition was not wasted as it would have been had we depended upon my powers with a rifle. The climate was almost perfect.

"Eventually I arrived at the end of my primary course and came, at the end of the last volume, to a message which read — 'First read volume one, case three. A complete catalogue of the contents of the library will also be found in this case.'

"This volume was soon secured, and without hesitation I plunged into it. It was written in a fairly simple style, and with the aid of an excellent dictionary I found in the same case, I was able to read right through. I read it in four days, hardly stopping to eat or sleep, nearly ruining my eyesight with the strain. After that I slackened up a bit and did manual work at intervals in order to get some exercise. I will outline the contents of this volume to you.

CHAPTER III

"'Hundreds of thousands of years before this story opens, intelligent life had dawned upon one of our nearest neighbors in space, the planet Mars; in much the same manner as we have supposed it to do on this Earth of ours, so that at the time this narrative was written civilization had reached a very high plane. The records show that they had reached what we might call the ideal state. Every being was intelligent enough to work under what I might call a system of social democracy.

"'Every member of the planet's teeming millions was an integral part of a smoothly working system in which no parasites existed, for when one, by some atavistic freak, did turn up who attempted to "throw a monkey-wrench into the machinery" he was simply exterminated.

"'Throughout the ages, while this system was slowly being built up, the race had been carefully developed by intelligent selection in mating and every undesirable feature had been slowly eliminated. The result was that at the time this narrative opens every man and woman on the planet was both mentally and physically perfect.

"'As time went on it became apparent that the life of the planet would be shortened by the loss of air and water vapor. The gravitation on the surface of Mars being much less than on the Earth, nearly one-half as great, the gases of its atmosphere would more readily escape. The Kinetic Theory of Gases shows that a velocity of seven miles a second is readily obtained by the faster moving molecules of water vapor. This is the critical speed for escape from the Earth's attraction. How much more readily will the water vapor escape from a planet like Mars.

"'Some scheme had to be developed then, in order to reduce this rapid escape of the planet's vital fluid, if life on the planet was to be possible in future ages.

"'Martian engineers set to work, after due deliberation, to construct gigantic underground reservoirs lined with an impervious material. After nearly a thousand years' labor the work was finished and the waters of the lakes and seas were impounded in these vast underground storage basins.

"'To conserve the precious liquid still further, that which was deposited as snow in the polar regions was carefully trapped as the summer sun melted it. Huge subterranean aqueducts led it back equator-wards, assisted by enormous pumping plants. These conduits were tapped at intervals by lateral lines in order to supply water to irrigate the fast drying surface, and at the time the record was written, the construction of an intricate system of conduits and pumping stations was well under way.

"Just as the late Professor Lowell hypothecated," I exclaimed, to which Hargraves added:

"And those oases, as Lowell called them, were the locations of the pumping stations, the intensely cultivated area around them causing them to show up as black dots on the planet's surface, as your observations showed.

"The prominent blue-green markings on our neighbor in space are of a heavier soil and are the old sea beds. The lighter sandy soils were abandoned, because of the large quantity of water necessary to make them fertile, save along the lines of the canals. But to continue —

"'With their highly developed instruments the Martians had ascertained that their neighboring planet, the Earth, was well suited to support life. Indeed it seemed a veritable land of promise to them, with its vast oceans and verdant continents. Encouraged by the thought of the possibilities this new world held for them, researches were instituted which resulted in a machine which would travel through interplanetary space. The method of propulsion was similar to that of the "Goddard Rocket"; gases formed by the combination of certain solid chemicals, escaping through specially shaped nozzles attached to the after part of the machine propelled it in exactly the same manner as our skyrockets are shot aloft.

"'Wing-shaped members supported it in the air until its velocity was high enough for it to leave the atmosphere, while a second series of nozzles in the bow of the craft retarded it when a landing had to be made.

"'A company of daring pioneers left one eventful day to commence the first interplanetary navigation our solar system has known, and after months of an uneventful journey, landed safely on the Earth. An unforeseen disaster overtook this adventurous company, however. Under the greater gravitational force to which they were subjected here, their relatively frail bodies broke down. Prolapse of their inner organs caused many to die in agony within a month of their landing, so the project was abandoned and the survivors returned to their native planet.

"'Undaunted by this failure they set to work to develop a race capable of withstanding the new conditions. After a lapse of nearly four hundred years a new expedition set forth. This

THE RETREAT TO MARS 37

second party was more successful than the first, and succeeded in founding a colony on the high plateau region where the cylinder was found. Their bodies were skillfully braced by a metal framework which relieved, to some extent, the strain to which they were subjected.

"'These first intelligent inhabitants of the Earth were giants compared with us. Their average height was about nine feet; their lungs, which were developed to accommodate the rarer atmosphere of Mars, were enclosed by a barrel-like chest, but their limbs were pitifully thin, though much better adapted to their new environment than those of their predecessors.

"'As time went on children were born into this new world and new arrivals came across the gulf every two years when Mars was in opposition. Then came another catastrophe. As the children born here grew, it was noticed that their intelligence was inferior to that of their parents. Bodily they were smaller and sturdier, but their mentality when they reached the adult stage was only equivalent to that of a Martian child half their age. (Ed. Note: Opposition. A planet is in opposition nearest to the earth when the Sun, Earth and the planet are in the same straight line with the Earth and the planet on the same side of the Sun.)

"'Immigration stopped while this new phase was anxiously watched. Everything within the Martians' power was done to check this effect, but without avail. Things went from bad to worse as the second generation was born, for these were still farther from the high mental standard of their forefathers. Instead of highly intelligent beings, the race was rapidly reverting to the primitive state.

"'The fourth generation was but a grotesque caricature of the original stock, and were already forming into bands of nomadic savages, leaving the center of their community to wander at large over the face of the Earth.

"'Everything within the power of the Martians having failed

to alleviate these conditions, the projected plan was abandoned. Before leaving this planet forever, to return to their own sphere, it was decided to build a monument to their endeavors, so that as time went on and intelligence again returned to this planet, a record of their attempt, and data of the most useful kind, would be available to those who found it.

"'Two other cylinders, similar in every respect to the one I found, were constructed of a tough noncorrosive metal which would withstand the destructive forces of the elements throughout the ages until intelligence again appeared. This period has been much longer than was anticipated by the builders, I can see from what I have read. The three monuments were placed where observation had showed cataclysms of nature, such as flood or earthquake, would be at a minimum. One where I found it, another somewhere on a continent over which the Atlantic now rolls, and the last in the continent which we know as Australia. This latter may yet be found. The cylinders were sealed in the manner I have described so that none but intelligent beings could gain access to them. They were so constructed that should they break they would do so midway between the dividing partitions of the cells, thus leaving each cell intact until someone should arrive who could solve the riddle of the system of numerals and make keys to fit the locks.

"'This planet and all their works were then abandoned. Practically all other traces of their sojourn have now vanished into dust, though here and there I found remains of their supporting harness, for which they had used this remarkable metal, which is, I believe, akin to aluminum.' "

CHAPTER IV

"BY the time my cursory survey of the contents of the library was completed, the natives had succeeded in clearing away the mass of earth around the cylinder, so that I was better able to understand its construction and what had happened to it throughout the ages.

"The walls of the object were approximately six feet thick with the top and bottom of convex form, better to withstand any great pressure to which it might be subjected. The whole structure was of one seamless piece, unbroken save where the manhole gave access to its interior. Four massive, equally spaced spokes, or ribs, radiated out from the cylinder, the object of these being to prevent the cylinder rolling over as the soil subsided. The cylinder was approximately forty feet high and sixty in diameter. The arrangement of the interior I have already described to you.

"Originally the structure had rested on the surface of a hard limestone formation, but the gradual weathering of this had caused it to sink downwards into the little valley which now exists there.

"Having completed my examination of the cylinder and satisfied myself that there was nothing more to be learned until other volumes were translated, I carefully sealed and locked the entrance, after selecting a few of what I deemed the most important records to take away with me. The keys I sewed into a canvas belt which I strapped about my waist and, packing the remaining trophies very carefully, we retraced our steps to the coast.

"Eight months after leaving the valley I was once more in Washington where I laid my discoveries before the departmental heads. It was decided to keep the thing secret until an expedition could go to Africa and return with the remainder of the library. I expect that we shall be hearing from them in a few months' time, if all goes well.

"Among the volumes I brought out with me was this one," Hargraves said, reaching for the package he had brought with him.

Unwrapping it, he handed me a lustrous metal box such as he had described. I took it and pressed the spring at the side. The cover, which I may liken to the front board of our books, flew back.

There before me, apparently floating in space, was the representation of a sphere. So real was the three-dimensional aspect of the thing that I could not resist passing my fingers over its surface to assure myself that it really was in one plane. It was an illustration of the planet of mystery — Mars. At the poles glistened twin polar caps, the northern one surrounded by a hazy outline while the southern was belted with a liquid-blue band. It was evidently the fall of the year in the planet's northern hemisphere.

I recognized some of the principal features — Utopia, the Syrtis Major and the Pseboas Lucus (Author's Note: The reader is recommended to read "The Planet Mars," "Mars and its Canals," and "Mars as the Abode of Life," — three volumes written by the late Professor Percival Lowell, who observed Mars systematically for twenty years, mostly at Flagstaff. Arizona, where the atmospheric conditions are, perhaps, better than those to be found at any other observatory. These books are well written, mostly in non-technical language.) — though there were other blue-green markings with which I was not familiar The desert areas, I saw at once, were much smaller than they are today and only a few canals were shown.

I stopped to examine the "page" on which it was depicted. Like the case, it was of metal, and appeared to pass over a roller, like the film of a camera. Afterwards I learned that it was on an endless belt arrangement, passing over a series of small rollers which kept the metal sheet from coming into contact with itself. Had this precaution not been taken there was a danger of the sheets cohering and being irreparably ruined.

Pressing the little lever-like arrangement at the lower end of

THE RETREAT TO MARS 41

the case as my companion directed, the picture flicked out of sight revealing another view of the planet. A series of such views gave details of every portion of the planet's surface and then I came to a different type of picture.

It was an illustration showing a gigantic engineering undertaking. A low range of hills formed the background and down their slope ran a great scar. At the foot was a vast building under construction, and leading from it to the foreground was an immense excavation at the bottom of which were what I took to be excavating machines, whose apparent size was enhanced by the diminutive, human-like figures I could see here and there among them.

Translating the legend below, Hargraves informed me that this illustrated one of the canals under construction and that the building at the foot of the hill housed the pumping mechanism which was to raise the water to its new level. This particular piece of work was at what we call the northern point of the Trivium Charontis (Ed. Note: Observations have shown that there are no great elevations on the surface of Mars— nothing that approaches mountainous size.)

Page after page flicked before me on the pressing of the lever. Great engineering works, maps and plans of districts and cities, and last of all views of the cities themselves. These latter illustrations are well worth describing. Unlike our canyon-like streets the ways received sunlight in abundance, for the buildings were pyramidal in form, each story being smaller than the one below, with a broad open space running around it. A reddish stone seemed to be used in their construction, with a trimming of dull green, well suiting the style of architecture, which had a Babylonian cast about it. Fancy carving or ornamentations were wholly absent.

A number of torpedo-shaped objects were evidently moving through the air above the ways between these massive piles, a host of others were "parked" on the broad galleries of the buildings, over which were what I supposed to be long windows which lighted their interiors.

This, Hargraves told me, was the metropolis of the planet, and these were the executive offices from which the affairs of this far-off world were directed. A symbol mounted on a staff at the top of each building marked the department to which it belonged. A flaming Sun, crossed parallel lines, a square and compass, and a cluster of fruits were among some of those I saw. I will leave it to the reader's imagination to solve the meanings of these symbols.

Another view showed the stages from which great aerial liners left for distant cities, or to which they came to discharge their living cargo. A few were resting upon their cradles, taking aboard freight and passengers, or discharging the products of distant districts into conveyors which took it rapidly underground. All heavy traffic was carried underground in the cities, I was informed, and came to the surface only at its destination.

"To think that this was taking place half-a-million years ago," I said to my companion. "I wonder what it is like there now."

"Some day we may learn," he replied. "They may have progressed but little and may be passively waiting until our intelligence is high enough to make it worth their while to communicate with us. Think of the difference in intelligence which must exist between us! Perhaps as much as between mankind and the apes. We would not think of establishing communication with monkeys, would we? Then we must not expect to hear from our neighbors until we begin to approach their standard of intelligence."

It was late that night when my visitor left, very kindly leaving the volume behind for my further perusal and with a promise to aid me by interpreting the accompanying text. Without his aid I would not have been able to make much of it, and would

THE RETREAT TO MARS

perhaps have come to many erroneous conclusions.

The following days, with Hargraves' assistance, I studied it thoroughly, comparing the maps with my own drawings and checking up much of my observational data.

I have written down this story so that time would not cause me to forget the finer details. Some day I may publish it, if I can obtain permission.

POSTSCRIPT

SINCE penning the above the remainder of the library has arrived in America, and my friend informs me that I am quite at liberty to publish this (which he has read). At present Hargraves, with a large staff of assistants, is engaged in the translation of the records, but it will be a long time before such a colossal work can be published. The expense will be enormous. The world has waited half-a-million years for this discovery, so I suppose we can be patient for a few more years until the story is given to us.

RADIO MATES
By Benjamin Witwer

"Think of it! A twist of a switch and the living, breathing piglet slowly dissolved before my eyes and vanished along a pair of wires to my aerial, whence it was transformed as a set of waves in the ether to the receiving apparatus—there to reincarnate into the living organism once more, alive and breathing, unharmed by its extraordinary journey!"

Introduction

FROM the telegraph to the telephone was but a step. From the telephone to radio constituted but another such step, and we are now enjoying radio broadcast from stations thousands of miles away. Every time you have an X-ray photograph taken you are bombarded, not by rays, but by actual particles that go right through the walls of the tube, which particles are just as real as if they were bullets or bricks, the only difference being that they are smaller. Thus our scientists lead up to the way of sending solids through space. While impossible of achievement, as yet, it may be possible, years hence, to send living beings through spare, to be received at distant points. At any rate, the author of this story weaves a fascinating romance around this idea. It makes excellent reading, and the plot is as unusual as is its entire treatment.

RADIO MATES
By Benjamin Witwer

IT was a large brown envelope, of the size commonly used for mailing pamphlets or catalogues. Yet it was registered, and had come by special messenger that afternoon, my landlady informed me. Probably it was a strain of that detective instinct which is present in most of us that delayed my opening the missive until I had carefully scrutinized the handwriting of the superscription. There was something vaguely familiar in its slanting exactitude, yet when I deciphered the postmark — "Eastport, N. Y.,"— I was still in the dark, for I could not remember ever having heard of the place before. As I turned the packet over, however, my pleasant tingle of anticipation was rudely chilled. Along the flap was a sinister row of black sealing wax blobs, which seemed to stare at me with a malignant fore-knowledge. On closer examination, I noticed that each seal retained the impression of a coat-of-arms, also elusively familiar.

With a strange sense of foreboding I dropped the missive on the table. Queer what ominous significance a few drops of wax can impart to an ordinary envelope. Deliberately I changed into smoking jacket and slippers, poked the well laid fire and lit a pipe before finally tearing open the seals.

There were many typewritten sheets, commencing in letter form:

54 Westervelt Ave.,
Eastport, New York,
February 15th.

Dear Cousin George:

Now that you have identified me by referring to my signature on the last page (which I had just done) you will no doubt wonder at the occasion for this rather effusive letter from one so long silent as I have been. The fact of the matter is that you are the only male relative with whom I can communicate at this time. My nephew, Ralph, is first officer of a freighter somewhere in the Caribbean, and Alfred Hutton, your mother's first cousin, has not been heard from since he embarked on that colonizing scheme in New Guinea, nearly a year ago.

I must do all in my power to prevent the bungling metropolitan police from implicating Howard Marsden in my disappearance. It would take no great stretch of the imagination to do just that, and were the State to require Marsden's life as forfeit for my own, then my carefully planned revenge would be utterly frustrated. I have been cultivating the village postmaster for some weeks, since this plan began to shape definitely in my mind. I am mailing this letter at three o'clock time this afternoon, for I have noticed that at that hour the postal section of the store is generally deserted. I shall ask him if his clock is correct, thus

RADIO MATES

fixing the time in his mind. Please remember these points. Then I shall register this letter, taking care to exhibit the unusual collection of seals on the back. I shall manage to inform him also that I stamped the seals with my ring and will show him the coat-of-arms, explaining its meaning in detail. These villagers are a curiosity-ridden lot. Upon returning home, I shall drop this same ring into the inkwell which stands upon my desk. Finally I shall proffer my friend the postmaster a fifty-dollar bill in paying for my registry. The registry slip itself will be found within the hatband of my brown hat, which I shall place in the wall safe of my study.

You are becoming more amazed as you proceed, no doubt asking yourself if this letter is the product of a madman or a faker. Before you have finished you will probably be assured that both assumptions are correct. It matters little, for I will at least have firmly established the fact that this letter was mailed by no one else but me. As for the rest, Howard Marsden will corroborate what follows.

To begin at the beginning. As you know, or perhaps you do not know, for I forget that our correspondence has been negligible of late, five years ago I accompanied the Rodgers expedition into Afghanistan. We were officially booked as a geological mission, but were actually in search of radium, among other things. When I left, I was practically engaged to Venice Potter, a distant relation of the Long Island Potters, of whom you have perhaps heard. I say "practically" engaged because the outcome of this expedition was to furnish me with the standing and position necessary for a formal demand for her hand. As I said, that was nearly five years ago.

Four months after my departure her letters ceased coming and mine were returned to me unopened. Two months later I received an announcement of her betrothal to Howard Marsden. Received it out there in Afghanistan, when I had returned to the coast for supplies. We'll skip that next year, during which I stuck with the expedition. We were successful. I returned.

Then I found out where the Marsdens were living, here in Eastport. I'd met Marsden once or twice in the old days, but paid him little attention at the time. He seemed but another of the moneyed idlers; had a comfortable income from his father's estate, and was interested in "gentleman farming,"—blooded stock and the rest. I decided at it was useless to dig into dead ashes for the time being, at least until I could determine the lay of the land, so to speak. Meanwhile I had my researches to make, a theory I had evolved as a sort of backfire to fill that awful void of Venice's loss,—out there on the edge of the world. Countless sleepless nights I had spent in a feverish attempt to lose myself in scientific speculation. At last I believed I had struck a clue to conclusions until now entirely overlooked by eager searchers. I decided to establish my laboratory here in Eastport, perhaps devoting any leisure hours to an unravelling of that mystery of my sudden jilting. With a two-year-old beard and sunbaked complexion there were few who would have recognized me under my real name, and none in my assumed role of "Professor Walters."

THUS it was that I leased an old house not half a mile from Marsden's pretentious "farm." I converted the entire ground floor into a laboratory, living in solitary state upon the upper floor. I was used to caring for myself, and the nature of my experiment being of such potentialities, I felt that I wanted no prying servants about me. Indeed, it has turned out to be of such international importance that I feel no compunction whatever in utilizing it for my own selfish ends. It could be a boon to humanity, yet its possibilities for evil in the hands of any individual or group is so great as to render it most dangerous to the happiness of the human kind on this small globe.

RADIO MATES

One day, some three months after I had taken up my residence in Eastport, I had a visitor. It was Marsden. He had been attracted by the sight of my novel aerial, just completed. By his own admission he was an ardent "radio fan," as they are popularly termed, I believe, and he spent the better part of an afternoon bragging of stations he had "logged" with his latest model radio set. Aside from my vague suspicions of his complicity in the alienation of my beloved Venice, I must admit that even then I felt an indefinable repulsion towards him. There was something intangibly unwholesome about him, a narrowness between the eyes which repelled me. Yet, although at that time I had no plan in mind, nevertheless I encouraged him in my most hospitable manner, for even thus early I felt, that at some time not far distant, I might be called upon to utilize this acquaintanceship to my own advantage.

This first visit was followed by others, and we discussed radio in all its phases, for the man had more than a smattering of technical knowledge on the subject and was eager to learn more. At last, one day, I yielded to his insistence that I inspect his set and agreed to dine at his house the following evening. By now I felt secure in my disguise, and although I dreaded the moment when I should actually confront my lost love once more, yet I longed for the sweet pain of it with an intensity which a hard-shelled bachelor like you will never understand. Enough. I arrived at the Marsden's the next evening and was duly presented to my hostess as "Thomas Walters." In spite of my private rehearsals I felt a wave of giddiness sweep over me as I clasped that small white hand in my own after the lapse of almost five years, for she was, if possible, lovelier than ever. I noted when my vision cleared that her eyes had widened as they met mine. I realized that my perturbation had been more apparent than I imagined and managed to mutter something about my alleged "weak heart," a grimmer jest by far than I intended. Frantically I fortified myself with remembrances of those barren days in Afghanistan, where I stayed on and on, impotent to raise a hand in the salvage of my heart's wreckage.

We chatted politely all through that interminable meal, no morsel of which aroused the faintest appreciation on my dry tongue. Finally the chairs were pushed back and my host excused himself to bring down some pieces of apparatus he had recently purchased, concerning which he professed to desire my invaluable opinion.

No sooner had he left the room than the polite smile dropped from Venice's face like a discarded mask.

"Dick," she cried, "what are you doing here?"

It was my first inkling that she suspected my true identity. I rallied quickly, however, and allowed my self-encouraged bitterness its outlet.

"Had I believed you would recognize me, *Mrs. Marsden,* I should not have inflicted my unwelcome presence upon you, I can assure you."

She bit her lips and her head raised with a jerk. Then her mouth softened again as her great eyes searched mine.

"Yes, but why—" she broke off at the sound of approaching footsteps. Suddenly she leaned forward. "Meet me in the pine grove to-morrow afternoon—four o'clock," she breathed. Then her husband entered.

The remainder of the evening I was forced to listen to Marsden's eager dissertation on the alleged "static eliminator" which had been foisted upon him on his last trip to the city. Mechanically I answered or grunted in simulated appreciation when a pause in his endless monologue warned me that some reply was expected of me; but my pulses were leaping in exultation because of the fleeting hope which those few words from my lost Venice had kindled. I could not imagine why the offer to bridge the breach of years should come from her so voluntarily, yet it was enough for me that she remembered and wished to see me. I cared not why.

I arrived nearly an hour early that next afternoon, for I had been unable either to sleep or work during the interim. I shall not bore you with the particulars of that meeting, even were I free to reveal such sacred details. Suffice to say that after the preliminaries of doubt and misunderstanding had been brushed away—and it was not the simple process this synopsis would seem to infer, I can assure you—I stood revealed as the victim of a most ingenious and thoroughly knavish plot. Boiled down, it resembles one of those early movie scenarios.

You remember I spoke of Venice as related to the Long Island Potters, a branch of the family highly rated in the Social Register? You will also remember that before I undertook that expedition I was never particularly certain whence my next year's expenses were to be derived, nor to what extent, if you understand what I mean. At about this time I was preparing for this expedition which I hoped would make me financially and scientifically independent, this wealthy branch of the family seriously "took up" my darling Venice, inviting her to live with them that summer. I remember now all too late, that even during that confusion of mind caused by the agony of leaving my loved one, coupled with the feverish preparations for departure, chill clouds of censure came from the aloof Potters. They made no effort to mask their disapproval of my humble self and prospects, yet in my blindness I had never connected them intimately with what followed.

It was, in short, the old story of the ingenious man-on-the-ground, the "good match," aided and abetted by the patronesses of the "poor relation." The discriminating Marsden naturally fell in love with Venice, and to his great surprise and chagrin, was decisively repulsed by her. Never before having been refused anything he really wanted in his comfortably arranged life, he became passionately desirous of possessing her. Accordingly, my darling was shown a letter, forged with such diabolical cleverness as to be almost indistinguishable from my own hand. It purported to intrigue me with a very ordinary female at a period coincident with the time I had been so fervently courting my dear one.

She refused to credit the document and dispatched of distance, she continued to write me for over a month. When no answer arrived after nearly three long months, she at length delivered a hastily planned ultimatum, to which she was later persuaded to adhere through the combined pressure of Marsden and her family, beating against the razed defences of her broken heart. Then it was that I received the betrothal announcement, the only communication her watchful family had permitted to escape their net of espionage.

AS the story unfolded, my heart pounded with alternate waves of exaltation and red rage at the treacherous Marsden. Because of selfish duplicity, he had robbed us both of five years' happiness, for I had forced my darling's admission that she had never loved him, and now despised him as a common thief. My brief moment of delirious joy was sharply curtailed, however, when I came to press her to separate from this selfish swine. After some demur she confided that he was a drug addict. She said that he had been fighting desperately to break this habit ever since their marriage, for his jealous love of her was the only remaining weapon with which to combat his deep rooted vice. Deprived of his one motive, my darling earnestly assured me that it would be a matter of but a few short years before the white powders wrote *Finis* to yet another life. I could see but a balancing of an already overdrawn account in such an event, and said so in no uncertain terms. She did not chide me, merely patiently explained with sweet, sad resignation that she held herself responsible for his very life for the present. That although she could not love and honor him as she had promised, yet she was bound to cleave to him during this, his "worse" hour. And so we left it for the time, our future clouded, yet with no locked door to bar the present from us.

We met almost daily, unless Marsden's activities interfered. At those times I was like a raging beast, unable to work, consumed with a livid hatred for the cunning thief who had stolen my love while my back was turned. I could not shake her resolution to terminate this loveless match, even though she now loathed the mate she had once tolerated. But in spite of the formlessness of our future, my work progressed as never before. Now my days were more than a mere procession of dates, for each was crowned with the glow of those few stolen moments with my darling Venice.

Came the day of my first complete success. Some weeks previously I had finally succeeded in transmitting a small wooden ball by radio. Perhaps I should say that I had "dissolved" it into its vibrations, for it was not until this later day that I had been able to materialize or "receive" it after it had been "sent." I see you start and re-read this last sentence. I mean just what I say, and Marsden will bear me out, for as you shall see, he has witnessed this and other such experiments here in my laboratory. I have explained to him as much as I wanted him to know of the process, in fact, just enough so that he believes that a little intensive research and experimentation on his part will make him master of my secret. But he is entirely ignorant of the most important element, as well as of the manner of its employment.

Yes, after years of study and interrupted experimental research I was enabled finally to disintegrate, without the aid of heat, a solid object into its fundamental vibrations, transmit these vibrations into the ether in the form of so-called "radio waves" which I then attracted and condensed in my "receiving" apparatus, slowly damping their short kinked vibration-rate until finally there was deposited the homogeneous whole, identical in outline and displacement,— entirely unharmed from its etheric transmigration!

My success in this, my life's dream, was directly the result of our discoveries on that bitter expedition into Afghanistan. All my life I had been interested in the study of vibrations, but had achieved no startling successes or keen expectations thereof until we stumbled upon that strange mineral deposit on what was an otherwise ill-fated trip for me. It was then that I realized that radioactive niton might solve my hitherto insurmountable difficulty in the transmission of material vibrations into electronic waves. My experiments thereafter, while successful to the degree that I discovered several entirely new principles of resonic harmonics, as well as an absolute refutation of the quantum theory of radiation, fell far short of my hoped-for goal. At that time I was including both helium and uranium in my improved cathode projectors, and it was not until I had effected a more sympathetic combination with thorium that I began to receive encouraging results. My final success came with the substitution of actinium for the uranium and the addition of Polonium, plus a finer adjustment which I was able to make in the vortices of my three modified Tesla coils, whose limitations I had at first underrated. I was then enabled to filter my resonance waves into pitch with my "electronic radiate rays," as I called them, with the success I shall soon describe.

Of course, all this is no clearer than a page of Sanscrit to you, nor do I intend that it shall be otherwise. As I have said, such a secret is far too potent to be unloosed upon a world of such delicately poised nations, whose jaws are still reddened from their recent ravening. It needs no explanation of mine to envision the terrible possibilities for evil in the application of this great discovery. It shall go with me—to return at some

RADIO MATES

future, more enlightened time after another equally single-minded investigator shall have stumbled upon it. It is this latter thought which has caused me to drop the hints that I have. My earnest hope is that you will permit the misguided Marsden to read the preceding paragraph. In it he will note a reference to an element which I have not mentioned to him before, and will enable him to obtain certain encouraging results,—encouraging but to further efforts, to more frantic attempts. But I digress.

With my success on inanimate objects, I plunged the more enthusiastically into my work. I should have lost all track of time but for my daily tryst with Venice. Her belief in me was the tonic which spurred me on to further efforts after each series of meticulously conducted experiments had crumbled into failure. It was the knowledge that she awaited me which alone upheld me in those dark moments of depression, which every searcher into the realms of the unknown must encounter.

Then came the night of November 28th, the Great Night. After countless failures, I finally succeeded in transmitting a live guinea pig through the atmosphere and "received" it, alive and well, in the corner of my laboratory. Think of it! A twist of a switch and the living, breathing piglet slowly dissolved before my eyes and vanished along a pair of wires to my aerial, whence it was transferred as a set of waves in the ether to the receiving apparatus,—there to reincarnate into the, living organism once more, alive and breathing, unharmed by its extraordinary journey! That night I strode out into the open and walked until dawn suddenly impressed the gray world upon my oblivious exaltation, for I was King of the Universe, a Weaver of Miracles.

Then it was that my great plan began to take shape. With renewed energy I began the construction of a mammoth transmitter. At intervals I "transmitted" stray cats and dogs of every description, filling several books with notes wherein I recorded minutely the varying conditions of my subjects before transmission. Invariably their condition upon being "cohered" in the receiving tube, was excellent. In some cases, indeed, minor ailments had entirely disappeared during their short passage through the ether. What a study for the medical profession!

I had, of course, told Venice the object of my researches long ago, but had never brought her to my laboratory for reasons of discretion. One afternoon, however, I slipped her in under cover of the heavy downpour. After I had warmed her with a cup of tea, before her astonished eyes I transmitted an old she-cat which was afflicted with some sort of rheumatism or paralysis of its hind legs. When its form began to reappear in the transparent receiving tube, my darling gasped in awed wonder. She was rendered utterly speechless, however, when I switched off the current and released the animal from its crystal prison. And no wonder, for it gambolled about like a young kitten, all trace of its former malady having entirely disappeared! The impression upon Venice was all that I had hoped for, and when I at length escorted her out into the dusk, I felt her quick, awed glances flickering over me like the reverence of a shy neophyte for the high priest.

ALL was set for the final act. I literally hurled myself into the completion of my improved set. The large quantities of certain minerals required caused me an unexpected delay. This I filled with demonstrations in the presence of Marsden, whom I was encouraging as a fellow radio enthusiast,—with considerable unexpected histrionic ability on my part. It was so hard to keep my fingers off his throat! I pretended to explain to him the important factors of my great secret, and drilled him in the mechanical operation of the sets. I had divulged to him also that my greatest desire was to demonstrate my principle on a human being, and like all great scientific explorers, proposed to offer myself as the

RADIO MATES   57

subject. Venice had strenuously opposed the proposal until the demonstration on the diseased cat, and even now viewed the entire proposition with alarm. Yet I insisted that unless applied to human beings my entire work went for naught, and I finally succeeded in quieting her fears to a great extent.

At last I am ready. I have told my darling how it is impossible to transmit anything metallic by the very nature of the conflicting rays encountered. I have bemoaned the fact that, due to the softness of my teeth since boyhood, my mouth is one mass of metallic fillings and crowns, rendering it impossible for me to test the efficiency of my life's work. As I had hoped, she has volunteered herself as the subject for the great experiment, for her white teeth are as yet innocent of fillings. I have demurred and refused to listen to the idea, permitting myself to be won over only after days of earnest argument on her part. We are not to tell Marsden, for there is no doubt that his fanatical love for her would refuse to tolerate the mere suggestion.

Tonight it shall be accomplished. There is no other way, for that accursed husband of hers seems to progress in neither direction. He will be nothing but a mud-buried anchor until the end of her days, while I—I love her. What other excuse need be offered?

But to the facts. At eight o'clock that drug-soaked love pirate comes to officiate at my transmission through space. I shall meet him with a chloroformed soaked rag. Later he will awake to find himself effectively gagged, with his hands and feet firmly shackled to the wall of a dark corner of my laboratory. These shackles consist of armatures across the poles of large electro-magnets which I have embedded in the walls. At 10:30, a time switch will cut off the current, releasing the wretch, for, above all things, he must live. I debated sending a message for his chauffeur to call for him here at the designated hour. I have decided rather to trust to, mechanical certitude than lay my plan open to frustration because of some human vagary.

At nine o'clock Venice comes for the great experiment. Marsden has told her that he will remain in the city over night, at my suggestion, so that in case I fail to materialize after being "sent" he cannot be held in connection with my disappearance. She does not know that I have had my teeth extracted and have been using India rubber plates for nearly a month. By the time she has arrived, the effects of the chloroform will have entirely worn off from my would-be assistant, and I shall have had plenty of time to introduce myself properly to him and explain the evening's program which has been so carefully arranged for his benefit.

Then he will have the excruciating pleasure of watching his beloved wife dissolve into—*nothingness!* Soon thereafter he will witness the same process repeated upon myself, for I have so adapted the apparatus that I need no outside assistance other than a time-clock to actuate the mechanism! Then, at the appointed hour, the current will be shut off and the frenzied wretch will rush to the distant switch controlling the receiving apparatus. As he throws the metal bars into their split receptacles there will come a blinding flash, and behold—the apparatus will have disappeared in a puff of crystalline particles! The secret has returned whence it came!

Then will come that personally prepared hell for my mean spirited forger. As I told you, he believes that he is in possession of enough of the details of my secret to reconstruct the apparatus and duplicate my success. The added details of this letter will assure him into an idiotic confidence which will lead him on and on through partially successful attempts. I know that no matter whether you sympathize with my actions or not (and I am sure that you do not, for you never have), your sense of justice will force you to show this letter to the proper authorities in order to prevent a fatal bungling.

Meanwhile that miserable sneak will be frenzied with the

knowledge that at last, the lover he so long cheated of his loved one is now with her, alone, —where he, her lawful husband, can never follow. And we shall be together, unchanged, awaiting the day when some other enlightened mortal solves Nature's riddle, when we shall once more assume our earthly forms, unhindered by other selfish man-beasts.

Farewell,
BROMLEY CRANSTON.

NEEDLESS to say, I hurried to Eastport. But my trip was unnecessary. I found Harold Marsden in a "private sanitarium" for the hopelessly insane. There all day, and as far into the night as the opiates would permit him, he is to be found seated before a radio set, the earphones clamped to his head—listening. His statements, methodically filed away by the head of the place, corresponded wildly with the prophecies of my strange letter. Now he was listening to fragmentary messages from those two he had seen precipitated into space, he maintained. Listening.

And they had disappeared, utterly. I found the large seal ring in the inkwell on the desk. Also the slip in the hatband of the hat which had been placed in the wall safe, unlocked. The postmaster remembered the seals on the letter my cousin had mailed, and the approximate time he had received it. I felt my own reason wavering.

That is why, fantastic as is the whole affair, I cannot yet bear the sound of one of those radio loud speakers. It is when that inarticulate sound they call "static" occurs, when fragments of words and sentences seem to be painfully attempting to pierce a hostile medium,—that I picture that hunched up figure with its spidery earphones,—listening. Listening. For what?

The Man with the Strange Head
By Dr. Miles J. Breuer

Anstruther leaped upon the hold-up man; the driver said he heard Anstruther's muscles crunch savagely, as with little apparent effort he flung the man over the Ford.

Introduction

HERE is one of the most fantastic bits of scientifiction we have ever read. This is a story so strange and amazing that it will keep your interest until the end. You are not permitted to know until at the very end what it is really all about, and you will follow the proceedings with keen interest.

THE MAN WITH THE STRANGE HEAD

By Miles J. Breuer, M.D.

A MAN in a gray hat stood halfway down the corridor, smoking a cigar and apparently interested in my knocking and waiting. I rapped again on the door of Number 216 and waited some more, but all remained silent. Finally my observer approached me.

"I don't believe it will do any good," he said. "I've just been trying it. I would like to talk to someone who is connected with Anstruther. Are you?"

"Only this." I handed him a letter out of my pocket without comment, as one is apt to do with a thing that has caused one no little wonderment:

"Dear Doctor": it said succinctly. "I have been under the care of Dr. Faubourg who has recently died. I would like to have you take charge of me on a contract basis, and keep me well, instead of waiting till I get sick. I can pay you enough to make you independent, but in return for that, you will have to accept an astonishing revelation concerning me, and keep it to yourself. If this seems acceptable to you, call on me at 9 o'clock, Wednesday evening. Josiah Anstruther, Room 216, Cornhusker Hotel."

"If you have time," said the man in the gray hat, handing me back the letter, "come with me. My name is Jerry Stoner, and I make a sort of living writing for magazines. I live in 316, just above here."

"By some curious architectural accident," he continued, as we reached his room, "that ventilator there enables me to hear minutely everything that goes on in the room below. I haven't ever said anything about it during the several months that I've lived here, partly because it does not disturb me, and partly because it has begun to pique my curiosity—a writer can confess to that, can he not? The man below is quiet and orderly, but seems to work a good deal on some sort of clockwork; I can hear it whirring and clicking quite often. But listen now!"

Standing within a couple of feet of the opening which was covered with an iron grill, I could hear footsteps. They were regular, and would decrease in intensity as the person walked away from the ventilator opening below, and increase again as he approached it; were interrupted for a moment as he probably stepped on a rug; and were shorter for two or three counts, no doubt as he turned at the end of the room. This was repeated in a regular rhythm as long as I listened.

"Well?" I said.

"You perceive nothing strange about that, I suppose," said Jerry Stoner. "But if you had listened all day long to just exactly that you would begin to wonder. That is the way he was going on when I awoke this morning; I was out from 10 to 11 this forenoon. The rest of the time I have been writing steadily, with an occasional stretch at the window, and all of the time I have heard steadily what you hear now, without interruption or

THE MAN WITH THE STRANGE HEAD   63

change. It's getting on my nerves.

"I have called him on the phone, and have rung it on and off for twenty minutes; I could hear his bell through the ventilator, but he pays no attention to it. So, a while ago I tried to call on him. Do you know him?"

"I know who he is," I replied, "but do not remember ever having met him."

"If you had ever met him you would remember. He has a queer head. I made my curiosity concerning the sounds from his room an excuse to cultivate his acquaintance. The cultivation was difficult. He is courteous, but seemed afraid of me."

We agreed that there was not much that we could do about it. I gave up trying to keep my appointment, told Stoner that I was glad I had met him, and went home. The next morning at seven he had me on the telephone.

"Are you still interested?" he asked, and his voice was nervous. "That bird's been at it all night. Come and help me talk to the hotel management." I needed no urging.

I found Beesley, the hotel manager, with Stoner; he was from St. Louis, and looked French.

"He can do it if he wants to," he said, shrugging his shoulders comically; "unless you complain of it as a disturbance."

"It isn't that," said Stoner; "there must be something wrong with the man."

"Some form of insanity—" I suggested; "or a compulsion neurosis."

"That's what I'll be pretty soon," Stoner said. "He is a queer gink anyway. As far as I have been able to find out, he has no close friends. There is something about his appearance that makes me shiver; his face is so wrinkled and droopy, and yet he sails about the streets with an unusually graceful and vigorous step. Loan me your pass key; I think I'm as close a friend of his as anyone."

Beesley lent the key, but Stoner was back in a few minutes, shaking his head. Beesley was expecting that; he told us that when the hotel was built, Anstruther had the doors made of steel with special bars, at his own expense, and the windows shuttered, as though he were afraid for his life.

"His rooms would be as hard to break into as a fort," Beesley said as he left us; "and thus far we do not have sufficient reason for wrecking the hotel."

"Look here!" I said to Stoner; "it will take me a couple of hours to hunt up the stuff and string up a periscope; it's an old trick I learned as a Boy Scout."

Between us we had it up in about that time; a radio aerial mast clamped on the window sill with mirrors at the top and bottom, and a telescope at our end of it, gave us a good view of the room below us. It was a sort of living room made by throwing together two of the regular-sized hotel rooms. Anstruther was walking across it diagonally, disappearing from our field of view at the further end, and coming back again. His head hung forward on his chest with a ghastly limpness. He was a big, well-built man, with a vigorous stride. Always it was the same path. He avoided the small table in the middle each time with exactly the same sort of side step and swing. His head bumped limply as he turned near the window and started back across the room. For two hours we watched him in shivering fascination, during which he walked with the same hideous uniformity.

"That makes thirty hours of this," said Stoner. "Wouldn't you say that there was something wrong?"

We tried another consultation with the hotel manager. As a physician, I advised that something be done; that he be put in a hospital or something. I was met with another shrug.

"How will you get him? I still do not see sufficient cause for destroying the hotel company's property. It will take dynamite

THE MAN WITH THE STRANGE HEAD 65

to get at him."

He agreed, however, to a consultation with the police, and in response to our telephone call, the great, genial chief, Peter John Smith was soon sitting with us. He advised us against breaking in.

"A man has a right to walk that way if he wants to," he said. "Here's this fellow in the papers who played the piano for 49 hours, and the police didn't stop him; and in Germany they practice making public speeches for 18 hours at a stretch. And there was this Olympic dancing fad some months ago, where a couple danced for 57 hours."

"It doesn't look right to me," I said, shaking my head. "There seems to be something wrong with the man's appearance; some uncanny disease of the nervous system—Lord knows I've never heard of anything that resembles it!"

We decided to keep a constant watch. I had to spend a little time on my patients, but Stoner and the chief stayed, and agreed to call me if occasion arose. I peeped through the periscope at the walking man several times during the next twenty-four hours; and it was always exactly the same, the hanging, bumping head, the uniformity of his course, the uncanny, machine-like exactitude of his movements. I spent an hour at a time with my eye at the telescope studying his movements for some variation, but was unable to be certain of any. That afternoon I looked up my neurology texts, but found no clues. The next day at 4 o'clock in the afternoon, after not less than 55 hours of it, I was there with Stoner to see the end of it; Chief Peter John Smith was out.

As we watched, we saw that he moved more and more slowly, but with otherwise identical motions. It had the effect of the slowed motion pictures of dancers or athletes; or it seemed like some curious dream; for as we watched, the sound of the steps through the ventilator also slowed and weakened. Then we saw him sway a little, and totter, as though his balance were imperfect. He swayed a few times and fell sidewise on the floor; we could see one leg in the field of our periscope moving slowly with the same movements as in walking, a slow, dizzy sort of motion. In five more minutes he was quite still.

The Chief was up in a few moments in response to our telephone call.

"Now we've got to break in," he said. Beesley shrugged his shoulders and said nothing. Stoner came to the rescue of the hotel property.

"A small man could go down this ventilator. This grill can be unscrewed, and the lower one can be knocked out with a hammer; it is cast-iron."

Beesley was gone like a flash, and soon returned with one of his window-washers, who was small and wiry, and also a rope and hammer. We took off the grill and held the rope as the man crawled in. He shouted to us as he hit the bottom. The air drew strongly downwards, but the blows of his hammer on the grill came up to us. We hurried down stairs. Not a sound came through the door of 216, and we waited for some minutes. Then there was a rattle of bars and the door opened, and a gust of cold wind struck us, with a putrid odor that made us gulp. The man had evidently run to open a window before coming to the door.

Anstruther lay on his side, with one leg straight and the other extended forward as in a stride; his face was livid, sunken, hideous. Stoner gave him a glance, and then scouted around the room—looking for the machinery he had been hearing, but finding none. The chief and I also went over the rooms, but they were just conventional rooms, rather colorless and lacking in personality. The chief called an undertaker and also the coroner, and arranged for a post-

THE MAN WITH THE STRANGE HEAD 67

mortem examination. I received permission to notify a number of professional colleagues; I wanted some of them to share in the investigation of this unusual case with me. As I was leaving, I could not help noting the astonished gasps of the undertaker's assistants as they lifted the body; but they were apparently too well trained to say anything.

That evening, a dozen physicians gathered around the figure covered with a white sheet on the table in the center of the undertaker's work room. Stoner was there; a writer may be anywhere he chooses. The coroner was preparing to draw back the sheet.

"The usual medical history is lacking in this case," he said. "Perhaps an account by Dr. B. or his author friend, of the curious circumstances connected with the death of this man, may take its place."

"I can tell a good deal," said Stoner; "and I think it will bear directly on what you find when you open him up, even though it is not technical medical stuff. Do you care to hear it?"

"Tell it! Go on! Let's have it!"

"I have lived above him in the hotel for several months," Stoner began. "He struck me as a curious person, and as I do some writing, all mankind is my legitimate field for study. I tried to find out all I could about him.

"He has an office in the Little Building, and did a rather curious business. He dealt in vases and statuary, book-ends and chimes, and things you put around in rooms to make them look artistic. He had men out buying the stuff, and others selling it, all by personal contact and on a very exclusive basis. He kept the stock in a warehouse near the Rock Island tracks where they pass the Ball Park; I do not believe that he ever saw any of it. He just sat in the office and signed papers, and the other fellows made the money; and apparently they made a lot of it, for he has swung some big financial deals in this town.

"I often met him in the lobby or the elevator. He was a big, vigorous man and walked with an unusually graceful step and an appearance of strength and vitality. His eyes seemed to light up with recognition when he saw me, but in my company he was always formal and reserved. For such a vigorous-looking man, his voice was singularly cracked and feeble, and his head gave an impression of being rather small for him, and his face old and wrinkled.

"He seemed fairly well known about the city. At the Eastridge Club they told me that he plays golf occasionally and excellently, and is a graceful dancer, though somehow not a popular partner. He was seen frequently at the Y.M.C.A. bowling alleys and played with an uncanny skill. Men loved to see him bowl for his cleverness with the balls, but wished he were not so formally courteous, and did not wear such an expression of complete happiness over his victories. Bridley, manager of Rudge & Guenzel's book department, was the oldest friend of his that I could find, and he gave me some interesting information. They went to school together, and Anstruther was poor in health as well as in finances. Twenty-five years ago, during the hungry and miserable years after his graduation from the University, Bridley remembered him as saying:

'My brain needs a body to work with. If I had physical strength, I could do anything. If I find a fellow who can give it to me, I'll make him rich!'

"Bridley also remembers that he was sensitive because girls did not like his debilitated physique. He seems to have found health later, though I can find no one who remembers how or when. About ten years ago he came back from Europe where he had been for several years, in Paris, Bridley thinks; and for several years after this, a Frenchman lived

THE MAN WITH THE STRANGE HEAD   69

with him. The city directory of that time has him living in the big stone house at 13th and 'G' streets. I went up there to look around, and found it a double house, Dr. Faubourg having occupied the other half. The present caretaker has been there ever since Anstruther lived in the house, and she says that his French companion must have been some sort of an engineer, and that the two must have been working on an invention, from the sounds she heard and the materials they had about. Some three or four years ago the Frenchman and the machinery vanished, and Anstruther moved to the Cornhusker Hotel. Also at about this time, Dr. Faubourg retired from the practice of medicine. He must have been about 50 years old, and too healthy and vigorous to be retiring on account of old age or ill health.

"Apparently Anstruther never married. His private life was quite obscure, but he appeared much in public. He was always very courtly and polite to the ladies. Outside his business he took a great interest in Y.M.C.A. and Boy Scout camps, in the National Guard, and in fact in everything that stood for an outdoor, physical life, and promoted health. In spite of his oddity he was quite a hero with the small boys, especially since the time of his radium hold-up. This is intimately connected with the story of his radium speculation that caused such a sensation in financial circles a couple of years ago.

"About that time, the announcement appeared of the discovery of new uses for radium; a way had been found to accelerate its splitting and to derive power from it. Its price went up, and it promised to become a scarce article on the market. Anstruther had never been known to speculate, nor to tamper with sensational things like oil and helium; but on this occasion he seemed to go into a panic. He cashed in on a lot of securities and caused a small panic in the city, as he was quite wealthy and had especially large amounts of money in the building-loan business. The newspapers told of how he had bought a hundred thousand dollars worth of radium, which was to be delivered right here in Lincoln—a curious method of speculating, the editors volunteered.

"It arrived by express one day, and Anstruther rode the express wagon with the driver to the station. I found the driver and he told the story of the hold-up at 8th and 'P' streets at eleven o'clock at night. A Ford car drove up beside them, from which a man pointed a pistol at them and ordered them to stop. The driver stopped.

'Come across with the radium!' shouted the big black bulk in the Ford, climbing upon the express wagon. Anstruther's fist shot out like a flash of lightning and struck the arm holding the pistol; and the driver states that he heard the pistol crash through the window on the second floor of the Lincoln Hotel. Anstruther pushed the express driver, who was in his way, backwards over the seat among the packages and leaped upon the hold-up man; the driver said he heard Anstruther's muscles crunch savagely, as with little apparent effort he flung the man over the Ford; he fell with a thud on the asphalt and stayed there. Anstruther then launched a kick at the man at the wheel of the Ford, who crumpled up and fell out of the opposite side of the car.

"The police found the pistol inside a room on the second floor of the Lincoln Hotel. The steering post of the Ford car was torn from its fastenings. Both of the hold-up men had ribs and collar-bones broken, and the gunman's forearm was bent double in the middle with both bones broken. These two men agreed later with the express driver that Anstruther's attack, for suddenness, swiftness, and terrific strength was beyond anything they had dreamed possible; he was like a thunderbolt; like some furious demon. When the two men were huddled in black heaps on the pavement,

THE MAN WITH THE STRANGE HEAD 71

Anstruther said to the driver, quite impersonally: "Drive to the police station. Come on! Wake up! I've got to get this stuff locked up!'

"One of the hold-up men had lost all his money and the home he was building when Anstruther had foreclosed a loan in his desperate scramble for radium. He was a Greek named Poulos, and has been in prison for two years; just last week he was released—"

Chief Peter John Smith interrupted.

"I've been putting two and two together, and I can shed a little light on this problem. Three days ago, the day before I was called to watch ' Anstruther pacing his room, we picked up this man Poulos in. the alleyway between Rudge & Guenzel's and Miller & Paine's. He was unconscious, and must have received a terrible licking at somebody's hands; his face was almost unrecognizable; several ribs and several fingers on his right hand were broken. He clutched a pistol fitted with a silencer, and we found that two shots had been fired from it. Here he is—"

A limp, bandaged, plastered man was pushed in between two policemen. He was sullen and apathetic, until he caught sight of Anstruther's face from which the chief had drawn a corner of the sheet. Terror and joy seemed to mingle in his face and in his voice. He raised his bandaged hand with an ineffectual gesture, and started off on some Greek religious expression, and then turned dazedly to us, speaking painfully through his swollen face.

"Glad he dead. I try to kill him. Shoot him two time. No kill. So close—" indicating the distance of a foot from his chest; "then he lick me. He is not man. He is devil. I not kill him, but I glad he dead!"

The Chief hurried him out, and came in with a small, dapper man with a black chin whisker. He apologized to the coroner.

"This is not a frame-up. I am just following out a hunch that I got a few minutes ago while Stoner was talking. This is Mr. Fournier. I found his address in Anstruther's room, and dug him up. I think he will be more important to you doctors than he will in a court. Tell 'em what you told me!"

While the little Frenchman talked, the undertaker's assistant jerked off the sheet. The undertaker's work had had its effect in getting rid of the frightful odor, and in making Anstruther's face presentable. The body, however, looked for all the world as though it were alive, plump, powerful, pink. In the chest, over the heart, were two bullet holes, not bloody, but clean-cut and black. The Frenchman turned to the body and worked on it with a little screw-driver as he talked.

"Mr. Anstruther came to me ten years ago, when I was a poor mechanic. He had heard of my automatic chess-player, and my famous animated show-window models; and he offered me time and money to find him a mechanical relief for his infirmity. I was an assistant at a Paris laboratory, where they had just learned to split radium and get a hundred horse-power from a pinch of powder. Anstruther was weak and thin, but ambitious."

The Frenchman lifted off two plates from the chest and abdomen of the body, and the flanks swung outward as though on hinges. He removed a number of packages that seemed to fit carefully within, and which were on the ends of cables and chains.

"Now—" he said to the assistants, who held the feet. He put his hands into the chest cavity, and as the assistants pulled the feet away, he lifted out of the shell a small, wrinkled emaciated body; the body of an old man, which now looked quite in keeping with the well-known Anstruther head. Its chest was covered with dried blood, and there were two bullet

THE MAN WITH THE STRANGE HEAD   73

holes over the heart. The undertaker's assistants carried it away while we crowded around to inspect the mechanism within the arms and legs of the pink and live-looking shell, headless, gaping at the chest and abdomen, but uncannily like a healthy, powerful man.

The PLAGUE of the LIVING DEAD
By A. Hyatt Verrill

Racing as fast as their old legs could carry them, the two fellows came dashing toward him, terror on their faces, panting and breathless, while at their heels came a mob of men and women, screaming, shouting incomprehensible words, waving their arms threateningly, and obviously hostile.

Introduction

If you should read this story by our well-known author with incredulity and feel inclined to lay it aside with the remark "impossible," please be apprised of the following facts:

At the Rockefeller Institute, in New York City, the famous surgeon, Dr. Alexis Carrel. for the last fifteen years, has retained a fragment of a chicken's heart in a special medium, in which it has not only stayed alive and pulsating but has continued growing also, so that it only needs to be trimmed every little while, to he kept alive.

Here, then, is immortality in the laboratory. Mr. Verrill's story, therefore, is not as fanciful as it might seem.

THE PLAGUE OF THE LIVING DEAD

By A. Hyatt Verrill

CHAPTER I

THE astounding occurrences which took place upon the island of Abilone many years ago, and which culminated in the most dramatic and most remarkable event in the history of the world, have never been made public. Even the vague rumours of what happened in the island republic were regarded as fiction or as the work of imagination, for the truth has been most zealously and carefully concealed. Even the press of the island co-operated with the officials in their desire to maintain absolute secrecy regarding what was taking place, and instead of making capital of the affair, the papers merely announced as the government had requested them to do that an unknown, contagious disease had broken out upon the island

and that a most rigid quarantine was being enforced.

But even if the incredible news had been blazoned to the world, I doubt if the public would have believed it. At any rate, now that it is for ever a thing of the past, there is no reason why the story should not be told in all its details.

When the world-famous biologist, Dr. Gordon Farnham, announced that he had discovered the secret of prolonging life indefinitely, the world reacted to the news in various ways. Many persons openly scoffed and declared that Dr. Farnham was either in his dotage or else had been misquoted. Others, familiar with the doctor's attainments and his reputation for conservative statements, expressed their belief that, incredible as it might seem, it must be true; while the majority were inclined to treat the matter as a joke. This was the attitude of nearly all the daily papers; the Sunday supplements had elaborately illustrated the entirely unfounded and ridiculous stories purporting to voice the doctor's views and statements on the subject.

Only one paper, the reliable, conservative, and somewhat out of date *Examiner* saw fit to print the biologist's announcement verbatim and without comment. Upon the vaudeville stage, and over the radio, jokes based on Dr. Farnham's alleged discovery were all the rage; a popular song in which immortality and the scientist were the leading themes was heard on every side and at length. In sheer desperation, Dr. Farnham was forced to make public a detailed statement of his discovery. In this, he clearly pointed out that he had not claimed to have learned the secret of prolonging human life indefinitely, for, in order to prove that he had done so it would be necessary to keep a human being alive for several centuries, and even then the treatment might merely have prolonged life for a certain period and not for ever. His experiments, he stated, had hitherto been confined to the lower animals and by his treatment of them be had been able to extend their normal span of life four to eight times. In other words, if the treatment worked equally well with human beings, a man would live for five to eight hundred years quite long enough to fulfill most persons' ideas of immortality. Certain persons, whose names he declined to reveal, had taken his treatment, the doctor stated, but of course its effect had not yet had time to prove his claims. He added that the treatment was harmless, that a chemical preparation injected into the system figured in it, and that he was willing to treat a limited number of persons if they wished to experiment and test the efficacy of his discovery. For Dr. Farnham, who was sparing of words both in conversation and writing, and who rarely gave out anything for publication, this statement was remarkable and, so his champions claimed, proved that he was sure of his stand. But such is the psychology of the average person, that the biologist's perfectly logical and straightforward explanation, instead of convincing the public or the press, served merely to bring an even greater storm of ridicule upon his head.

Curious crowds gathered about his laboratory. Wherever he went he was stared at, laughed at and watched. At every turn press photographers snapped cameras at him. Hardly a day passed without some new and humorous or sarcastic article appearing in the press and his pictures appeared along with those of crooks, murderers, society divorcees and prize-fighters in the illustrated tabloid newspapers. To a man of Dr. Farnham's retiring habits, self-consciousness and modesty, all this was torture, and finally, unable to endure his unwelcome publicity longer, he packed up his belongings and slipped quietly and secretly away from the metropolis, confiding the secret of his destination to only a few of his most intimate scientific friends. For a space his disappearance created something of a stir, and further sensational news for press and public; but in a short time, he and his alleged discovery were forgotten.

Doctor Farnham, however, had no intention of abandoning

his researches and experiments and, together with his supposedly immortal menagerie, as well as three aged derelicts who had offered themselves for treatment, and who had agreed to remain with the scientist indefinitely at larger salaries than they had ever received before be moved to Abilone Island. Here he was wholly unknown, and scarcely an inhabitant had ever heard of him or his work. He purchased a large abandoned sugar estate and here, he thought, he could carry on his work unnoticed and unmolested. But he did not take into consideration his three human experiments.

These worthies, finding that their treatment was having its effects and that they were remaining, as it were, steadfast in years and vigour, and quite convinced that they would continue to live on for ever, could not resist boasting of the fact to those whom they met. The white residents listened and laughed, deeming the fellows a little mad, while the coloured population regarded the doctor's patients with superstitious awe, and were convinced that Doctor Farnham was a most powerful and greatly to be feared "Obeah man".

The fact that his secret and his reasons for being on the island had leaked out, did not, however, interfere with Doctor Farnham's work as be had dreaded. The intelligent folk, who were in the minority, of course, jokingly referred to what they had heard when they met the scientist, but never asked him seriously if there was any truth in the story, while the majority avoided him as they would Satan himself and gave his grounds a wide berth, for which he was thankful. But, on the other hand, he had no opportunities to try out his immortality treatment on human beings, and hence was obliged to carry on his experiments with the lower animals.

Quite early in the course of his experiments, he had discovered that while his treatment halted the ravages of time on vertebrates, and the creatures or human beings treated gave every promise of living on indefinitely, yet it did not restore them to youth. In other words, a subject treated with his serum remained in the same condition, physically and mentally, as existed when the treatment was administered, although, to a certain extent, there was an increase in the development of muscles, an increased flexibility of joints, a softening of hardened arteries and a greater activity, due perhaps, to the fact that the vital organs were not being worked to their limit to stave off advancing age.

Thus the oldest in point of years of the doctor's human experiments was to all external appearances over ninety (his exact age was ninety-three when he had taken the treatment) or precisely as he had appeared when, two years previously, he had submitted his ancient frame to the doctor's injections. His gums were toothless, his scanty hair was snow white, his face was as seamed and gnarled as a walnut, and he was bent, stoop-shouldered and scrawny-necked. But he had thrown aside his glasses, he could see as well as any man, his hearing was acute, and he was as lively as a cricket and physically stronger than he had been for years, and he ate like a sailor. For all he or the scientist could see he would go on in this state until the crack of doom, barring accidents, for each day his blood pressure, his temperature, his pulse and his respiration were carefully noted, microscopic examinations were made of his blood, and so far, not the least sign of any alteration in his condition, and not the least indication of any increase in age, had been detected.

CHAPTER II

BUT Doctor Farnham was not satisfied with this. If his discovery was to be of real value to the human race, he would have to learn how to restore at least a little of lost youth, as well as to check age; and day and night he worked trying to discover how to accomplish the impossible.

Countless rabbits, guinea pigs, dogs, monkeys and other creatures were treated, innumerable formulae were worked out and tested, endless and involved experiments were made, and volumes of closely written and methodically tabulated observations filled the shelves of Doctor Farnham's library.

But still, he seemed as far from the desired result as ever. He was not, in his own estimation, trying to perform a miracle, nor was he striving to bring about the impossible. The human system, or that of any creature, was, he argued, merely a machine, a machine which, through marvellously perfected and most economical means, utilized fuel in the form of food to produce heat, power, and motion, and which in addition constantly replaced the worn parts of its own mechanism. The presence of a soul or spirit, as anything divine or incomprehensible, the biologist would not admit, although he willingly granted that life, which actuated the machine, was something which no man could explain or could create. But, he argued, this did not necessarily mean that, sooner or later, the secret of life might not be discovered. Indeed, he affirmed, it was the machine of the body which produced life, rather than life which actuated the machine. And, following this line of reasoning, he would hold that the spirit or soul, or as he preferred to call it, "the actuative intelligence", was the ultimate product, the goal so to speak, of the entire machinery of the organic body.

"The unborn embryo," he once said, "is capable of independent motion, but not of independent thought. It does not breathe, it does not produce sounds, it neither sleeps nor wakes, and it does not obtain nourishment by eating. Neither does it pass excrement. In other words, it is a completed machine as yet inoperative by its own power, a mechanism like an engine with banked fires, ready to be set in motion and to produce results when the steam is turned on. This moment is the time of birth. With the first breath, the machinery starts in motion; cries issue from the vocal organs; food is demanded, waste matter is thrown off and steadily, ceaselessly, the machine continues gradually forming and building up the intelligence until it has reached its highest state, whereupon, the machine, having accomplished its purpose, begins to slow down, to let its worn out parts remain worn, until at last, it is clogged, erratic and finally fails to function."

So having decided, to his entire satisfaction, that any living creature was in its basic principles a machine, Doctor Farnham felt that in order to keep the machine running for ever it was only necessary to provide for the replacement of worn out units and to provide an inducement for the "actuative intelligence" to keep the mechanism going after it had fulfilled its original purpose. And to all intents and purposes, the scientist had accomplished this. Animals which he had treated, and which under his care and observation had lived on for several times their normal span of life, at no time showed any signs of hardening of the blood vessels, or the accumulation of lime in the system, or of glandular deterioration.

Moreover, the doctor had discovered that creatures which had been treated could propagate their race, although normally they would have been sterile through age, and he grew wildly excited over this, for, if his conclusions were correct, the young of these supposedly immortal animals would inherit immortality. But here Doctor Farnham ran against a seemingly insurmountable obstacle to propagating a race of immortals. A litter of young rabbits remained, for month after month, the same helpless, blind, naked, embryonic things they had been at birth. No doubt they would have continued in that state for ever had not the mother, perhaps growing impatient or disgusted with her offspring, devoured the entire litter. However, it proved that the power of inheriting the results of the treatment existed, and Doctor Farnham felt sure that in time he could work out some scheme by which the young would develop to any desired stage of life before the cessation of age took effect, and they would then remain indefinitely in that state. Herein, he felt assured, lay the solution to the restoration of youth. Not that he could restore old age to youth, but that, provided he discovered the means, all future generations would if they desired attain vigorous manhood or womanhood and would then cease to increase in age and would forever remain at the very pinnacle of mental and physical power. It was while conducting his researches in this direction that Doctor Farnham accidentally made a most amazing discovery which quite altered his plans.

He had been working on an entirely new combination of the constituents of his original product, and in order to test its penetrative peculiarities, he injected a little of the fluid into a chloroformed guinea pig, so as to determine the progress of the material through the various organs. To his utmost astonishment the supposedly dead animal at once began to move, and, before the astounded doctor's eye, was soon running about as lively as ever. Doctor Farnham was speechless. The little creature had been supposedly dead for hours its body had even been stiff, and yet here it was obviously very much alive.

Could it be that the guinea pig had merely been in a state of anaesthesia? Or was it possible and Doctor Farnham trembled with excitement at the idea that his serum had actually restored life to the animal?

Scarcely daring to hope that this was the case, the scientist quickly secured a rabbit from his stock, and placing it under a bell glass administered enough ether to have killed several men. Then, forcing himself to be patient, he waited until the rabbit's body was cold and *rigor mortis* had set in. Even then the doctor was not satisfied. He examined the rabbit's eyes. Listened with a most delicate stethoscope for possible heart beats, and even opened a vein in the animal's leg. There could be no question, the rabbit was dead. Then, with nervous but steady fingers, the doctor inserted the point of his hypodermic needle in the rabbit's neck and injected a small quantity of the new liquid. Almost immediately the rabbit's legs twitched, its eyes opened, and as the doctor gazed incredulously, the creature rose to its feet and hopped off.

CHAPTER III

HERE *was* a discovery! The serum with its new constituents would not only check the inroads of age but it would restore life!

But Doctor Farnham was a hard-headed scientist and not a man given to imaginative romancing, and he fully realized that there must be limitations to his discovery. It could not, he felt sure, restore life to a creature which had met a violent death through injury to a vital organ, nor to a creature which bad died from some organic disease. In coming to this conclusion he was unconsciously comparing living things with machinery, as usual. "One might stop the pendulum of a clock," he wrote, "and the mechanism will cease to function until the pendulum is again put in motion; but if the clock stops through loss of a wheel or broken spring or cogs, it cannot be made to function again unless the broken parts are replaced or repaired."

But would his treatment revive animals which had succumbed to death by other means than anaesthetics? That was a most important matter to settle, and Doctor Farnham immediately proceeded to settle it. For his first experiment, a kitten was sacrificed to the cause of science, and was humanely and very thoroughly drowned. In order that his experiment might be the more conclusive, the biologist decided to delay his attempted resurrection until all possibility of ordinary means of resuscitation were at an end; he set four hours as the time which he would permit to elapse before he injected his serum in the defunct cat. In the meantime, he prepared for another test. He had mentally checked off the various causes of premature death, apart from those by organic disease and violence, and found that drowning, freezing, gas-poisoning, and poisoning by non-irritant poisons led the list; after these came fright, shock, and various other rare causes.

It might be difficult to provide subjects killed by all of these means, but he could test the efficacy of his treatment on the more important ones, so he proceeded to prepare subjects by freezing, gassing, and poisoning a number of animals. By the time these corpses had been made ready, the dead cat had reposed upon his laboratory table for the allotted four hours, and, with pulse quickened in a wholly unscientific manner, Doctor Farnham forced a dose of his compound into the kitten's neck. In exactly fifty-eight seconds by the doctor's watch, the cat's muscles twitched, its lungs began to breathe, its heart commenced to resume its interrupted functions, and at the expiration of two minutes and eighteen seconds, the kitten was sitting up and licking its damp and bedraggled fur. The experiments with the frozen, gassed and poisoned subjects were equally successful, and Doctor Farnham was thoroughly convinced that, barring injuries, deterioration of vital organs, or excessive loss of blood, any dead animal could be brought back to life by his process. Naturally, he was most anxious to test the marvelous compound on human beings, and he at once hurried to the coroner's office with a request that he might try a new form of resuscitation on the next person drowned or poisoned on the island. Then he visited the hospital in the hopes of finding some unfortunate who had expired through some cause which had not wrought injury to the vital organs, but was again disappointed. However, the authorities promised to notify him if such a case as he desired turned up; he returned to his laboratory to carry on more extensive tests.

THE PLAGUE OF THE LIVING DEAD

Among other matters, he wished to determine how long a creature could remain dead and yet be revived, and, with this end in view, he began a wholesale slaughter of his menagerie intending to label each body and carry on a progressive series of experiments, each animal being allowed to remain dead a certain number of hours, until his injections failed to restore life, thus enabling him to determine the exact limits of its efficacy.

It so happened that, in the excitement and interest of his discovery, he had neglected to place the resurrected kitten in a cage; during his absence from the laboratory, his servant the youngest of the three human immortals found the creature loose and, thinking it had escaped from its pen, replaced it with the other cats. And later, when the doctor selected half a dozen healthy-looking cats as martyrs to science, he inadvertently included the animal which, a few hours previously, he had brought back from death.

Together with its fellow felines, the resurrected kitten was placed in an airtight chamber into which lethal gas was forced, and wherein the cats were allowed to remain for nearly an hour. Feeling certain the deadly fumes had most thoroughly done their work, the doctor, wearing a gasmask, opened the chamber preparatory to removing the bodies of the deceased creatures. Imagine his amazement when, as the cover was removed, a bristling, meowing cat sprang from within and, racing across the room, leaped upon a table, spitting and snarling and most obviously very much alive.

"Extraordinary! Most extraordinary!" exclaimed the scientist, as he cautiously peered into the chamber and saw the other cats stretched lifeless within. "A most remarkable example of natural immunity to the effects of hydrocyanic acid gas. I must make a note of the fact."

After considerable difficulty in mollifying the irate creature. Doctor Farnham examined her most carefully. In doing so he noticed a small wound upon the cat's neck and uttered a surprised ejaculation. This was the very cat he had resuscitated! The mark upon its neck was where he had inserted his hypodermic needle, and across his brain flashed a wild, impossible thought. The cat was immortal! Not only would it resist death by age indefinitely, but it could not be killed!

But the next instant, the scientist's common sense came to his rescue. "Of course," he reasoned, "that is impossible; absolutely preposterous."

But, after all, he thought, was it any more preposterous than bringing dead creatures back to life? There might be some unknown effect of his treatment which rendered creatures subjected to it immune to certain poisons. But if so, then other means would destroy the cat's life, and, anxious to prove this theory, he secured the cat and proceeded to drown her the second time. Having left her immersed in water for a full hour, Doctor Farnham lifted the wire basket containing the supposedly defunct kitten from the tank, and the next second leaped back as if he had been struck. Within the close-meshed container the cat was scratching, yowling, fighting like a fury to escape, and evidently very much alive and most highly indignant at having been immersed in the cold water.

CHAPTER IV

UNABLE to believe his senses, Doctor Farnham sank into a chair and mopped his forehead while the cat, having at last freed itself, dashed like a mad thing about the room and finally sought refuge under a radiator.

Presently, however, the doctor recovered his accustomed self-possession, and considered the seeming miracle more calmly. After all, he thought, the cat had been restored to life after drowning, so why was it not possible that having once been resuscitated, it could not thereafter be drowned, even though subject to death through other means? But then again, the creature had also survived the gas. Here was something that must be investigated. He would try freezing the cat he chuckled to himself as he thought of the time-honoured saying that cats had nine lives and if the beast still refused to succumb he would test every other means. But the cat had other ideas on the subject and, having had quite enough of the doctor's experiments, it eluded the scientist's grasp, and with arched back and fluffed-out tail sprang through a partly-opened window and vanished for ever in the shrubbery of the open spaces.

Doctor Farnham sighed. Here was a most valuable and interesting experiment lost, but he soon consoled himself. He recollected that he still had a rabbit and a guinea pig which had also been revived from an apparently dead state, and he could carry out his tests on these.

And the doctor became more and more astounded as his tests proceeded. The two creatures were frozen as stiff as boards, but no sooner had they thawed out than they were as healthy and lively as before; they were gassed, chloroformed, poisoned, and electrocuted but all to no purpose. They could not be put to sleep by anaesthetics and they could not be killed. At last the scientist was forced to believe that his treatment literally rendered living things immortal.

And when at last he was convinced, and had assured himself that he was still sane, he threw himself into a chair and roared with laughter.

What would the papers back in the States say to this? Not only could human beings live on for ever, so far as age was concerned, but they would be immune from the most common causes of accidental death. Persons going on sea voyages would have no dread of disaster for they could not be drowned. Electricians need have no fear of live wires or third rails for they could not be killed by any current. Arctic explorers could be frozen solid but would revive when thawed out. And half the terrors of war, the deadly gases on which such vast sums had been spent and to which so many years of research had been devoted, now meant nothing, for an army treated with the marvelous compound would be immune to the effects of the most fatal gases.

The doctor's head fairly whirled with the ideas that crowded his brain, but still he was not entirely satisfied. He had proved his amazing discovery by testing it on the lower animals, but was he positive that it would perform the same miracles on human beings? He thought of trying it on his three companions, but hesitated. Supposing he drowned, poisoned, or gassed one of the three old men and the fellow failed to revive? Would he not be guilty of murder in the eyes of the law, even if the subject had willingly submitted to the test? And dared he actually take the risk? Doctor Farnham shook his head as he thought on this. No, he admitted to himself, he would not dare risk it. Many times, he knew, experiments which were perfectly successful with the lower animals, were anything but successful when applied to men. And then again, if he could not test his discovery on human beings, how would he ever be sure mat it would or would not render mankind immortal?

Possibly, he decided, by dissecting one of his immortal creatures, he might discover something which would throw light on the matter. And then a puzzled, troubled frown wrinkled his forehead. He was thoroughly antagonistic to vivisection; and yet, bow could be dissect one of his creatures without practising vivisection? Of course, he thought, he could kill the rabbit by a blow on the back of the bead, by piercing the brain painlessly with a lancet or by decapitating it. But in that case he might be destroying the very thing which he was in search of.

Still, that was the only way: not even in the interests of science, nor to set his mind at rest, would he willingly torture

THE PLAGUE OF THE LIVING DEAD 89

any living thing. But he could kill the rabbit by injuring its brain and kill the guinea pig by an equally painless death by way of its heart, and thus be reasonably sure of having both the nervous and circulatory systems uninjured.

So, rather regretfully, he picked up the unsuspecting rabbit, and with the utmost care and precision, he thrust a slender-bladed scalpel into the base of the creature's brain.

The next instant his instrument fell from his hand, he felt faint and weak, and he sat staring with gaping jaw and unbelieving eyes. Instead of becoming instantly limp in death at the thrust, the rabbit was quite unconcernedly nibbling a bit of carrot, and appeared as much alive and as healthy as before!

Doctor Farnham now felt convinced that he had gone mad. The excitement, the nerve strain, his long hours of experimenting had caused him to have hallucinations, for he well knew that no matter how remarkable his discovery had actually proved, no warm-blooded vertebrate could survive a scalpel thrust in its brain.

CHAPTER V

HE shook himself, rubbed his eyes, pinched himself. He looked about his laboratory, gazed at the palm trees and shrubbery of the grounds about his dwelling, perused a few pages of a book, and put himself to a dozen tests. In every respect he seemed in his normal senses.

Something, he reasoned, must have gone wrong. By some error he had failed to reach a vital spot, and forcing himself to calmness, and steadying his nerves by a tremendous effort, he again picked up his lancet, and holding the rabbit's head immovable, he ran the full length of the razor-edged blade into the animal's brain.

And then he almost screamed and, limp and faint, slumped into his chair, while the rabbit, shaking its head and wiggling its ears as if a bit uncomfortable, hopped from the table and began sniffing about for bits of carrot which had dropped to the floor!

For fully half an hour the biologist remained, inert, entirely overcome, his nerves shaken, his brain in a whirl. How could such a thing be possible?

At last, slowly, almost fearfully, Doctor Farnham rose, and with determination written on his features, he secured the guinea pig and, by an almost superhuman exercise of will power, he stretched the animal upon a table and deliberately ran a scalpel through its heart. But, apart from a small amount of blood which issued from the wound, the creature appeared absolutely uninjured. Indeed it did not seem to suffer any pain and made no effort to escape when released.

For the first time in his life. Doctor Farnham swooned.

When, nearly an hour later, his assistant, frightened half out of his wits, managed to revive the scientist, darkness had fallen, and, trembling and utterly unnerved. Doctor Farnham staggered from his laboratory, scarcely daring to look about and wondering if it had all been some nightmare or the hallucination of his fainting fit.

It was a long time before he recovered his usual calm, and having forced himself to view the two animals which, by all accepted theories and scientific facts, should be stiff in death, enjoying excellent health, and having braced himself by a hearty meal and some fifty-year-old rum, the doctor set himself to face incontrovertible facts and to determine the reasons therefore.

From the time he had entered his senior year at college, he had devoted himself to the study of biology. No other biologist living had won such an enviable reputation as a master of the science. No other biologist had made more important or world-famous discoveries. No other scientist could boast of such a voluminous and complete library or a more valuable and perfect collection of instruments, apparatus, and paraphernalia for studying in his chosen field, for Doctor Farnham was fortunate

THE PLAGUE OF THE LIVING DEAD

in being immensely wealthy, and he devoted all his income to his science. Although thoroughly revolutionary and unconventional in his theories, his experiments and his beliefs, yet he was willing to admit that no man can know everything, and that the most exact and careful persons will at times make mistakes. Hence, even if he did not entirely agree with them, he consulted all available works of other biologists, and, very often, he would find much of value in their monographs, and reports. Also, on more than one occasion, he had seized upon some statement or apparently unimportant data which had been passed by with cursory mention, and built meaningfully upon it, giving full credit to his source.

So now, faced with an impossible fact. Doctor Farnham proceeded to get at basic facts. To describe in detail all his deductions, to analyse his reasoning, or to mention the authoritative confirmations in a dozen languages, which led to his final conclusions would be impossible. But, as transcribed in his notes, which he jotted down as he worked, they were as follows:

"No one can exactly define life and death. What is fatal to one form of animal life may be innocuous to other forms. A worm or an amoeba, as well as many invertebrates, may be subdivided, cut into several pieces, and each fragment will continue to survive and will suffer no inconvenience. Moreover, under certain conditions, two or more of these fragments may join and heal together in their original form. Some vertebrates, such as lizards and turtles, may survive injuries which would destroy life in other creatures, but which, in their cases, produce no ill effects. Cases are numerous in which such organs as hearts or even brains have been removed from tortoises, and yet the creatures survived and were able to move about and eat for considerable periods. We speak of vital organs, but can we say which organs *are* vital? An accidental injury to the brain, heart, or lungs may cause death, and yet even more serious injuries may be inflicted by surgeons and the patient will survive. A human nose, ear or even a finger, if severed, may be made to grow to the stump, but a limb once severed cannot be rejoined. But why not? Why should it be possible to graft certain organs or portions of anatomy and not others? One man may be shot through the brain or heart and may be instantly killed, while another may have several bullets fired through his brain or may be shot or stabbed through the heart and may live in perfect health for years thereafter. Even so-called vital organs may be removed by surgery without visibly affecting the patient's health, whereas an injury to a non-essential organ may produce death in another. It is not uncommon for persons to die of hemorrhage from a pin prick or a superficial abrasion of the skin, while it is equally common for persons to survive the loss of a limb by an accident or the severing of an artery.

"Life is customarily defined as a condition wherein the various organs are functioning, when the heart beats and the respiratory system is in operation. Conversely, a person or other animal is ordinarily considered dead when the organs cease to function and heart and lung actions cease. But, in innumerable cases of suspended animation, all organs cease functioning and there are no audible or visible traces of heart or lung action. In cases of immersion or drowning, the same conditions exist, the blood ceases to flow through arteries and veins, and the victim, if left to himself, will never revive. But by artificial respiration and other means he may be resuscitated. Is the drowned person alive or dead?

"To sum up: It is impossible to define life or death in exact or scientific terms. It is impossible to state definitely when death takes place until decomposition sets in. It is impossible to say what causes life or produces death. No one has ever yet determined the uses or functions of many glands, and no one can explain the precise action of stimulants, narcotics, sedatives or anaesthetics.

"Is it not possible or even probable that, under certain conditions, life may continue uninterrupted despite causes which

THE PLAGUE OF THE LIVING DEAD

ordinarily would result in death? Is it unreasonable to suppose that certain chemical reactions may be produced which will so act upon the vital organs and tissues that they resist all attempts to destroy their functions?

"My contention is that such things are possible. That, scientifically speaking, there is no more reason for an animal surviving the removal of its kidney, stomach, spleen or ductless glands, or injuries to these organs, than for surviving similar injuries to or the removal of the heart, brains or lungs."

Here the doctor dropped his pen, pushed aside his pad and books, and became buried in thought. He had, after all, learned nothing he did not already know. He had come back to his starting point. In fact, he had already answered his own queries and had proved his contention. But his studies and researches had started new trains of thought. Never before had he been so close to the mystery of life and death. Never before had it occurred to him that life might be a thing entirely apart from the mere physical organism the machine, as he called it. An if his theories were correct, if his deductions were sound, could he not then restore life to a creature killed by violence or whose organs were injured or diseased? And where might his discovery not lead? If a creature could be so treated that it could resist death by drowning, by gassing, poisoning, freezing and electrocution, and the perforation of heart or brains, would it be possible to deprive that creature of life by any means? Even if the animal were cut into pieces, if its head were severed from its body, would it die? Or would it, like the earthworm or the amoeba, continue to life, and living, would the parts reunite and function as before?

Suddenly the scientist leaped from his chair as if a spring had been released beneath him. He had it at last! That was the solution! No one had been able to explain why certain forms of life could be subdivided without injury, while other forms succumbed to comparatively slight injuries.

But whatever the reason, whatever the difference between the lower and higher animals as regards life and death, he had bridged the gap. By his discovery the warmblooded invertebrates were rendered as indestructible as animalcules.

Yes, it must be so; it must be that by his treatment a mammal could survive the same mutilation as an earthworm. Doctor Farnham rushed to his laboratory, seized the rabbit and, without the least qualms or hesitation, severed the head from the body.

And although he had been prepared for it, although he was confident of the result, yet he paled, and staggered back, grasped a chair for support, when the headless creature continued to hop about, erratically and aimlessly, but fully alive, while the bodiless head wiggled its nose, waved its ears and blinked its eyes as if wondering what had become of its body. Hastily picking up the living body and the living head he placed them together, sewed and splinted them securely in position and, elated at the success of his experiment, placed the apparently contented and non-suffering rabbit in its cage. But there was still one experiment Doctor Farnham had not tried. Could he resuscitate a creature killed by violence? He would soon find out; and securing a healthy hare he mercifully and painlessly killed it by a thrust in its brain, and immediately prepared to inject a dose of his almost magical preparation into the dead animal's veins. But the test was never made...

CHAPTER VI

AS everyone knows, Abilone Island is of volcanic formation and is subject to frequent earthquakes. Hence, while during the past few days earth tremors had been felt, no one paid much attention to them, and even Doctor Farnham, who subconsciously noted that one or two tremors had been unusually severe, was merely disturbed because they interfered with his work and the adjustment of his delicate instruments.

Now, as he bent above the dead body of the hare, his hypodermic syringe in hand, a terrific quake shook the earth; the floor or the laboratory rose and fell; the walls cracked; glass came slithering down from the skylight; beakers, bell-glasses, retorts, test-tubes, jars and porcelain dishes toppled to the floor in a clash of shattered fragments; tables and chairs were overturned, and the doctor was thrown violently against the wall. It was no time for hesitating, no time for scientific experiments, and Doctor Farnham, being thoroughly human and quite alive to his own danger, dashed from the wrecked laboratory to the open air, still grasping his syringe in one hand and a vial of his preparation in the other. Quite forgetting that they were supposedly immortal, his three aged companions rushed screaming with terror from the crumbling dwelling and, scarcely able to keep to their feet, nauseated and dizzy from the rocking, oscillating earth shocks which followed one another in rapid succession, the four gazed speechless and awed as the buildings were reduced to shapeless ruins before their eyes.

But the worst was yet to come. Following upon quakes, came a deafening, awful roar the sound of a terrific explosion that seemed to rend the universe. The sky grew black; bright daylight gave way to twilight; the palm trees bent with a howling gale, and, unable to stand, the four men threw themselves flat upon their faces.

"An eruption!" shouted the doctor, striving to make himself heard above the howling wind, the explosive concussions that sounded like the detonations of shell-fire, and the thrashing of palm-fronds. "The volcano is in eruption," he repeated. "The crater of Sugar Loaf has burst into activity. We are probably out of danger, but thousands of people may have been destroyed. God pity the villagers upon the mountain slopes!"

Even while he spoke, dust and ashes began to fall, and soon, the earth, the vegetation, the ruins of the buildings and the men's clothing were covered with a grey coating of the volcanic ash. But presently the dust ceased to fall, the wind died down, the explosions grew fainter and occurred at longer intervals and the four shaken and terrified men rose to their feet and gazed about upon a landscape they would never have recognized.

The houses, outbuildings, laboratory and library were utterly destroyed, for fire had broken out and had completed the destruction of the earthquake, and Doctor Farnham's priceless books, his invaluable instruments, his work of years were gone for ever. Somewhere under the heap of blazing ruins lay the formulae and ingredients for his elixir of immortality; somewhere in the smoking pile reposed the bodies of the creatures which had proved its efficacy, and sadly, unable to voice the immensity of his loss, Doctor Farnham stood regarding what had so shortly before been his laboratory. Suddenly, from beneath the piles of debris, a brown and white creature appeared, and with a confused glance about, scuttled off into the weeds and brush. The scientist stared, rubbed his eyes and gasped. That any living thing could have survived that catastrophe seemed impossible. And then he broke into hysterical laughter. Of course! He had forgotten! It was the immortal guinea pig! And scarcely had his explanation dawned upon him when, from another pile of blackened, shattered masonry and timbers, a second animal appeared. Like a man bereft of reason the doctor stared incredulously at the apparition a large white rabbit, its neck swathed in bandages and adhesive tape. There could be no doubt of it. It was the rabbit whose head had been severed from its body and then replaced! All of the biologist's scientific ardour came back with a rush at sight of this incredible demonstration of the miraculous nature of his discovery, and leaping forward, he attempted to capture the little rodent. But he was too late. With a bound, the rabbit

THE PLAGUE OF THE LIVING DEAD 97

gained a clump of hibiscus and vanished as completely as if the earth had swallowed him up.

For a moment Doctor Farnham stood irresolute, and then he gave vent to a shout which startled his three companions almost out of their immortal senses. Across his brain had flashed an inspiration. There must be scores, hundreds, perhaps thousands of men and women killed or badly injured by the earthquake and eruption. He still possessed enough of his anti-death preparation to treat hundreds of persons. He would hurry to the stricken districts near the volcano, and would use the last drop of his priceless compound in restoring fife to the dead and dying. At last he could test his discovery on human beings to the limit of his desires, and he would be carrying on a work of humanity and incalculable scientific value at one and the same time. If nothing were gained, nothing would be lost, whereas, if the treatment proved efficacious with human beings, he would have saved countless lives and would have rendered those he treated immortal and for ever safe from subsequent eruptions and earthquakes. Partly owing to chances and partly owing to carelessness, the doctor's shabby but thoroughly serviceable car was uninjured, having been left standing in the drive at some distance from the buildings. Leaping into it and followed by the uncomprehending three, Doctor Farnham stepped on the gas and dashed towards the mountain slopes above which hung a dense black smoke cloud lit by vivid flashes of lightning, intermittent bursts of flaming gas, and outbursts of incandescent lava-bombs.

"Not so serious an eruption as I thought," commented the scientist, as the car, bumping over the earthquake-disrupted roads and across cracked culverts and bridges, drew nearer and nearer to the hills. "Apparently largely of local extent," he continued, "No signs of mud flows on this side of the cone probably ejected on the opposite side towards the sea.

And it must be admitted that, as Doctor Farnham drew near to the still active and threatening volcano, be became somewhat disappointed at finding the catastrophe had been no worse. Not that he was sorry the eruption had caused such a comparatively small amount of damage and loss of life, but because he began to fear that he would have no opportunity to test out his discovery on human beings.

But he need not have worried. Although, as he had assumed, the crater had erupted on the northern side, and the stupendous masses of red-hot lava and lava-bombs had flowed down the almost uninhabited seaward slopes into the ocean, still several small villages and many isolated houses had been utterly wiped out of existence; scores of persons, both white and black, had been burned to cinders or buried under many feet of ashes and mud; thousands of acres of cultivated fields and gardens bad been transformed into barren, desolate steaming seas of mud, and an incalculable amount of damage had been done.

Close to the crater, which since time immemorial had been considered wholly extinct, the destruction, where it had occurred at all, had been complete. Beyond this zone of scalding steam, red-hot cinders and blazing gases, even greater fatalities had occurred through the action of heavy deadly gases which, descending from the upper strata of air, had left hundreds of asphyxiated human beings in its wake.

But as is almost always the case with volcanic eruptions and phenomena, the death-dealing fumes had taken their toll in a most erratic and inexplicable manner. People had fallen in their tracks by scores in one spot, while within a few yards, none had suffered. One side of a village street had been swept by the noxious gas, while the opposite side of the narrow thoroughfare had been unaffected, and, when later intelligible reports had been made, it was found that in several instances a man had been overcome and killed while conversing with a friend who

THE PLAGUE OF THE LIVING DEAD 99

had escaped without injury. Of all the settlements which had thus been made the target for the deadly gases, that of San Marco had suffered the most, and as Doctor Farnham and his companions drove into the stricken village the scientist knew that the opportunity of his lifetime had come. Everywhere, the crumpled-up, inert bodies of men and women lay where they had fallen when overcome by the gas from the volcano. They were stretched on the pavements and in the streets, they lay sprawled on steps and in doorways; the market place and tiny plaza were filled with them, and less than a dozen of the inhabitants of the town remained alive and unhurt. And as these had fled from the gas-stricken village, Doctor Farnham and his three men were the sole living beings in San Marco. Naturally, the scientist was immensely pleased. There was nobody to interfere with him or to raise foolish and wholly unjustifiable objections to his work. There was a superabundance of material to work on, and subjects of the most desirable kind for, at his first glance, Doctor Farnham knew that the people had been killed by gas or shock, and that the deaths had not been caused by injuries to vital organs, in which case he would have had less confidence in his treatment. And we cannot blame him for his elation at finding the village strewn with corpses. Why should behave felt sorrow, pity or regret when, in his own mind, he felt positive that he could bring the stricken people back to life, yes, more than life, to a state of immortality? To him they were not dead, but merely in a temporary state of suspended animation, from which they would awaken never to die.

Leaping from his car, and assisted by his three ancient, but lively and energetic companions. Doctor Farnham proceeded methodically to inject the minimum dose of his precious elixir of life into each body in turn. At the very outset, however, he realized that he could not by any possibility restore all the dead in the village to life. He did not possess half enough of his compound for that, and he was in a quandary. In the first place, he most ardently desired to retain enough of his material to test it on the bodies of those who, he felt sure, must have met violent deaths nearer the volcano. In the second place, how could he decide whom to save and bless with immortality and whom to leave?

It was a difficult, hard question to solve, for never before had any one man possessed the power of life and death over so many of his fellows. But he could not devote much time to deciding. He did not know how long a human being could remain dead and be resuscitated, and much precious time had already elapsed since the villagers had been struck down by the gas. Some decision must be made at once, and he made it. Life, he decided, was more important to the younger and more vigorous persons than to the aged, and more desirable to the intelligent and educated individuals than to the ignorant and illiterate. He knew that, broadly speaking, his treatment would result in the persons treated remaining indefinitely in the physical state in which they were at the time of treatment, that even with the slightly renewed vigour and strength which followed, an old man or woman would remain physically old, and, he reasoned, it was very probable that an infant or a child would remain for ever undeveloped mentally and physically. Hence, for the good of the world, he would treat the bodies of those who had died in the prime of life but for the sake of science a few of the children would be treated as well permitting the old, the diseased, the maimed and the decrepit to remain dead. In this, he felt he was not acting inhumanely or callously. He could only save a certain number anyway, and those whom he passed by would be no worse off than they were at present, for he had assured himself, by a rapid examination, that according to all medical and known standards the victims were as dead as doornails.

CHAPTER VII

SO, having come to his decision, he hurried about, injecting his compound into the veins of those he deemed worthy to survive, and in the meantime filled with visions of the future, of a race of immortal people developing from the nucleus he had started. Anxious to know the results of his treatment, and to find out how long it took for a dead person to come back to life. Doctor Farnham ordered his three companions to remain behind and watch the bodies of those treated, and to report to him the moment any of the dead showed signs of reviving. He had commenced his work at the plaza, and here he stationed one of the three; at the market he left another, and the third was to be stationed a few blocks farther on. By the time Doctor Farnham reached the market he had treated several hundred bodies, and yet no word had come from the fellow watching for results at the plaza. Doubts began to assail the scientist as he continued on his way. Perhaps, after all, human beings would not respond to his treatment. Possibly the effects of this particular and unknown gas rendered his treatment valueless. It might be...

Terrifying sounds from the rear suddenly interrupted his thoughts. From the direction of the plaza came screams, shouts, a babel of sounds. It had worked! Where a moment before was the silence of death now could be heard the unmistakable sounds of life. The dead had been raised. The impossible had been accomplished, and, forgetting all else in his anxiety to witness the resurrection. Doctor Farnham dropped syringe and vial beside the body he had been about to treat, and hurried towards the plaza.

The sounds were increasing and coming nearer. Of course, he thought, the dead in the market were coming to life. But why, he wondered, had his two men failed to report?

The answer came most unexpectedly. Racing as fast as their old legs could carry them, the two fellows came dashing around a corner, terror on their faces, panting and breathless, while at their heels came a mob of men and women, screaming, shouting incomprehensible words, waving their arms threateningly, and obviously hostile.

Gasping, hurriedly, the two men tried to explain. They're mad," exclaimed he who had been stationed at the plaza, "murderin' mad! Lord knows why, but they set on me like tigers. Mauled me something dreadful. How I lived through it I dunno. Cracked me over the head with stones and beat me up."

"Me, too," chimed in the fellow who had been at the market place. "Stuck a machete in me, one fellow did. Looka here!" As he spoke he bared his chest and revealed a three-inch incision over his heart. The doctor, despite the approaching and obviously dangerous mob, gasped. The wound should have killed the fellow, and yet he appeared in no way inconvenienced. Then it dawned upon him. Of course be had not been killed. How could he be killed when he was immortal!

The two men were in no danger. No matter what the mob did they would survive, and Doctor Farnham had a fleeting, instantaneous vision of the two fellows being chopped into bits or torn to pieces and each separate fragment of their anatomies continuing to live, or perhaps even reuniting to form a complete man again. And bitterly he regretted that he had never tried the treatment on himself. Why hadn't he? For the life of him he didn't know. But there was no time for introspection or regrets. The mob was close now, something must be done. "You can't be hurt," he shouted to his companions. "You are immortal. Nothing can kill you. Don't run, don't be afraid. Face the mob."

But the fellows' confidence in the scientist's treatment and words was not great enough to make them obey, and furtively glancing about for a refuge, they prepared to flee. For a brief

THE PLAGUE OF THE LIVING DEAD 103

instant the doctor thought of facing the mob, of reasoning with them, of explaining why he was there, of quieting them, for he had reasoned that, in all probability, their actions were due to terror and nervous strain; that, reviving, they had been filled with the mad terror of the eruption which had been their last conscious sensations; that seeing many of their fellow men still lying dead they had become panic-stricken, and that their attack on the two watchmen had been merely the unreasoning, unwarranted act of half-crazed, fear-maddened men.

But the scientist's half-formed idea of facing the mob was abandoned almost as soon as conceived. No one could reason with the crowd. In time the mob would calm down; once they realized the eruption was over they would forget their terrors and would busy themselves burying the remaining dead. For the present, discretion was the better part of valour, and seizing his three companions, for the third fellow had now arrived on the scene. Doctor Farnham ducked around the nearest building and the four raced like mad for the car. But even as they fled, shouts, curses and screams came from the other direction; men and women appeared from streets and dwellings, and scores of resuscitated people rushed forward and fell madly, fiendishly upon the mob from the plaza. Instantly pandemonium reigned, and the four fugitives stood, transfixed with the horror of the scene. Fighting, clawing, biting, stabbing, the people fell upon one another, and the watching four shuddered as they saw men and women, minus arms or hands, faces shapeless masses of pulp, bodies slashed, pierced and torn, still leaping, springing about; still struggling and wholly oblivious to their terrible wounds, for being immortal nothing could destroy them.

Heedless of the dead bodies which had not been resuscitated, the struggling mob swayed here and there, while now and then and Doctor Farnham and his men felt faint and sick at the sight some panting man or woman would leave the milling mob, and springing like a beast on one of the trampled corpses, would tear and devour the flesh.

It was too much! Madly the four raced to the car, leaped in, and unheeding the peril of the road drove towards the distant town.

As they tore along, Doctor Farnham gradually calmed himself and forced his mind to function in its accustomed manner. He could not fully account for the savagery of the resurrected inhabitants of the village, but he could formulate reasonable theories to account for it. "Reversion to ancestral types under stress of great mental strain," he mentally classified it. "Suddenly finding themselves alive and safe after the impression that they were being destroyed, released inhibitions and gave dormant, savage instinct full rein. A mental explosion as it were. Probably normal calm and other conditions will follow."

But was it not possible and the scientist trembled at the thought was it not possible that while his treatment restored life, it did not restore mentality? He had hitherto experimented only with the lower animals, and who could say whether a rabbit or a guinea pig possessed normal or abnormal mentality after being retrieved from death? Then, through Doctor Farnham's mind came thoughts of the actions of the kitten which he had first resuscitated by his discovery, and he remembered how the beast had spit and scratched and yowled, finally escaping and taking to the brush like a wild thing. Perhaps only the physical organism could be restored to life, and the mental processes remained dead. Perhaps, after all, there was such a thing as a soul or spirit and this fled from the body at death and could not be restored. Doctor Farnham shivered despite the sweltering heat of the sun. If this were so, if all the soul or spirit or reason or whatever it was that kept the balance of a human being or an animal, if this inexplicable unknown thing were absent when the dead were revived, then God help the world.

THE PLAGUE OF THE LIVING DEAD 105

CHAPTER VIII

NO one could visualize the results. The resurrected dead must continue. They could not even destroy one another.

Then, more calmly, and feeling vastly relieved, he tried to cheer himself with the thought that, after all, there might be no basis for his fears. Perhaps the actions of the savage beings back in the village were merely temporary, and possibly, even if mentality or the soul was lacking at first, it would return in time and again fit itself to the resurrected body. No one could say, no one could do more than theorize; but whatever the ultimate result, Doctor Farnham had made up his mind that he would report the matter to the authorities, that regardless of what the consequences might be for him, he would make a clean breast of it, and would do all in his power, would devote all of his fortune and his time to trying to right what he had done, if, as be feared, matters were as bad as they might be.

In this manner came the Plague of the Living Dead, as it was afterwards known. At first, the authorities at Abilone believed that Doctor Farnham and his three companions had gone temporarily mad through the effects of the earthquake and the eruption, and they tried to calm the four and to soothe them. But when, a few hours later the survivors of a relief party reported that the village and the neighbourhood was filled with wild blood-mad savages and that three members of the party had been attacked, killed and torn to pieces, the authorities took action, although they still had no faith in Doctor Farnham's tale, and scoffed at the idea that he had resuscitated the dead or that the savages were immortal, and considered these the hallucinations of an overwrought mind.

No doubt, they said, the survivors of the catastrophe had been driven mad by the eruption and had reverted to savagery, but it would be a simple matter to round them up, confine them in an asylum and gradually cure them.

But the force of police sent to the vicinity of the village found that neither Doctor Farnham nor the relief party had exaggerated matters in the least. In fact, only two policemen managed to escape, and with terror-filled eyes they told a story of horror beyond any imagination. They had seen their fellows destroyed before their eyes. They had poured bullets into the bodies of the savage villagers at close range, but with no effect. They had fought hand-to-hand and had seen their short swords bury themselves in their antagonist's flesh without result, and they shuddered as they told of seeing armless, yes, even headless, men fighting like demons.

At last the officials were convinced that something entirely new and inexplicable had occurred. Incredible as it might seem, the doctor's story must be true, and something must be done without delay to rid the island of its curse -this Plague of the Living Dead. Far into night, and throughout the following day, all the officials of the island sat in conference with the scientist, for, being sensible men, the authorities realized that no one would be so likely to offer a solution of the problem as the man who had brought it about. And very wisely, too. The first suggestion that was made and acted upon was to establish a strict censorship on everything leaving the island. To let the outside world know what had occurred would be most unwise. The press would get hold of it; reporters and others would rush to the island to secure the facts; Abilone would be made the butt of incredulous ridicule or a place accursed, according to whether or not the press and public believed in the reports. But how to establish a censorship, how to prevent outsiders from visiting the island or to prevent the islanders from leaving was the question. This was solved by Doctor Frisbie, the medical inspector of the port. It would be announced that a virulent contagious disease had

THE PLAGUE OF THE LIVING DEAD

broken out in a remote village which was in a way no more than the truth and that until further notice no vessels would be allowed to enter or leave the ports. Of course, this would entail some hardships, but the available supplies of food were sufficient to support the population for at least several months, and long before the expiration of that period it was hoped that the Living Dead would be eliminated. But as time passed, those upon Abilone began to fear that no human power could conquer the soulless automatons in human form who cursed the land and could not be destroyed. Luckily, being absolutely lacking in intelligence and with no reasoning powers, the things did not wander far, and showed no inclination to leave their original district to attack persons who did not bother them. And to prevent any possibility of their spreading, immense barriers of barbed wire were erected about the locality where the Living Dead held sway. As Doctor Farnham had pointed out, the barbed wire would not deter the things through the pain or injuries caused by its jagged points, and hence the fence was erected for strength and height, and formed a barrier which even elephants could scarcely have broken through. This, however, took time, and long before it was completed innumerable attempts had been made to surround and capture or to destroy the soulless beings, for so fixed are certain ideas in the human brain that the officials could not believe that the Living Dead could not be killed, despite the arguments of Doctor Farnham who, over and again, declared that it was a waste of money and life to attempt to annihilate the beings, he had resurrected. But, of course, every attempt was futile. Bullets had no effect upon them, and when, after many arguments and innumerable protests, it was decided that, as the beings were no better than wild beasts and, therefore, a menace to the world, any means were justifiable, preparations were made to burn them out. Innumerable fires were kindled, and before a fresh wind the flames swept across the entire area occupied by the Living Dead and reduced the last vestiges of their former village to ashes. But, when, the fire over, a detachment of police was sent into the district to count the bodies, they were attacked, almost annihilated and driven back by the horde of singed, mutilated, ghastly beings who, had survived powder and ball, poison gases, and every other means to destroy them. Next, it was suggested that they be drowned, and although Doctor Farnham openly scoffed at the idea and the expense involved, no one could be made to believe that the things were really immune to death in any form whatsoever. Hence, at a terrific expense, a dam was built across the river flowing through the district, and for days the entire area was flooded. But at the end of the time the Living Dead were as lively, as savage, as unreasoning and as great a plague as ever. Strangely enough, too, not one of the beings had ever been captured. On two occasions, to be sure, members of the band had been seized, but on each occasion the beings had literally torn themselves free, leaving a dismembered arm or hand in possession of their captors. And these fragments of flesh, to everyone's horror and amazement, had continued to live.

It was indescribably gruesome to see the dismembered arm twisting and writhing about, to see the muscles flexing and the fingers opening and closing. Even when placed in jars of alcohol for formaldehyde, the limbs continued to retain their life and movement, and at last, in sheer desperation, the officials buried them in masses of concrete where, so far as they were concerned, the immortal fragments of anatomy might continue to survive and writhe until the crack of doom.

CHAPTER IX

INTENSIVE studies and observations of the Living Dead had been made, however, and at last it was conceded that Doctor Farnham had been right and had not in the

THE PLAGUE OF THE LIVING DEAD 109

least overestimated the attributes of the beings. And it was also admitted that his theories regarding their condition and actions were in the main correct. They could not be killed by any known means; that had been conclusively proved. They could exist without apparent ill effects even when horribly mutilated and even headless. They could literally be cut to pieces and each fragment would continue to live, and if two of these pieces came into contact, they would reunite and grow into monstrous, nightmarish, terrible things. Watching the area within the barrier through powerful glasses, the observers saw many of these things. Once, a head which had joined to two arms and a leg went racing across an open space like a monstrous spider. On another occasion a body appeared minus legs, and with two additional heads growing from the shoulders from which the original arms had been severed. And many of the fairly whole beings had hands, fingers, feet or other portions of anatomy growing from wounds upon various parts of their bodies. For the Living Dead, having no reasoning powers, yet instinctively sought to replace any portions of their bodies which they had lost, and picked up the first human fragment they found and grafted it into any wound or raw surface of their flesh. Strangely enough too. although it was perfectly logical once the matter was given thought, those individuals who were minus heads appeared fully as well off as those whose heads remained upon their shoulders, for without any glimmerings of intelligence, without reason and merely flesh and blood machines uncontrolled by brains, the Living Dead had no real need of heads. Nevertheless, they seemed to have some strange subconscious idea that heads were desirable, and fierce battles took place over the possession of a head which two of the things discovered simultaneously. Very frequently, the head, when re-established upon a body, was back to front, and a large percentage of the beings wore heads which did not originally belong to them. Moreover, the beings became head-hunters, and lopping off one another's heads became their chief diversion or occupation.

The amazing speed with which the most ghastly wound healed, and the incredibly short period of time required for a limb or head to graft itself firmly in place, were downright uncanny, but were accounted for by Doctor Farnham who explained that whereas, ordinarily, the tissues of normal human beings partially die and must be replaced by new growths, the tissues of the Living Dead remained alive, active and with all their cells intact, and hence instantly re-united, while at the same time, septic infection and injurious microbes could find no opportunity to act upon healthy living tissues. Although at first the beings had struggled and fought night and day, yet as time passed, they became more peaceable and seldom battled among themselves. When this was first observed, the authorities were hopeful of the beings eventually becoming rational, but Doctor Farnham disillusioned them and was borne out in his statement by the island's medical and scientific men.

"It is the logical and to-be-expected result," he declared. "In the first place, being without reason or the powers of deduction, and not being able to profit by experience, they have merely exhausted their powers of fighting. And, in the second place, a large proportion of their numbers are composites. That is, they have arms, limbs, heads or other portions of their anatomy belonging to other individuals. Hence to attack another being would be equivalent to attacking themselves. It is not a question of either instinct or brain, but merely the reaction of muscles and nerves to the inexplicable but long recognized cellular recognition or affinity existing in all organic matter."

At first, too, it had been thought that the Living Dead could be starved to death, or if truly immortal, that they could be so weakened by lack of food that they could easily be captured. But here again, the authorities had overlooked the basic features

THE PLAGUE OF THE LIVING DEAD

of the case. Although the creatures now and then devoured one another and Doctor Farnham wondered what happened when an unkillable being was devoured by his fellows yet this cannibalism seemed more a purely instinctive act than a necessity. The headless members of the community could not, of course, eat, but they got along just as well, and at last it dawned upon the officials that when a creature is truly immortal, nothing mortal can affect it.

Meanwhile, the island was getting perilously short of provisions and the people were being put on rations. Very soon, all knew, it would be necessary to allow a vessel to enter the port to bring in supplies, and the quarantine, moreover, could not much longer be maintained without arousing suspicion. Of course, long before this, the government had come to a realization of the fact that the terrible secret of the island could not be kept indefinitely. But the authorities had hoped that the Plague of the Living Dead might be for ever removed before it became necessary to apprise the world at large of the curse which had fallen upon Abitone.

Had it not been for its isolated position, and the fact that news of the eruption had reached the outer world and the public had assumed that the reported epidemic was the direct result of this, the true facts of the case would have become public property long ago.

Now, however, the authorities were at their wits' end. They had tried every means to exterminate the Living Dead without success. They had devoted a fortune and had sacrificed many lives trying to capture the terrible things, all without avail. And Doctor Farnham had, so far, been unable to suggest a means of ridding the island and the world of the incubus he had so unfortunately put upon it.

This, then, was the state of affairs when, on a certain night, the officials bad garnered in conference to consider the question of lifting the quarantine and giving up in despair, trusting to keeping the Living Dead confined indefinitely within the wire barrier.

"That," declared Colonel Shoreham, the military commandant, "is, or rather will be, impossible. So far, thank God, the things have made no attempt to tear down or scale the barrier, but sooner or later, they will. If they possessed reason they would have done so long ago, but some day perhaps tomorrow, perhaps not for a century they will decide to move, and the stoutest barricade man can erect will not hold them in check. Why, one of those spider-like monsters, consisting of legs and arms, could clamber over the wire as readily as a fly can walk on yonder wall. And do not forget, gentlemen, that water is no barrier to these terrible beings. They cannot be drowned, and hence they may be carried by sea to distant lands and may spread to the uttermost ends of the earth. Terrible and blasphemous as it may sound, I wish to God that another eruption might occur and that a volcano might break forth under the Living Dead and blow them into space. Personally -"

He was interrupted by a shout from Doctor Farnham, who, leaping to his feet, excitedly drew the attention of everyone to himself.

"Colonel!" he cried, "to you belongs the credit of having solved the problem. You spoke of blowing the Living Dead into space. That, gentlemen, is the solution. We will not need to invoke Divine aid in creating the volcano to do this, but we will provide the means ourselves."

The others looked at one another and at the enthusiastic scientist in utter amazement. Had his worries driven him mad? What was he driving at?

CHAPTER X

BUT Doctor Farnham was most evidently sane and most obviously in earnest. "I quite realize how visionary the idea may appear to you, gentlemen." he said, striving

THE PLAGUE OF THE LIVING DEAD

to speak calmly. "But I think you will accept it after my most unfortunate discovery, which resulted, it is true, in our present predicament, but which, nevertheless, proved that the most visionary and seemingly impossible things may be possible. I feel sure, I repeat, that after what you have all seen, you will agree with me that my present scheme is neither visionary nor impossible. Briefly, gentlemen, it is to construct an immense cannon, or perhaps better, an artificial crater, beneath the Living Dead and blow every one of the beings into space. In fact, blow them to such an immense distance that they will be beyond the attraction of Earth and will for ever revolve, like satellites, about our planet."

As he finished, silence fell upon those present. A few weeks previously they would have jeered, scoffed, ridiculed the idea or would have felt sure he was mad. But too many seemingly insane things had occurred to warrant a hasty judgement, and all were thinking deeply. At last, a dignified white-haired gentleman rose to his feet and cleared his throat. He was Senor Martinez, a descendent of one of the old Spanish families who had originally owned the island, and a retired engineer of world-wide fame.

"I feel," he began, "that Doctor Farnham's suggestion might be carried out. I have only two questions in my mind as to its feasibility. First; the cost of the undertaking which would be prodigious far more than the somewhat depleted treasury of Abilone would permit. And second; by what form of explosive the force could be generated which would project the beings so far that they would not fall back upon Earth, and being immortal, still be living things?"

"The expense," announced Doctor Farnham, as Senor Martinez resumed his seat, "will be borne by me. My fortune, which originally amounted to something over three millions, has remained practically untouched for the past forty-five years, for I have expended but a small fraction of the income. As it was entirely due to my work that the Plague of the Living Dead has been brought upon your island, I feel that it is no more than just that I should devote my last cent and my last effort to righting the wrong. As for the explosive, Senor Martinez, that will be a combination of nature's forces and modern high-powered explosives. Beneath the area occupied by the Living Dead is a deep-seated fissure connecting, in all probability, with the Sugar Loaf volcano. By excavating and tunneling we will enlarge that fissure to form an immense hollow under the area we desire to destroy, and we will fill the hollow with all the highest explosives known to science, and which can be purchased with my wealth. In the meantime, the San Marco River will be diverted from its present course and will be led to a tunnel which will be cut through the rim of the old crater. By means of electricity we will arrange to explode the charge under the Living Dead at the precise instant when the water of the river is released, and emptying into the crater, creates a steam pressure sufficient to produce an eruption. That pressure, gentlemen, being released by the detonation of the explosives will unquestioningly follow the line of least resistance and will burst forth as a violent sporadic eruption coincidentally with the force of the explosives, and will, I feel sure, project the Living Dead beyond the attraction of our planet."

For a brief instant silence followed the scientist's words, and then the hall echoed to uproarious applause.

When the demonstrations had at last subsided, the elderly engineer again spoke. "As an engineer, I approve most heartily of Doctor Farnham's ideas," he announced. "A few years ago such an undertaking would have been impossible, but science in many lines has advanced by leaps and bounds. We know the exact pressure generated by water in contact with molten igneous rocks at various depths thanks to the researches

THE PLAGUE OF THE LIVING DEAD   115

of Sigoor Baroardi and Professor Svenson, who devoted several years to intensive studies of volcanic activities in their respective countries of Italy and Iceland. We now know the exact pressure of steam essential to produce a volcanic eruption, and we also know the precise temperature at that steam pressure. Hence it will be a comparatively simple matter to devise means of detonating explosives coincidentally with the eruptive forces, as Doctor Farnham has outlined. Also, the modern explosives, which I presume would be the recently discovered YLT, and the even more powerful Mozanite, have already proved to possess sufficient force to project a missile several thousand miles beyond Earth's atmosphere, and in all probability, beyond the attractive forces of our sphere. The one really great difficulty which I foresee will be to calculate the exact diameter and depth of the excavation and to confine the Living Dead to the area immediately above it. I am most happy, gentlemen, to offer my poor services in this cause, and if you desire it, I will most gladly place my knowledge of engineering at the disposal of the government and will be honoured to collaborate with Doctor Farnham."

Amid vociferous applause Senor Martinez took his chair, and the governor rose and thanked him and accepted his offer. He was followed by Colonel Shoreham, who expressed his gratification in having inadvertently suggested the means of destroying the Living Dead, and who offered a plan for confining the beings to the restricted area desired. "It is possible, I think," he said, "to gradually push the wire barrier nearer and nearer the selected spot. It will, I take it, require some considerable time to complete excavations and prepare for the grand finale, and in the interim we can move the barrier forward an inch or two at a time. As the Living Dead have no intelligence they will never notice the change, and even if they do they will not understand what it means. As soon as Doctor Farnham and Senor Martinez have decided upon the exact spot, and the extent of the area to be blown up, I will commence moving the barrier."

This suggestion appeared to solve the last difficulty, and, vastly relieved that at last there seemed to be hopes of for ever destroying the Plague of the Living Dead, the meeting broke up after voting carte blanche to those who had volunteered to see the scheme through.

There is little more to be told. Everything proceeded smoothly. The precise area which was to be blown into space was determined, and true to his word, Colonel Shoreham moved the steel barrier forward until the inhuman, though human, monsters within were confined to the selected spot. Meanwhile, with millions at their disposal, the engineer and his assistants diverted the San Marco River, cut a tunnel through the base of the thin outer rim of the crater, and held the pent-up stream in check by a dam which could be destroyed by a single explosion set off by an electrical connection and detonator. Beneath the doomed beings, great electrically-driven machines were tunneling deep into the bowels of the mountain slope, and each hour, as the excavation deepened, the heat increased and scalding steam jets were more frequently met, all of which was most promising as proving that the active crater was not many feet below the spot wherein the work was going on. At last Senor Martinez feared to go deeper. Beneath the vast hole the roaring and rumbling of the volcano's forces could be heard; the steam issued from every crevice and crack in the rocks, and the temperature registered over two hundred degrees. Carefully, hundreds of tons of the most powerful of up-to-date explosives were piled within the vast excavation tons of the recently discovered YLT, which had entirely superseded TNT and was nearly one hundred times as powerful, and tons of the even more powerful Mozanite until the cavity was completely filled with the explosives. At last all was in

THE PLAGUE OF THE LIVING DEAD 117

readiness. Delicate instruments had been placed deep within the crater, instruments which at pre-determined temperatures would send a charge of electricity to the detonating caps in the explosive-filled excavations, and instruments which would accomplish the same result when the steam pressure reached a pre-arranged pressure.

CHAPTER XI

FOR weeks, the inhabitants had been warned away from the vicinity of activities, though there was little need for this, for few people cared to visit that portion of the island. And in order that persons in distant parts of the island might not be unduly alarmed, notices had been posted stating that at any time a stupendous explosion might occur, but which would cause no damage to outlying districts. Far more excited and nervous than they had ever been in their lives, the officials, together with the engineer and Doctor Farnham, waited within their bomb-proof shelter several miles from the area of the Living Dead, for the last stupendous drama.

Without a hitch the dam was blown-up, and the vast torrent of water rushed in a mighty cataract through the crater wall and into the depths of the volcano. Even from where they watched, the officials could see the far-flung white cloud of steam that instantly arose from the towering mountain top. One minute passed, two, three with a roar that seemed to split heaven and earth, with a shock that threw every man to the ground, the entire side of the mountain seemed to rise into the air. A blinding glare that dulled the midday sun clove the sky; a pillar of smoke that shot upward to the zenith blotted sun and sky from sight, and for miles around the earth was split, rent and riven. Streams overflowed their banks; landslides came crashing down mountain sides; forest trees were splintered into matchwood. Birds were killed in mid-air by the concussion, and for days afterwards, dead fish floated by thousands upon the surface of the sea. To those in the bombproof shelter, it seemed as if the explosion would never end, as if the mightiest of the volcano's forces had been conjured from the bowels of the earth and might never cease to erupt. And for what seemed hours, no debris, no stones or pulverized earth and rocks came tumbling back to earth. But at last — in reality but a few moments after the explosion thousands of tons of broken rock, of splintered trees, of ash and mud, of impalpable dust came crashing, pattering, until at last all was still not a sound was heard.

Awed and shaken, the watchers, accompanied by a band of armed troops, made their way to the devastated area.

A vast new crater yawned where the Living Dead had been. For half a dozen miles about, the island was littered with debris; but nowhere could a trace be found of the terrible beings.

And as no one, anywhere, has ever reported finding one of the monsters, or any fragments of their immortal bodies, it is safe to assume that somewhere, far beyond Earth's attraction, the Living Dead, blown to infinitesimal atoms, are doomed to for ever remain suspended in space.

The terrific explosion, which was reported by ships at sea and which was plainly heard at Roque over fifty miles distant, was passed off as a natural, but harmless eruption of Sugar Loaf volcano.

As for Doctor Farnham, with the several thousands of dollars left from his fortune, he built a church and a hospital, and he still resides quietly in Abilone, devoting his talents and his knowledge to healing the sick and relieving the suffering. His three human experiments are still with him. Never have they divulged what they know, and never do they mention the fact that they were subjected to the doctor's treatment, for they have got the idea that if the officials should discover they are immortal, they would meet the same fate as the Living Dead.

THE PLAGUE OF THE LIVING DEAD

As far as can be seen or determined, they are as lively and chipper as ever, but whether they are fated to live on for ever, or whether their span of life has merely been extended, no one can say. At any rate, the oldest fellow has made his will, and the other two are in constant dread of being killed by motor cars. So, being immortal does not, apparently, rid a person of the fear of death.

ADVANCED CHEMISTRY
~By Jack G. Huekels~

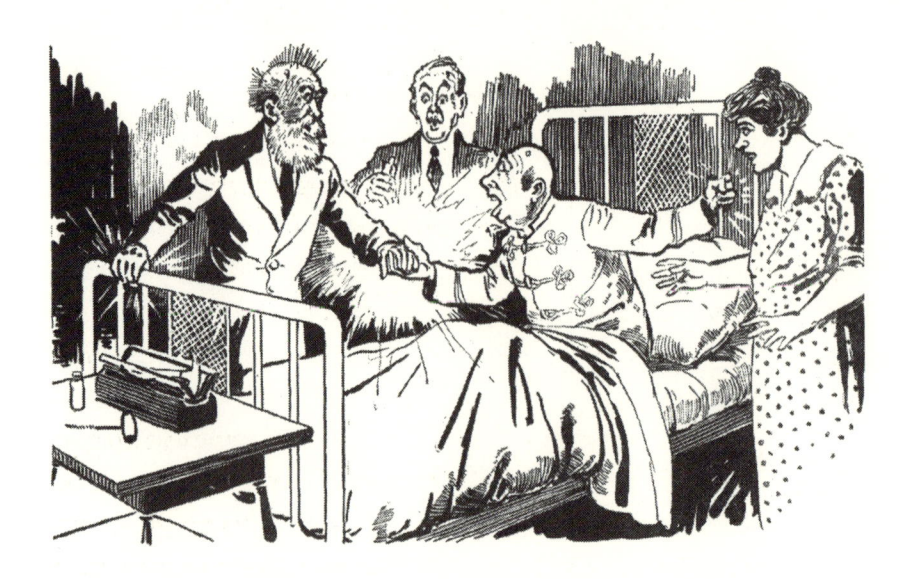

He grasped the brass bed post with one hand and stretched out the other to aid the staggering man. He caught his hand; both bodies stiffened; a slight crackling sound was audible and simultaneously a blue flash shot from where their hands made contact with the bed post.

Introduction

IN this story, like in many other .satires, there will be found a whole it of truth. Every day brings the modern student nearer to the conviction that the world really is electrical in every sense of the word. If you wish a few moments of good entertainment, we recommend this story to you.

ADVANCED CHEMISTRY
By Jack G. Huekels

Professor Carbonic was diligently at work in his spacious laboratory, analyzing, mixing and experimenting. He had been employed for more than fifteen years in the same pursuit of happiness, in the same house, same laboratory, and attended by the same servant woman, who in her long period of service had attained the plumpness and respectability of two hundred and ninety pounds.

"Mag Nesia," called the professor. The servant's name was Maggie Nesia—Professor Carbonic had contracted the title to save time, for in fifteen years he had not mounted the heights of greatness; he must work harder and faster as life is short, and eliminate such shameful waste of time as putting the "gie" on Maggie.

"Mag Nesia!" the professor repeated.

The old woman rolled slowly into the room.

"Get rid of these and bring the one the boy brought today."

He handed her a tray containing three dead rats, whose brains had been subjected to analysis.

"Yes, Marse," answered Mag Nesia in a tone like citrate.

The professor busied himself with a new preparation of zinc oxide and copper sulphate and sal ammoniac, his latest concoction, which was about to be used and, like its predecessors, to be abandoned.

Mag Nesia appeared bringing another rat, dead. The professor made no experiments on live animals. He had hired a boy in the neighborhood to bring him fresh dead rats at twenty-five cents per head.

Taking the tray he prepared a hypodermic filled with the new preparation. Carefully he made an incision above the right eye of the carcass through the bone. He lifted the hypodermic, half hopelessly, half expectantly. The old woman watched him, as she had done many times before, with always the same pitiful expression. Pitiful, either for the man himself or for the dead rat. Mag Nesia seldom expressed her views.

Inserting the hypodermic needle and injecting the contents of the syringe, Professor Carbonic stepped back.

Prof. Carbonic Makes a Great Discovery

"Great Saints!" His voice could have been heard a mile. Slowly the rat's tail began to point skyward; and as slowly Mag Nesia began to turn white. Professor Carbonic stood as paralyzed. The rat trembled and moved his feet. The man of sixty years made one jump with the alacrity of a boy of sixteen, he grabbed the enlivened animal, and held it high above his head as he jumped about the room.

Spying the servant, who until now had seemed unable to move, he threw both arms around her, bringing the rat close to her face. Around the laboratory they danced to the tune of the woman's shrieks. The professor held on, and the woman yelled. Up and down spasmodically on the laboratory floor came the two hundred and ninety pounds with the professor thrown in.

Bottles tumbled from the shelves. Furniture was upset. Precious liquids flowed unrestrained and unnoticed. Finally the professor dropped with exhaustion and the rat and Mag Nesia made a dash for freedom.

ADVANCED CHEMISTRY 123

Early in the morning pedestrians on Arlington Avenue were attracted by a sign in brilliant letters.

Professor Carbonic early in the morning betook himself to the nearest hardware store and purchased the tools necessary for his new profession. He was an M.D. and his recently acquired knowledge put him in a position to startle the world. Having procured what he needed he returned home.

Things were developing fast. Mag Nesia met him at the door and told him that Sally Soda, who was known to the neighborhood as Sal or Sal Soda generally, had fallen down two flights of stairs, and to use her own words was "Putty bad." Sal Soda's mother, in sending for a doctor, had read the elaborate sign of the new enemy of death, and begged that he come to see Sal as soon as he returned.

Bidding Mag Nesia to accompany him, he went to the laboratory and secured his precious preparation. Professor Carbonic and the unwilling Mag Nesia started out to put new life into a little Sal Soda who lived in the same block.

Reaching the house they met the family physician then attendant on little Sal. Doctor X. Ray had also read the sign of the professor and his greeting was very chilly.

"How is the child?" asked the professor.

"Fatally hurt and can live but an hour." Then he added, "I have done all that can be done."

"All that *you* can do," corrected the professor.

With a withering glance, Doctor X. Ray left the room and the house. His reputation was such as to admit of no intrusion.

"I am sorry she is not dead, it would be easier to work, and also a more reasonable charge." Giving Mag Nesia his instruments he administered a local anesthetic; this done he selected a brace and bit that he had procured that morning. With these instruments he bored a small hole into the child's head.

Inserting his hypodermic needle, he injected the immortal fluid, then cutting the end off a dowel, which he had also procured that morning, he hammered it into the hole until it wedged itself tight.

Professor Carbonic seated himself comfortably and awaited the action of his injection, while the plump Mag Nesia paced or rather waddled the floor with a bag of carpenter's tools under her arm.

The fluid worked. The child came to and sat up. Sal Soda had regained her pep.

"It will be one dollar and twenty-five cents, Mrs. Soda," apologized the professor. "I have to make that charge as it is so inconvenient to work on them when they are still alive."

Having collected his fee, the professor and Mag Nesia departed, amid the ever rising blessings of the Soda family.

At 3:30 P.M. Mag Nesia sought her employer, who was asleep in the sitting room.

"Marse Paul, a gentleman to see you."

The professor awoke and had her send the man in.

The man entered hurriedly, hat in hand. "Are you Professor Carbonic?"

"I am, what can I do for you?"

"Can you——?" the man hesitated. "My friend has just been killed in an accident. You couldn't——" he hesitated again.

"I know that it is unbelievable," answered the professor. "But I can."

Professor Carbonic for some years had suffered from the effects of a weak heart. His fears on this score had recently been entirely relieved. He now had the prescription—Death no more! The startling discovery, and the happenings of the last twenty-four hours had begun to take effect on him, and he did not wish to make another call until he was feeling better.

"I'll go," said the professor after a period of musing. "My

ADVANCED CHEMISTRY 125

discoveries are for the benefit of the human race, I must not consider myself."

He satisfied himself that he had all his tools. He had just sufficient of the preparation for one injection; this, he thought, would be enough; however, he placed in his case, two vials of different solutions, which were the basis of his discovery. These fluids had but to be mixed, and after the chemical reaction had taken place the preparation was ready for use.

He searched the house for Mag Nesia, but the old servant had made it certain that she did not intend to act as nurse to dead men on their journey back to life. Reluctantly he decided to go without her.

"How is it possible!" exclaimed the stranger, as they climbed into the waiting machine.

"I have worked for fifteen years before I found the solution," answered the professor slowly.

"I cannot understand on what you could have based a theory for experimenting on something that has been universally accepted as impossible of solution."

"With electricity, all is possible; as I have proved." Seeing the skeptical look his companion assumed, he continued, "Electricity is the basis of every motive power we have; it is the base of every formation that we know." The professor was warming to the subject.

"Go on," said the stranger, "I am extremely interested."

"Every sort of heat that is known, whether dormant or active, is only one arm of the gigantic force electricity. The most of our knowledge of electricity has been gained through its offspring, magnetism. A body entirely devoid of electricity, is a body dead. Magnetism is apparent in many things including the human race, and its presence in many people is prominent."

"But how did this lead to your experiments?"

"If magnetism or motive force, is the offspring of electricity, the human body must, and does contain electricity. That we use more electricity than the human body will induce is a fact; it is apparent therefore that a certain amount of electricity must be generated within the human body, and without aid of any outside forces. Science has known for years that the body's power is brought into action through the brain. The brain is our generator. The little cells and the fluid that separate them, have the same action as the liquid of a wet battery; like a wet battery this fluid wears out and we must replace the fluid or the sal ammoniac or we lose the use of the battery or body. I have discovered what fluid to use that will produce the electricity in the brain cells which the human body is unable to induce."

"We are here," said the stranger as he brought the car to a stop at the curb.

"You are still a skeptic," noting the voice of the man. "But you shall see shortly."

The man led him into the house and introduced him to Mrs. Murray Attic, who conducted him to the room where the deceased Murray Attic was laid.

Without a word the professor began his preparations. He was ill, and would have preferred to have been at rest in his own comfortable house. He would do the work quickly and get away.

Selecting a gimlet, he bored a hole through the skull of the dead man; inserting his hypodermic he injected all the fluid he had mixed. He had not calculated on the size of the gimlet and the dowels he carried would not fit the hole. As a last resource he drove in his lead pencil, broke it off close, and carefully cut the splinters smooth with the head.

"It will be seventy-five cents, madam," said the professor as he finished the work.

Mrs. Murray Attic paid the money unconsciously; she did not know whether he was embalming her husband or just trying the keenness of his new tools. The death had been too much for her.

ADVANCED CHEMISTRY

The minutes passed and still the dead man showed no signs of reviving. Professor Carbonic paced the floor in an agitated manner. He began to be doubtful of his ability to bring the man back. Worried, he continued his tramp up and down the room. His heart was affecting him. He was tempted to return the seventy-five cents to the prostrate wife when—THE DEAD MAN MOVED!

The professor clasped his hands to his throat, and with his head thrown back dropped to the floor. A fatal attack of the heart.

He became conscious quickly. "The bottles there," he whispered. "Mix—, make injection." He became unconscious again.

The stranger found the gimlet and bored a hole in the professor's head, hastily seizing one of the vials, he poured the contents into the deeply made hole. He then realized that there was another bottle.

"Mix them!" shrieked the almost hysterical woman.

It was too late, the one vial was empty, and the professor's body lay lifeless.

In mental agony the stranger grasped the second vial and emptied its contents also into the professor's head, and stopped the hole with the cork.

Miraculously Professor Carbonic opened his eyes, and rose to his feet. His eyes were like balls of fire; his lips moved inaudibly, and as they moved little blue sparks were seen to pass from one to another. His hair stood out from his head. The chemical reaction was going on in the professor's brain, with a dose powerful enough to restore ten men. He tottered slightly.

Murray Attic, now thoroughly alive, sat up straight in bed. He grasped the brass bed post with one hand and stretched out the other to aid the staggering man.

He caught his hand; both bodies stiffened; a slight crackling sound was audible; a blue flash shot from where Attic's had made contact with the bed post; then a dull thud as both bodies struck the floor. Both men were electrocuted, and the formula is still a secret.

The FATE of the POSEIDONIA

By CLARE WINGER HARRIS

...and before my startled vision a scene presented itself. I seemed to be inside a bamboo hut looking toward an opening which afforded a glimpse of a wave-washed sandy beach and a few palm trees... While my fascinated gaze dwelt on the scene before me, a shadow fell athwart the hut's entrance and the figure of a man came toward me.

Introduction

As a rule, women do not make good scientifiction writers, because their education and general tendencies on scientific matters are usually limited. But the exception, as usual, proves the rule, the exception in this case being extraordinarily impressive. The story has a great deal of charm, chiefly because it is not overburdened with science, but whatever science is contained therein is not only quite palatable, but highly desirable, due to its plausibility. Not only this, but you will find that the author is a facile writer who keeps your interest unto the last line. We hope to see more of Mrs. Harris's scientifiction in *Amazing Stories*.

THE FATE OF THE POSEIDONIA
By Clare Winger Harris

CHAPTER I

THE first moment I laid eyes on Martell I took a great dislike to the man. There sprang up between us an antagonism that as far as he was concerned might have remained passive, but which circumstances forced into activity on my side.

How distinctly I recall the occasion of our meeting at the home of Professor Stearns, head of the Astronomy department of Austin College. The address which the professor proposed giving before the Mentor Club of which I was a member, was to be on the subject of the planet, Mars. The spacious front rooms of the Stearns home were crowded for the occasion with rows of chairs, and at the end of the double parlors a screen was erected for the purpose of presenting telescopic views of the ruddy planet in its various aspects.

As I entered the parlor after shaking hands with my hostess, I felt, rather than saw, an unfamiliar presence, and the impression I received involuntarily was that of antipathy. What I saw was the professor himself engaged in earnest conversation with a stranger. Intuitively I knew that from the latter emanated the hostility of which I was definitely conscious.

He was a man of slightly less than average height. At once I noticed that he did not appear exactly normal physically and yet I could not ascertain in what way he was deficient. It was not until I had passed the entire evening in his company that I was fully aware of his bodily peculiarities. Perhaps the most striking characteristic was the swarthy, coppery hue of his flesh that was not unlike that of an American Indian. His chest and shoulders seemed abnormally developed, his limbs and features extremely slender in proportion. Another peculiar individuality was the wearing of a skullcap pulled well down over his forehead.

Professor Stearns caught my eye, and with a friendly nod indicated his desire that I meet the new arrival.

"Glad to see you, Mr. Gregory," he said warmly as he clasped my hand. "I want you to meet Mr. Martell, a stranger in our town, but a kindred spirit, in that he is interested in Astronomy and particularly in the subject of my lecture this evening."

I extended my hand to Mr. Martell and imagined that he responded to my salutation somewhat reluctantly. Immediately I knew why. The texture of the skin was most unusual. For want of a better simile, I shall say that it felt not unlike a fine dry sponge. I do not believe that I betrayed any visible surprise, though inwardly my whole being revolted. The deep, close-set eyes of the stranger seemed searching me for any manifestation of antipathy, but I congratulate myself that my outward poise was undisturbed by the strange encounter.

The guests assembled, and I discovered to my chagrin that I was seated next to the stranger, Martell. Suddenly the lights were

THE FATE OF THE POSEIDONIA

extinguished preparatory to the presentation of the lantern-slides. The darkness that enveloped us was intense. Supreme horror gripped me when I presently became conscious of two faint phosphorescent lights to my right. There could be no mistaking their origin. They were the eyes of Martell and they were regarding me with an enigmatical stare. Fascinated, I gazed back into those diabolical orbs with an emotion akin to terror. I felt that I should shriek and then attack their owner. But at the precise moment when my usually steady nerves threatened to betray me, the twin lights vanished. A second later the lantern light flashed on the screen. I stole a furtive glance in the direction of Martell. He was sitting with his eyes closed.

"The planet Mars should be of particular interest to us," began Professor Stearns, "not only because of its relative proximity to us, but because of the fact that there are visible upon its surface undeniable evidences of the handiwork of man, and I am inclined to believe in the existence of mankind there not unlike the humanity of the earth."

The discourse proceeded uninterruptedly. The audience remained quiet and attentive, for Professor Stearns possessed the faculty of holding his listeners spell-bound. A large map of one hemisphere of Mars was thrown on the screen, and simultaneously the stranger Martell drew in his breath sharply with a faint whistling sound.

The professor continued, "Friends, do you observe that the outstanding physical difference between Mars and Terra appears to be in the relative distribution of land and water? On our own globe the terrestrial parts lie as distinct entities surrounded by the vast aqueous portions, whereas, on Mars the land and water are so intermingled by gulfs, bays, capes and peninsulas that it requires careful study to ascertain for a certainty which is which. It is my opinion, and I do not hold it alone, for much discussion with my worthy colleagues has made it obvious, that the peculiar land contours are due to the fact that water is becoming a very scarce commodity on our neighboring planet. Much of what is now land is merely the exposed portions of the one-time ocean bed; the precious life-giving fluid now occupying only the lowest depressions. We may conclude that the telescopic eye, when turned on Mars, sees a waning world; the habitat of a people struggling desperately and vainly for existence, with inevitable extermination facing them in the not far distant future. What will they do? If they are no farther advanced in the evolutionary stage than a carrot or a jelly-fish, they will ultimately succumb to fate, but if they are men and women such as you and I, they will fight for the continuity of their race. I am inclined to the opinion that the Martians will not die without putting up a brave struggle, -which will result in the prolongation of their existence, but not in their complete salvation."

Professor Stearns paused. "Are there any questions?" he asked.

I was about to speak when the voice of Martell boomed in my ear, startling me.

"In regard to the map, professor," he said, "I believe that gulf which lies farthest south is not a gulf at all but is a part of the land portion surrounding it. I think you credit the poor dying planet with even more water than it actually has!"

"It is possible and even probable that I have erred," replied the learned man, "and I am sorry indeed if that gulf is to be withdrawn from the credit of the Martians, for their future must look very black."

"Just suppose," resumed Martell, leaning toward the lecturer with interested mien, "that the Martians were the possessors of an intelligence equal to that of terrestrials, what might they do to save themselves from total extinction? In other words to bring it home to us more realistically, what would we do were we threatened with a like disaster?"

'That is a very difficult question to answer, and one upon

THE FATE OF THE POSEIDONIA

which merely an opinion could be ventured," smiled Professor Stearns. "'Necessity is the mother of invention', and in our case without the likelihood of the existence of the mother, we can hardly hazard a guess as to the nature of the offspring. But always, as Terra's resources have diminished, the mind of man has discovered substitutes. There has always been a way out, and let us hope our brave planetary neighbors will succeed in solving their problem."

"Let us hope so indeed," echoed the voice of Martell.

CHAPTER II

AT the time of my story in the winter of 1894-1895, I was still unmarried and was living in a private hotel on E. Ferguson Ave., where I enjoyed the comforts of well furnished bachelor quarters. To my neighbors I paid little or no attention, absorbed in my work during the day and paying court to Margaret Landon in the evenings.

I was not a little surprised upon one occasion, as I stepped into the corridor, to see a strange yet familiar figure in the hotel locking the door of the apartment adjoining my own. Almost instantly I recognized Martell, on whom I had not laid eyes since the meeting some weeks previous at the home of Professor Stearns. He evinced no more pleasure at our meeting than I did, and after the exchange of a few cursory remarks from which I learned that he was my new neighbor, we went our respective ways.

I thought no more of the meeting, and as I am not blessed or cursed (as the case may be) with a natural curiosity concerning the affairs of those about me, I seldom met Martell, and upon the rare occasions when I did, we confined our remarks to that ever convenient topic, the weather.

Between Margaret and myself there seemed to be growing an inexplicable estrangement that increased as time went on, but it was not until after five repeated futile efforts to spend an evening in her company that I suspected the presence of a rival. Imagine my surprise and chagrin to discover that rival in the person of my neighbor Martell! I saw them together at the theatre and wondered, even with all due modesty, what there was in the ungainly figure and peculiar character of Martell to attract a beautiful and refined girl of Margaret Landon's type. But .attract her he did, for it was plainly evident, as I watched them with the eyes of a jealous lover, that Margaret was fascinated by the personality of her escort.

In sullen rage I went to Margaret a few days later, expressing my opinion of her new admirer in derogatory epithets. She gave me calm and dignified attention until I had exhausted my vocabulary, voicing my ideas of Martell, then she made reply in Martell's defense.

"Aside from personal appearance, Mr. Martell is a forceful and interesting character, and I refuse to allow you to dictate to me who my associates are to be. There is no reason why we three can not all be friends."

"Martell hates me as I hate him," I replied with smoldering resentment. "That is sufficient reason why we three can not all be friends."

"I think you must be mistaken," she replied curtly. "Mr. Martell praises your qualities as a neighbor and comments not infrequently on your excellent virtue of attending strictly to your own business."

I left Margaret's presence in a down-hearted mood.

"So Martell appreciates my lack of inquisitiveness, does he?" I mused as later I reviewed mentally the closing words of Margaret, and right then and there doubts and suspicions arose in my mind. If self-absorption was an appreciable quality as far as Martell was concerned, there was reason for his esteem of that phase of my character. I had discovered the presence of a mystery; Martell had something to conceal!

It was New Year's Day, not January 1st as they had it in the old

THE FATE OF THE POSEIDONIA

days, but the extra New Year's Day that was sandwiched as a separate entity between two years. This new chronological reckoning had been put into use in 1938. The calendar had previously contained twelve months varying in length from twenty-eight to thirty-one days, but with the addition of a new month and the adoption of a uniformity of twenty-eight days for all months and the interpolation of an isolated New Year's Day, the world's system of chronology was greatly simplified. It was, as I say, on New Year's Day that I arose later than usual and dressed myself. The buzzing monotone of a voice from Martell's room annoyed me. Could he be talking over the telephone to Margaret? Right then and there I stooped to the performance of a deed of which I did not think myself capable. Ineffable curiosity converted me into a spy and an eavesdropper. I dropped to my knees and peered through the keyhole. I was rewarded with an unobstructed profile view of Martell seated at a low desk on which stood a peculiar cubical mechanism measuring on each edge six or seven inches. Above it hovered a tenuous vapor and from it issued strange sounds, occasionally interrupted by remarks from Martell uttered in an unknown tongue. Good heavens! Was this a newfangled radio that communicated with the spirit world? For only in such a way could I explain the peculiar vapor that enveloped the tiny machine. Television had been perfected and in use for a generation, but as yet no instrument had been invented which delivered messages from the "unknown bourne!"

I crouched in my undignified position until it was with difficulty that I arose, at the same time that Martell shut off the mysterious contrivance. Could Margaret be involved in any diabolical schemes? The very suggestion caused me to break out in a cold sweat. Surely Margaret, the very personification of innocence and purity, could be no partner in any nefarious undertakings! I resolved to call her up. She answered the phone and I thought her voice showed agitation.

"Margaret, this is George," I said. "Are you all right?"

She answered faintly in the affirmative.

"May I come over at once?" I pled. "I have something important to tell you."

To my surprise she consented, and I lost no time in speeding my volplane to her home. With no introductory remarks, I plunged right into a narrative of the peculiar and suspicious actions of Martell, and ended by begging her to discontinue her association with him. Ever well poised and with a girlish dignity that was irresistibly charming, Margaret quietly thanked me for my solicitude for her well-being but assured me that there was nothing to fear from Martell. It was like beating against a brick wall to obtain any satisfaction from her, so I returned to my lonely rooms, there to brood in solitude over the unhappy change that Martell had brought into my life.

Once again I gazed through the tiny aperture. My neighbor was nowhere to be seen, but on the desk stood that which I mentally termed the devil-machine. The subtle mist that had previously hovered above it was wanting.

The next day upon arising I was drawn as by a magnet toward the keyhole, but my amazement knew no bounds when I discovered that it had been plugged from the other side, and my vision completely barred!

"Well I guess it serves me right," I muttered in my chagrin. "I ought to keep out of other people's private affairs. But," I added as an afterthought in feeble defense of my actions, "my motive is to save Margaret from that scoundrel." And such I wanted to prove him to be before it was too late!

CHAPTER III

THE sixth of April, 1945, was a memorable day in the annals of history, especially to the inhabitants of Pacific coast cities throughout the world. Radios buzzed with

THE FATE OF THE POSEIDONIA

the alarming and mystifying news that just over night the ocean line had receded several feet. What cataclysm of nature could have caused the disappearance of thousands of tons of water inside of twenty-four hours? Scientists ventured the explanation that internal disturbances must have resulted in the opening of vast submarine fissures into which the seas had poured.

This explanation, stupendous as it was, sounded plausible, enough and was accepted by the world at large, which was too busy accumulating gold and silver to worry over the loss of nearly a million tons of water. How little we then realized that the relative importance of gold and water was destined to be reversed, and that man was to have forced upon him a new conception of values which would bring to him a complete realization of his former erroneous ideas.

May and June passed marking little change in the drab monotony that had settled into my life since Margaret Landon had ceased to care for me. One afternoon early in July I received a telephone call from Margaret. Her voice betrayed an agitated state of mind, and sorry though I was that she was troubled, it pleased me that she had turned to me in her despair. Hope sprang anew in my breast, and I told her I would be over at once.

I was admitted by the taciturn housekeeper and ushered into the library where Margaret rose to greet me as I entered. There were traces of tears in her lovely eyes. She extended both hands to me in a gesture of spontaneity that had been wholly lacking in her attitude toward me ever since the advent of Martell. In the role of protector and advisor, I felt that I was about to be reinstated in her regard.

But my joy was short-lived as I beheld a recumbent figure on the great davenport and recognized it instantly as that of Martell. So he was in the game after all! Margaret had summoned me because her lover was in danger! I turned to go but felt a restraining hand.

"Wait, George," the girl pled. "The doctor will be here any minute."

"Then let the doctor attend to him," I replied coldly. "I know nothing of the art of healing."

"I know, George," Margaret persisted, "but he mentioned you before he lost consciousness and I think he wants to speak to you. Won't you wait please?"

I paused, hesitant at the supplicating tones of her whom I loved, but at that moment the maid announced the doctor, and I made a hasty exit.

Needless to say I experienced a sense of guilt as I returned to my rooms.

"But," I argued as I seated myself comfortably before my radio, "a rejected lover would have to be a very magnanimous specimen of humanity to go running about doing favors for a rival. What do the pair of them take me for anyway — a fool?"

I rather enjoyed a consciousness of righteous indignation, but disturbing visions of Margaret gave me an uncomfortable feeling that there was much about the affair that was incomprehensible to me.

"The transatlantic passenger-plane, *Pegasus*, has mysteriously disappeared," said the voice of the news announcer. "One member of her crew has been picked up who tells such a weird, fantastic tale that it has not received much credence. According to his story the *Pegasus* wag winging its way across mid-ocean last night keeping an even elevation of three thousand feet, when, without any warning, the machine started straight up. Some force outside of itself was drawing it up, but whither? The rescued mechanic, the only one of all the fated ship's passengers, possessed the presence of mind to manipulate his parachute, and thus descended in safety before the air became too rare to breathe, and before he and the parachute

THE FATE OF THE POSEIDONIA 139

could be attracted upwards. He stoutly maintains that the plane could not have fallen later without his knowledge. Scouting planes, boats and submarines sent out this morning verify his seemingly mad narration. Not a vestige of the *Pegasus* is to be found above, on the surface or below the water. Is this tragedy in any way connected with the lowering of the ocean level? Has someone a theory? In the face of such an inexplicable enigma the government will listen to the advancement of any theories, in the hope of solving the mystery. Too many times in the past have the so-called level-headed people failed to give ear to the warnings of theorists and dreamers, but now we know that the latter are often the possessors of a sixth sense that enables them to see that to which the bulk of mankind is blind."

I was awed by the fate of the *Pegasus*. I had had two flights in the wonderful machine myself three years ago, and I knew that it was the last word in luxuriant air-travel.

How long I sat listening to brief news bulletins and witnessing scenic flashes of worldly affairs I do not know, but there suddenly came to my mind and persisted in staying there, a very disquieting thought. Several times I dismissed it as unworthy of any consideration, but it continued with unmitigating tenacity.

After an hour of mental pros and cons I called up the hotel office.

"This is Mr. Gregory in suite 307," I strove to keep my voice steady. "Mr. Martell of 309 is ill at the house of a friend. He wishes me to have some of his belongings taken to him. May I have the key to his rooms?"

There was a pause that to me seemed interminable, then the voice of the clerk. "Certainly, Mr. Gregory, I'll send a boy up with it at once."

I felt like a culprit of the deepest dye as I entered Martell's suite a few moments later and gazed about me. I knew I might expect interference from any quarter at any moment so I wasted no time in a general survey of the apartment but proceeded at once to the object of my visit. The tiny machine which I now perceived was more intricate than I had supposed from my previous observations through the keyhole, stood in its accustomed place upon the desk. It had four levers and a dial, and I decided to manipulate each of these in turn. I commenced with the one at my extreme left. For a moment apparently nothing happened, then I realized that above the machine a mist was forming.

At first it was faint and cloudy but the haziness quickly cleared, and before my startled vision a scene presented itself. I seemed to be inside a bamboo hut looking toward an opening which afforded a glimpse of a wave-washed sandy beach and a few palm trees silhouetted against the horizon. I could imagine myself on a desert isle. I gasped in astonishment, but it was nothing to the shock which was to follow. While my fascinated gaze dwelt on the scene before me, a shadow fell athwart the hut's entrance and the figure of a man came toward me. I uttered a hoarse cry. For a moment I thought I had been transplanted chronologically to the discovery of America, for the being who approached me bore a general resemblance to an Indian chief. From his forehead tall, white feathers stood erect. He was without clothing and his skin had a reddish cast that glistened with a coppery sheen in the sunlight. Where had I seen those features or similar ones, recently? I had it! Martell! The Indian savage was a natural replica of the suave and civilized Martell, and yet was this man before me a savage? On the contrary, I noted that his features displayed a remarkably keen intelligence.

The stranger approached a table upon which I seemed to be, and raised his arms. A muffled cry escaped my lips! The feathers that I had supposed constituted his headdress were attached permanently along the upper portion of his arms to

THE FATE OF THE POSEIDONIA

a point a little below each elbow. *They grew there.* This strange being had feathers instead of hair.

I do not know by what presence of mind I managed to return the lever to its original position, but I did, and sat weakly gazing vacantly at the air, where but a few seconds before a vivid tropic scene had been visible. Suddenly a low buzzing sound was heard. Only for an instant was I mystified, then I knew that the stranger of the desert-isle was endeavoring to summon Martell.

Weak and dazed I waited until the buzzing had ceased and then I resolutely pulled the second of the four levers. At the inception of the experiment the same phenomena were repeated, but when a correct perspective was effected a very different scene was presented before my startled vision. This time I seemed to be in a luxuriant room filled with costly furnishings, but I had time only for a most fleeting glance, for a section of newspaper that had intercepted part of my view, moved, and from behind its printed expanse emerged a being who bore a resemblance to Martell and the Indian of the desert island. It required but a second to turn off the mysterious connection, but that short time had been of sufficient duration to enable me to read the heading of the paper in the hands of a copper-hued man. It was *Die Münchener Zeitung*.

Still stupefied by the turn of events, it was with a certain degree of enjoyment that I continued to experiment with the devil-machine. I was startled when the same buzzing sound followed the disconnecting of the instrument.

I was about to manipulate the third lever when I became conscious of pacing footsteps in the outer hall. Was I arousing the suspicion of the hotel officials? Leaving my seat before the desk, I began to move about the room in semblance of gathering together Martell's required articles. Apparently satisfied, the footsteps retreated down the corridor and were soon inaudible.

Feverishly now I fumbled with the third lever. There was no time to lose and I was madly desirous of investigating all the possibilities of this new kind of television-set. I had no doubt that I was on the track of a nefarious organization of spies, and I worked on in the self-termed capacity of a Sherlock Holmes.

The third lever revealed an apartment no less sumptuous than the German one had been. It appeared to be unoccupied for the present, and I had ample time to survey its expensive furnishings which had an oriental appearance. Through an open window at the far end of the room I glimpsed a mosque with domes and minarets. I could not ascertain for a certainty whether this was Turkey or India. It might have been any one of many eastern lands, I could not know. The fact that the occupant of this oriental apartment was temporarily absent made me desirous of learning more about it, but time was precious to me now, and I disconnected. No buzzing followed upon this occasion, which strengthened my belief that my lever manipulation sounded a similar buzzing that was audible in the various stations connected for the purpose of accomplishing some wicked scheme.

The fourth handle invited me to further investigation. I determined to go through with my secret research though I died in the effort. Just before my hand dropped, the buzzing commenced, and I perceived for the first time a faint glow near the lever of No. 4. I dared not investigate 4 at this time, for I did not wish it known that another than Martell was at this station. I thought of going on to dial 5, but an innate love of system forced me to risk a loss of time rather than to take them out of order. The buzzing continued for the usual duration of time, but I waited until it had apparently ceased entirely before I moved No. 4.

My soul rebelled at that which took form from the emanating

mist. A face, another duplicate of Martell's, but if possible more cruel, confronted me, completely filling up the vaporous space, and two phosphorescent eyes seared a warning into my own. A nauseating sensation crept over me as my hand crept to the connecting part of No. 4. When every vestige of the menacing face had vanished, I arose weakly and took a few faltering steps around the room. A bell was ringing with great persistence from some other room. It was mine! It would be wise to answer it. I fairly flew back to my room and was rewarded by the sound of Margaret's voice with a note of petulance in it.

"Why didn't you answer, George? The phone rang several times."

'Couldn't. Was taking a bath," I lied.

'Mr. Martell is better," continued Margaret. "The doctor says there's no immediate danger."

There was a pause and the sound of a rasping voice a little away from the vicinity of the phone, and then Margaret's voice came again.

"Mr. Martell wants you to come over, George. He wants to see you."

"Tell him I have to dress after my bath, then I'll come," I answered.

CHAPTER IV

THERE was not a moment to spare. I rushed back into Martell's room determined to see this thing through. I had never been subject to heart attacks, but certainly the suffocating sensation that possessed me could be attributed to no other cause.

A loud buzzing greeted my ears as soon as I had closed the door of Martell's suite. I looked toward the devil-machine. The four stations were buzzing at once! What was I to do? There was no light near dial 5, and that alone remained uninvestigated.

My course of action was clear; try out No. 5 to my satisfaction, leave Martell's rooms and go to Margaret Landon's home as I had told her I would. They must not know what I had done. But it was inevitable that Martell would know when he got back to his infernal television and radio. He must not get back! Well, time enough to plan that later; now to the work of seeing No. 5.

When I turned the dial of No. 5 (for, as I have stated before, this was a dial instead of a lever) I was conscious of a peculiar sensation of distance. It fairly took my breath away. What remote part of the earth's surface would the last position reveal to me?

A sharp hissing sound accompanied the manipulation of No. 5 and the vaporous shroud was very slow in taking definite shape. When it was finally at rest, and it was apparent that it would not change further, the scene depicted was at first incomprehensible to me. I stared with bulging eyes and bated breath trying to read any meaning into the combinations of form and color that had taken shape before me.

In the light of what has since occurred, the facts of which are known throughout the world, I can lend my description a little intelligence borrowed, as it were, from the future. At the time of which I write, however, no such enlightenment was mine, and it must have been a matter of minutes before the slightest knowledge of the significance of the scene entered my uncomprehending brain.

My vantage-point seemed to be slightly aerial, for I was looking down upon a scene possibly fifty feet below me. Arid red cliffs and promontories jutted over dry ravines and crevices. In the immediate foreground and also across a deep gully, extended a comparatively level area which was the scene of some sort of activity. There was about it a vague suggestion of a shipyard, yet I saw no lumber, only great mountainous piles of dull metal, among which moved thousands of agile figures. They were men and women, but how strange they appeared!

THE FATE OF THE POSEIDONIA

Their red bodies were minus clothing of any description and their heads and shoulders were covered with long white feathers that when folded, draped the upper portions of their bodies like shawls. They were unquestionably of the same race as the desert-island stranger — and Martell! At times the feathers of these strange people stood erect and spread out like a peacock's tail. I noticed that when spread in this fan-like fashion they facilitated locomotion. I glanced toward the sun far to my right and wondered if I had gone crazy. I rubbed my hands across my eyes and peered again. Yes, it was our luminary, but it was little more than half its customary size! I watched it sinking with fascinated gaze. It vanished quickly beyond the red horizon and darkness descended with scarcely a moment of intervening twilight. It was only by the closest observation that I could perceive that I was still in communication with No. 5.

Presently the gloom was dissipated by a shaft of light from the opposite horizon whither the sun had disappeared. So rapidly that I could follow its movement across the sky, the moon hove into view. But wait, was it the moon? Its surface looked strangely unfamiliar, and it too seemed to have shrunk in size.

Spellbound, I watched the tiny moon glide across the heavens the while I listened to the clang of metal tools from the workers below. Again a bright light appeared on the horizon beyond the great metal bulks below me. The scene was rapidly being rendered visible by an orb that exceeded the sun in diameter. Then I knew. Great God! There were two moons traversing the welkin! My heart was pounding so loudly that it drowned out the sound of the metal-workers. I watched on, unconscious of the passage of time.

Voices shouted from below in great excitement. Events were evidently working up to some important climax while the little satellite passed from my line of vision and only the second large moon occupied the sky. Straight before me and low on the horizon it hung with its lower margin touching the cliffs. It was low enough now so that a few of the larger stars were becoming visible. One in particular attracted my gaze and held it. It was a great bluish-green star and I noticed that the workers paused seemingly to gaze in silent admiration at its transcendent beauty. Then shout after shout arose from below and I gazed in bewilderment at the spectacle of the next few minutes, or was it hours?

A great spherical bulk hove in view from the right of my line of vision. It made me think of nothing so much as a gyroscope of gigantic proportions. It seemed to be made of the metal with which the workers were employed below, and as it gleamed in the deep blue of the sky it looked like a huge satellite. A band of red metal encircled it with points of the same at top and bottom. Numerous openings that resembled the port-holes of an ocean-liner appeared in the broad central band, from which extended metal points. I judged these were the "eyes" of the machine. But that which riveted my attention was an object that hung poised in the air below the mighty gyroscope, held in suspension by some mysterious force, probably magnetic in nature, evidently controlled in such a manner that at a certain point it was exactly counter-balanced by the gravitational pull. The lines of force apparently traveled from the poles of the mammoth sphere. But the object that depended in mid-air, as firm and rigid as though resting on terra-firma, was the missing *Pegasus*, the epitome of earthly scientific skill, but in the clutches of this unearthly looking marauder it looked like a fragile toy. Its wings were bent and twisted, giving it an uncanny resemblance to a bird in the claws of a cat.

In my spellbound contemplation of this new phenomenon I had temporarily forgotten the scene below, but suddenly a great cloud momentarily blotted out the moon, then another and another and another, in rapid succession. Huge bulks of air-craft were eclipsing the moon. Soon the scene was all but obliterated by the machines whose speed accelerated as they reached the upper air. On and on they sped in endless procession while the green star gazed serenely on! The green star, most sublime of the starry host! I loved its pale beauty though I knew not why. Darkness. The moon had set, but I knew that still those frightfully gigantic and ominous shapes still sped upward and onward. Whither?

The tiny moon again made its appearance, serving to reveal once more that endless aerial migration. Was it hours or days? I had lost all sense of the passage of time. The sound of rushing feet, succeeded by a pounding at the door brought me back to my immediate surroundings. I had the presence of mind to shut off the machine, then I arose and assumed a defensive attitude as the door opened and many figures confronted me. Foremost among them was Martell, his face white with rage, or was it fear?

"Officers, seize that man," he cried furiously. "I did not give him permission to spy in my room. He lied when he said that." Here Martell turned to the desk clerk who stood behind two policemen.

"Speaking of spying," I flung back at him, "Martell, you ought to know the meaning of that word. He's a spy himself," I cried to the two apparently unmoved officers, "why he — he—"

From their unsympathetic attitudes, I knew the odds were against me. I had lied, arid I had been found in a man's private rooms without his permission. It would be a matter of time and patience before I could persuade the law that I had any justice on my side.

I was handcuffed and led toward the door just as a sharp pain like an icy clutch at my heart overcame me. I sank into oblivion.

CHAPTER V

WHEN I regained consciousness two days later I discovered that I was the sole occupant of a cell in the State hospital for the insane. Mortified to the extreme, I pled with the keeper to bring about my release, assuring him that I was unimpaired mentally.

"Sure, that's what they all say," the fellow remarked with a wry smile.

"But I must be freed," I reiterated impatiently, "I have a message of importance for the world. I must get into immediate communication with the Secretary of War."

"Yes, yes," agreed the keeper affably. "We'll let you see the Secretary of War when that fellow over there," he jerked his thumb in the direction of the cell opposite mine, "dies from drinking hemlock. He says he's Socrates, and every time he drinks a cup of milk he flops over, but he always revives."

I looked across the narrow hall into a pair of eyes that mirrored a deranged mind, then my gaze turned to the guard who was watching me narrowly. I turned away with a shrug of despair.

Later in the day the man appeared again but I sat in sullen silence in a corner of my cell. Days passed in this manner until at last a plausible means of communication with the outside world occurred to me. I asked if my good friend Professor Stearns might be permitted to visit me. The guard replied that he believed it could be arranged for sometime the following week. It is a wonder I did not become demented, imprisoned as I was, in solitude, with the thoughts of the mysterious revelations haunting me continually.

One afternoon the keeper, passing by on one of his customary rounds, thrust a newspaper between the bars of my cell. I grabbed it eagerly and retired to read it.

THE FATE OF THE POSEIDONIA

The headlines smote my vision with an almost tactile force.

"Second Mysterious Recession of Ocean. The *Poseidonia* is lost!"

I continued to read the entire article, the letters of which blazed before my eyes like so many pinpoints of light.

"Ocean waters have again receded, this time in the Atlantic. Seismologists are at a loss to explain the mysterious cataclysm as no earth tremors have been registered. It is a little over three months since the supposed submarine fissures lowered the level of the Pacific ocean several feet, and now the same calamity, only to a greater extent, has visited the Atlantic.

"The island of Madeira reports stranded fish upon her shores by the thousands, the decay of which threatens the health of the island's population. Two merchant vessels off the Azores, and one fifty miles out from Gibraltar, were found total wrecks. Another, the *Transatlantia* reported a fearful agitation of the ocean depths, but seemed at a loss for a plausible explanation, as the sky was cloudless and no wind was blowing.

"'But despite this fact,' wired the *Transatlantia*, 'great waves all but capsized us. This marine disturbance lasted throughout the night.'

"The following wireless from the great ocean liner, *Poseidonia*, brings home to us the realization that Earth has been visited with a stupendous calamity. The *Poseidonia* was making her weekly transatlantic trip between Europe and America, and was in mid-ocean at the time her message was flashed to the world.

"'A great cloud of flying objects of enormous proportions has just appeared in the sky blotting out the light of the stars. No sound accompanies the approach of this strange fleet. In appearance the individual craft resemble mammoth balloons. The sky is black with them and in their vicinity the air is humid and oppressive as though the atmosphere were saturated to the point of condensation. Everything is orderly. There are no collisions. Our captain has given orders for us to turn back toward Europe — we have turned, but the dark dirigibles are pursuing us. Their speed is unthinkable. Can the *Poseidonia*, doing a mere hundred miles an hour, escape? A huge craft is bearing down upon us from above and behind. There is no escape. Pandemonium reigns. The enemy—'

"Thus ends the tragic message from the brave wireless operator of the *Poseidonia*."

I threw down the paper and called loudly for the keeper. Socrates across the hall eyed me suspiciously. I was beginning to feel that perhaps the poor demented fellow had nothing on me; that I should soon be in actuality a raving maniac.

The keeper came in response to my call, entered my cell and patted my shoulders reassuringly.

"Never mind, old top," he said, "it isn't so bad as it seems."

"Now look here," I burst forth angrily, "I tell you I am not insane!" How futile my words sounded! "If you will send Professor Mortimer Stearns, teacher of Astronomy at Austin, to me at once for an hour's talk, I'll prove to the world that I have not been demented."

"Professor Stearns is a very highly esteemed friend of mine," I continued, noting the suspicion depicted on his countenance. "If you wish, go to him first and find out his true opinion of me. I'll wager it will not be an uncomplimentary one!"

The man twisted his keys thoughtfully, and I uttered not a word, believing a silent demeanor most effective in the present crisis. After what seemed an eternity:

"All right," he said, "I'll see what can be done toward arranging a visit from Professor Mortimer Stearns as soon as possible."

I restrained my impulse toward a too effusive expression of gratitude as I realized that a quiet dignity prospered my cause more effectually.

THE FATE OF THE POSEIDONIA   151

The next morning at ten, after a constant vigil, I was rewarded with the most welcome sight of Professor Stearns striding down the hall in earnest conversation with the guard. He was the straw and I the drowning man, but would he prove a more substantial help than the proverbial straw? I surely hoped so.

A chair was brought for the professor and placed just outside my cell. I hastily drew my own near it.

"Well, this is indeed unfortunate," said Mortimer Stearns with some embarrassment, "and I sincerely hope you will soon be released."

"Unfortunate!" I echoed. "It is nothing short of a calamity."

My indignation voiced so vociferously startled the good professor and he shoved his chair almost imperceptibly away from the intervening bars. At the far end of the hall the keeper eyed me suspiciously. Hang it all, was my last resort going to fail me?

"Professor Stearns," I said earnestly, "will you try to give me an unbiased hearing? My situation is a desperate one, and it is necessary for some one to believe in me before I can render humanity the service it needs."

He responded to my appeal with something of his old sincerity, that always endeared him to his associates.

"I shall be glad to hear your story, Gregory, and if I can render any service, I'll not hesitate—"

"That's splendid of you," I interrupted with emotion, "and now to my weird tale."

I related from the beginning, omitting no details, however trivial they may have seemed, the series of events that had brought me to my present predicament.

"And your conclusion?" queried the professor in strange, hollow tones.

"That Martian spies, one of whom is Martell, are

superintending by radio and television, an unbelieveably well-planned theft of Earth's water in order to replenish their own dry ocean beds!"

"Stupendous!" gasped Professor Stearns. "Something must be done to prevent another raid. Let's see," he mused, "the interval was three months before, was it not? Three months we shall have for bringing again into use the instruments of war that praise God! have lain idle for many generations. It is the only way to deal with a formidable foe from outside."

CHAPTER VI

PROFESSOR STEARNS was gone, but there was hope in my heart in place of the former grim despair. When the guard handed the evening paper to me I amazed him with a grateful "thank you." But my joy was short-lived. Staring up at me from the printed passenger-list of the ill-fated *Poseidonia* were the names of Mr. and Mrs. T. M. Landon and daughter Margaret!

I know the guard classed me as one of the worst cases on record, but I felt that surely Fate had been unkind.

"A package for Mr. George Gregory," bawled a voice in the corridor.

Thanks to the influence of Professor Stearns, I was permitted to receive mail. When the guard saw that I preferred unwrapping it myself, he discreetly left me to the mystery of the missive.

A card just inside bore the few but insignificant words, "For Gregory in remembrance of Martell."

I suppressed an impulse to dash the accursed thing to the floor when I saw that it was Martell's radio and television instrument. Placing it upon the table I drew a chair up to it and turned each of the levers, but not one functioned. I manipulated the dial No. 5. The action was accompanied by the same hissing sound that had so startled my overwrought nerves upon the previous

THE FATE OF THE POSEIDONIA 153

occasion. Slowly the wraithlike mist commenced the process of adjustment. Spellbound I watched the scene before my eyes.

Again I had the sensation of a lofty viewpoint. It was identical with the one I had previously held, but the scene — was it the same? It must be — and yet! The barren red soil was but faintly visible through a verdure. The towering rocky palisades that bordered the chasm were crowned with golden-roofed dwellings, or were they temples, for they were like the pure marble fanes of the ancient Greeks except in color. Down the steep slopes flowed streams of sparkling water that dashed with a merry sound to a canal below.

Gone were the thousands of beings and their metal aircraft, but seated on a grassy plot in the left foreground of the picture was a small group of the white-feathered, red-skinned inhabitants of this strange land. In the distance rose the temple-crowned crags. One figure alone stood, and with a magnificent gesture held arms aloft. The great corona of feathers spread following the line of the arms like the open wings of a great eagle. The superb figure stood and gazed into the deep velvety blue of the sky, the others following the direction of their leader's gaze.

Involuntarily I too watched the welkin where now not even a moon was visible. Then within the range of my vision there moved a great object — the huge aerial gyroscope — and beneath it, dwarfed by its far greater bulk, hung a modern ocean-liner, like a jewel from the neck of some gigantic ogre.

Great God — it was the *Poseidonia*! I knew now, in spite of the earthly appearance of the great ship, that it was no terrestrial scene upon which I gazed. I was beholding the victory of Martell, the Martian, who had filled his world's canals with water of Earth, and even borne away trophies of our civilization to exhibit to his fellow-beings.

I closed my eyes to shut out the awful scene, and thought of Margaret, dead and yet aboard the liner, frozen in the absolute cold of outer space!

How long I sat stunned and horrified I do not know, but when I looked back for another last glimpse of the Martian landscape, I uttered a gasp of incredulity. A face filled the entire vaporous screen, the beloved features of Margaret Landon. She was speaking and her voice came over the distance like the memory of a sound that is not quite audible and yet very real to the person in whose mind it exists. It was more as if time divided us instead of space, yet I knew it was the latter, for while a few minutes of time came between us, millions of miles of space intervened!

"George," came the sweet, far-away voice, "I loved you, but you were so suspicious and jealous that I accepted the companionship of Martell, hoping to bring you to your senses. I did not know what an agency for evil he had established upon the earth. Forgive me, dear."

She smiled wistfully. "My parents perished with hundreds of others in the transportation of the *Poseidonia*, but Martell took me from the ship to the ether-craft for the journey, so that I alone was saved."

Her eyes filled with tears. "Do not mourn for me, George, for I shall take up the thread of life anew among these strange but beautiful surroundings. Mars is indeed lovely, but I will tell you of it later for I cannot talk long now."

"I only want to say," she added hastily, "that Terra need fear Mars no more. There is a sufficiency of water now — and I will prevent any—"

She was gone, and in her stead was the leering, malevolent face of Martell. He was minus his skullcap, and his clipped feathers stood up like the ruff of an angry turkey-gobbler.

I reached instinctively for the dial, but before my hand touched it there came a sound, not unlike that of escaping steam, and instantaneously the picture vanished. I did not

THE FATE OF THE POSEIDONIA

object to the disappearance of the Martian, but another fact did cause me regret; from that moment, I was never able to view the ruddy planet through the agency of the little machine. All communication had been forever shut off by Martell.

Although many doubt the truth of my solution to the mystery of the disappearance of the *Pegasus* and of the *Poseidonia*, and are still searching beneath the ocean waves, I know that never will either of them be seen again on Earth.

The FOUR-DIMENSIONAL ROLLER-PRESS
~ By Bob Olsen ~

After carefully adjusting the machine, the young inventor picked up the baboon...and placed it on the platform in front of the machine. He had the same difficulty in forcing the animal's head between the rollers...but no doubt it would have been harder had not Jocko become accustomed to the appearance and noise of moving machinery.

Introduction

We have once heard science defined as the measurement of things. Though that may be an overly simple definition, it is certainly true when it comes to the experiments upon which scientific discoveries are based. Measurement is the basis of all these discoveries—change in weight or size or color of one thing due to something else—this is all measurement. To measure accurately we must follow all the dimensions of an object, and to do that we must know all there is to know about dimensions: length, breadth, thickness...and others. It's the "others" that are the subject of this very fascinating story of a young genius, his pet monkey, and the unexpected result of a remarkable invention.

THE FOUR-DIMENSIONAL ROLLER-PRESS

By Bob Olsen

ACTING on the suggestion of my attorney I am writing a complete account of all I know concerning the unparalleled disappearance of William James Sidelburg.

Though his childhood and early education have an important bearing on the case, it is hardly necessary for me to remind anyone who has kept up with modern periodicals that he was son of a well-known professor of psychology, and that his early training was carried on in accordance with certain revolutionary and original theories. The success of these experiments was attested by the fact that he entered Harvard University at the age of eleven; and, when he was only a boy of thirteen, delivered before a body of eminent mathematicians a scholarly lecture on the fourth dimension.

My acquaintance with young Sidelburg began about a year after the mathematical lecture which brought him so much newspaper fame. I had just secured my M.E. degree from a well-known engineering school, and had registered with an employment agency conducted by the college faculty. One day, early in the summer, I received from the agency a notice requesting me to apply in person to Mr. Sidelburg.

Of course I had heard of Sidelburg through the papers, and was prepared to meet a young man; but I was genuinely surprised to find that he was not only young but extremely boyish in appearance and in dress. When he spoke, the childish treble of the voice seemed strangely out of keeping with his learned vocabulary and well ordered phrases.

He explained briefly that he was planning the construction of some new psychological apparatus, and required the assistance of a man familiar with machinery,—especially one who was a skilled wood-turner and pattern-maker. He had made careful inquiries into the records of a large number of candidates, and had selected me, because I had distinguished myself particularly in electricity, mathematics, and pattern-making, and also because I was one of the younger members of my class. The matter of salary, hours, and so forth were easily disposed of; and I went to work for him the following Monday.

His father owned a residence in Brookline, Massachusetts, with grounds covering several acres. In a remote corner of the estate, at some distance from the house, stood the building which young Sidelburg used as his private workshop. It was remarkably well equipped, with an electric switchboard, giving a large range of currents, both direct and alternating and at high and low voltage. There were lathes and other machines for working in wood and metal; and everything was of the best and latest design.

THE FOUR-DIMENSIONAL ROLLER-PRESS 159

Sidelburg had already prepared a set of blue-prints, and he put me to work turning out some of the parts. I found that his drawings called for several thousand pieces of maple turned out in the form of perfect spheres, about six inches in diameter. At my suggestion he ordered these spheres from a firm which made a specialty of work of that sort, and this left me free to spend most of my time on the gear wheels and other metal parts of the machine.

During all this time, I had absolutely no idea of the purpose, or even the general outlines of the invention. My work had been confined to the individual parts, and all the assembling was done by Sidelburg himself. As soon as enough of the parts were ready, he began setting up the device, not inside the laboratory but out-of-doors in an open space adjoining the shop. He explained that for certain reasons it would work better in the open air, where it would be free from the restricting influence of the ceiling and the four walls.

To protect it from occasional showers, and from the more frequent prying eyes of inquisitive neighbors, he erected a flimsy awning and two screens of canvas. Though resembling a tent, it could hardly be called one, since it was completely open on the sides which faced the workshop and the dwelling-house. It was connected electrically with the laboratory, and had four powerful arc lights for use in case he wished to work at night — which, by the way, was very seldom.

Judging that he had good reasons for his strict observance of secrecy concerning the purpose of his invention, I discreetly forbore asking any questions pertaining to this subject. The information, when it finally came, was entirely voluntary on his part.

We had been working for about three months, and the machine had at last assumed tangible shape, when he called me from my work one day and asked me to come and inspect the device.

"I suppose you wonder what it's for," he suggested.

I admitted that the mystery of its purpose had given me some concern.

"Well, I suppose it's time I told you all about it. I'll need your help to operate it, and you may as well begin now to study the principles' underlying the contrivance. I'm going to call this a four-dimensional roller-press. As the name implies, it is a device for compressing or expanding the amount of an object's fourth dimension."

Then he gave me a very scholarly and detailed account of the inception of his idea, and the theories which he had formulated and was now trying to prove. He first showed me a clipping from a magazine article giving a review of a paper by Mr. A. G. Blake, fellow of the Royal Astronomical Society of London. The theory propounded by Mr. Blake is that the density of an object may be regarded as its extension in a fourth dimension.

I have taken the liberty of quoting a few passages directly from the article, expressed in Mr. Blake's own words:

"Our ideas of the dimensions of a body are largely derived from the circumstances in which these dimensions may undergo variation. Thus we speak of a piece of paper as being of two dimensions because of the greater difficulty of changing its thickness compared with the difficulty of changing its length and breadth.

"In 'Flatland'—a hypothetical region where only motion confined to two dimensions is possible—it is quite conceivable—nay it is a necessary assumption if we are to allow the possibility of concrete bodies in it—that the bodies should have a certain thickness in a third dimension which would be invariable in individual bodies, but not necessarily uniform among different bodies. Thus the sum total thickness of bodies in 'Flatland' would be fixed and invariable. To the inhabitants, who would

THE FOUR-DIMENSIONAL ROLLER-PRESS 161

be incapable of realizing thickness, this would result in the conservation of some physical attribute peculiar to bodies of two-dimensional space.

"In seeking evidence of a fourth dimension we must draw our inference from the conservation of some physical attribute peculiar to "In our three-dimensional universe every body has a thickness in a fourth dimension, which is variable in different bodies but invariable in the same body, and that thickness is the body's density.

"Though we can not directly change the extent of a body in its fourth dimension, we can do so indirectly by taking advantage of the principle of the conservation of mass and compressing the body in three dimensions. This always increases its density. The two-dimensional equivalent to this is that in two-dimensional space it is impossible to alter the third dimension, yet by compressing it in two dimensions, the third will be increased while the volume will remain constant."

Though rather technical, this sounded perfectly consistent to me; but in order to be sure of my complete comprehension, young Sidelburg elucidated, amplified, and illustrated the discussion of the subject of hyper-space, somewhat as follows:

"Suppose we start with a point and move it a unit distance, say a foot, in any definite direction. This is exactly what we do when we draw a line with the point of a lead pencil. The line which results is an object of one dimension, which is length. If, however, we move our line at right angles to itself for any distance, a plane having two dimensions, length and width, is generated. For instance, if I draw out this curtain, which looks like a mere stick or line, a flat surface or plane is formed. Now, if our plane is moved at right angles to both its dimensions, a three-dimensional solid or cube is produced. We might illustrate this by the opening of an opera hat or Japanese lantern. Let us continue the process one step further, moving our solid cube its own length at right angles to each of its three dimensions. Then we should have a four-dimensional unit which mathematicians call a hypercube or tesseract. As you doubtless know, I have worked out the mathematical formulas of several other regular four-dimensional objects. To these I have given appropriate names such as polyhedragons, sextacosiahedragons, and hecatonicosiahedragons.

"Here is another conception of a four-dimensioned object, based on the circle rather than the cube, and on rotation rather than movement at right angles. Let us go back to our one-dimensional line and rotate it about a point midway between its extremities. What is formed? Clearly, a circle, which has extension in two dimensions. Next, we rotate our circle (a plane) about one of its diameters (a line) as an axis, and we get a three-dimensional solid, it may be a sphere. Now, the question arises, what will happen if we rotate our sphere about a plane which passes through its center? This would mean rotation through a fourth dimension, and a four-dimensional hyper-sphere would result. Can you not easily imagine such a thing?"

I confessed that I could not conceive of rotating a solid object about a plane and through a fourth dimension.

"Of course," he continued, "such an idea is contrary to our common-sense notions, since we are constantly hedged about with three-dimensional objects and three-dimensional concepts. If we could actually move in a fourth dimension, many strange things would be possible. We could pass out of a locked cell without touching door, window, or wall; we could take out the inside of a watermelon without disturbing the rind; a doctor could remove an appendix without cutting the patient's skin.

"These things sound like miracles; but, after all, what are miracles but phenomena which, on account of our ignorance, we cannot explain? The submarine and the airplane would have been miracles to our great grandfathers; and what are these inventions but the first feebly successful steps in man's efforts to conquer the *third* dimension? It wasn't so long ago that man was like the restricted inhabitants of Mr. Blake's imaginary 'Flatlands'—confined to the two-dimensional surface of the land or ocean. Subways, elevated railroads, mines, and skyscrapers are other examples of man's efforts to branch out in a third dimension. When our conquests of the air and of the submarine and subterranean regions are complete, the next step will be that of wresting from nature the secrets of the fourth dimension.

"Evidence of the existence of such a dimension are abundant in nature. Take, for example, the left and right symmetry of almost any natural object, such as the human body, for instance. Just as the two halves of a symmetrical two-dimensional object, such as a leaf, will fit if folded over along the line of the midrib, through the third dimension, so the human body if rotated on a plane through a fourth dimension, would fit part on part.

"It is a simple matter to find out how you would appear if you turned around through the fourth dimension. Just look at your image in a mirror. Suppose you part your hair on the left side. The image man has his parted on the right side. Hold out your right hand, as if to shake hands with your image. The looking-glass man extends his left hand. Your hands are directly opposite each other, instead of being crossed in front as they would be if you shook hands with a real person.

"Now to return to Mr. Blake's theories. Suppose I cut a circle out of paper. Since its thickness is practically zero, we may consider this a two-dimensional object; but if I pile several thousand of these disks of paper one on top of the other, a solid with a definite thickness is formed. This cylindrical rolling-pin which I have in my hand was actually made that way.

"Mr. Blake calls attention to the familiar fact that compressing an object in three dimensions increases its density. This is exactly what would happen if density were a fourth dimension. My idea is to reverse the process. By applying pressure to an object in the direction of its fourth dimension, its four-dimensional extension will be diminished, and all its other dimensions will be increased. In other words, the volume would be enlarged and the density decreased.

"Let me illustrate with an example from two-dimensional space; I have prepared a quantity of biscuit dough, and you will notice that I have cut out several objects of varying thicknesses. I can increase the thickness of any of these little squares by pressing them with my hands around the edges. If I apply pressure from above, by means of this rolling-pin, the thickness is greatly lessened, but a corresponding increase in the length and width has taken place.

"Here is a two-dimensional man, which I cut out with a form such as our grandmothers used for making gingerbread men. If I roll him out flat, he still retains the same general form, but he has expanded in his two-dimensional world, while his third dimension has been diminished.

"If an ordinary human body were compressed in the direction of a fourth dimension his volume would increase and his density decrease. This would greatly lessen the labor of walking, would make it as easy for a person to float on fresh water as on the waters of the Great Salt Lake, and might realize the dreams of Darius Green, who, you remember, tried to fly by means of wings propelled by his own muscles.

"Of course, in order to produce pressure in a fourth dimension, it is necessary to have a four-dimensional object. This I have succeeded in accomplishing with the aid of my mathematical formulas. Just as I built up a three-dimensional cylinder by piling together a large number of circles, so I have constructed a hyper-cylinder, or four-dimensional roller by

THE FOUR-DIMENSIONAL ROLLER-PRESS

joining together a large number of spheres."

He then called my attention to certain parts of the mechanism which had interested me particularly, since they were the most distinctive features of the machine. I can think of no better way of describing one of these four-dimensional rollers than by comparing it to a cluster of toy balloons, a bunch of grapes, or a blackberry. Of course, it was more regular in shape than either of these objects, and was composed of the six-inch spheres which I have mentioned before.

Thus Sidelburg continued: "Just as a solid is bounded by surfaces, so a four-dimensional object is bounded by solids. Bear in mind that in grouping these spheres together they cannot be placed side by side, one in front of the other, or one on top of the other, as any one of these methods of joining would simply be extending the object in one of its three dimensions. They cannot be arranged next to each other, but must be put through each other or around each other. It doesn't matter much which way you look at it, but perhaps the term 'around' is easier to comprehend than 'through'."

The rollers were eight in number, and were arranged in the form of an octagon surrounding an open space about six feet across. That is, the space looked open. The youthful inventor explained that owing to a considerable, but invisible, extension of each of the rollers in the fourth dimension, the space was really full, except for a very small aperture to admit the object to be compressed.

At his suggestion, I tried to thrust my hand through this space, which, as far as visible evidence was concerned, was totally vacant. Much to my astonishment, my hand encountered something palpably hard and solid, nor could I force my arm through the six-foot opening.

By an ingenious arrangement of gears, operated by a powerful electric motor, the eight rollers could be made to rotate in unison. The amount of opening between them could be adjusted within a fraction of a centimeter by means of a very accurate micrometer screw turned by a wheel about the size of the steering wheel of an automobile. This wheel could either be operated by hand; or, if any especially large

force were desired, could be put in gear with the electric motor by the simple expedient of throwing over a handle very much like the controller of a trolley car.

Having thus explained the theoretical and mechanical principles underlying his invention, Sidelburg proceeded to test it. I could see that he was very nervous and excited when the final moment arrived which would determine whether he had wasted an enormous amount of money and labor, or had made a revolutionary discovery.

The first object run through the press was a cylinder of steel about two feet long and three inches in diameter. It was a waste piece sawn from a longer bar which had formed one of the shafts of the machine. He placed it on the table in front on the rollers, adjusted it so that it came exactly in the center of the octagon, and directed me to throw the switch. With the jerky motion of a mechanism operated for the first time, the rollers began to rotate. As he pushed the cylinder forward it seemed to be caught by invisible claws and sucked slowly into the open space.

Sidelburg darted around to the other side, and breathlessly waited for it to emerge. A cry of joy escaped his trembling lips: "Eureka! It works!" And he seized the piece of metal and held it out for me to inspect. It had expanded to more than twice its original size, but except for the apparent decrease in density, still preserved the appearance of steel.

"Think what this will mean to the construction of aeroplanes, or any other machinery, for that matter," Sidelburg enthused. "It will be an easy matter to make steel

THE FOUR-DIMENSIONAL ROLLER-PRESS 167

which is lighter than aluminum."

"But will it have the same strength, volume for volume?"

"Probably not. That we can easily determine by making the usual tests; but if my theories are correct it will be possible to make an enormous decrease in the weight with only a slight diminution in strength. Now I'm going to see what will happen if I press it to the limit."

He started the machine once more, and as soon as the rollers had taken hold on the steel rod he threw over the controller handle, thus starting the mechanism which pressed the rollers together with great force. The severe strain which this put on the machine was shown by the ripping, grinding noise which it emitted.

The result was probably anticipated by Sidelburg, but to me it was a considerable surprise to see the solid chunk of metal swell up like an enormous toy balloon, and go sailing away into space, carrying with it the canvas awning which covered our outdoor machine shop.

"That illustrates another possibility," exulted the inventor. "Think of a dirigible balloon made of solid steel! No expensive silk covering, no dangerous explosive gas, just a piece of expanded metal with a propeller and rudder and elevating planes to direct it in whatever direction you desire. Now I'm going to try the effect on a living being. Jocko will have the honor of being the first living subject to go through the four-dimensional roller-press."

Jocko was the name of Sidelburg's pet monkey, a very droll creature which he kept chained to one of the poles of his outdoor laboratory. I had always regarded its presence as but one of the many indications of Sidelburg's natural boyishness; and the idea that he was contemplating using it to experiment upon had never entered my mind.

After carefully adjusting the machine, the young inventor

picked up the baboon (I should judge that it weighed about fifty pounds) and placed it on the platform in front of the machine. He had some difficulty in forcing the animal's head between the rollers, but I have no doubt that it would have been much harder had not Jocko become accustomed to the appearance and noise of moving machinery.

As we expected, Jocko appeared on the other side, somewhat augmented in size; though the machine had purposely been adjusted so that only a slight diminution in the fourth dimension or density would take place. Since the monkey seemed in no wise disturbed by the operation, and gave no indication that he had suffered any pain, we decided to repeat the process. The wheel of the micrometer was turned a fraction of a revolution, and this was repeated several times, until Jocko had assumed the proportions of a good sized man. When placed upon the ground, he behaved in a perfectly normal manner, except that his motions were extremely rapid, and when he moved about it was with surprisingly long leaps and bounds. Sidelburg explained that this was due to the removal of some of the inhibiting effects of gravity.

So elated was he with the manifest success of his invention, that he forgot to chain Jocko again, and the transformed animal was allowed to jump around at will and enjoy his new freedom.

Then nothing would do but that Sidelburg must try the machine on himself. In vain I pleaded with him to await a time when the experiment could be performed with other witnesses than myself. I told him I did not feel like bearing the responsibility alone; and in answer to this he hastily wrote and signed a note absolving me of all blame in case anything went wrong. This paper I have filed with the police authorities of Brookline.

Realizing at last that he was determined to experiment on

THE FOUR-DIMENSIONAL ROLLER-PRESS 169

his own body in spite of all my pleadings to postpone the test, I grudgingly consented to assist him. All the details of adjustment, however, I insisted that he should attend to himself. I merely waited until he had taken his position on the platform; and when he gave the word, threw in the switch.

The effect on Sidelburg was very much like that produced on the monkey the first time it went through the press—namely a slight increase in bulk. I believe I hinted before that he was rather small in stature. His original height was about five feet and four inches, and he couldn't have weighed much more than a hundred pounds. After passing through the machine, however, his height was approximately five feet and eight inches; and one would have estimated his weight to be about a hundred and fifty pounds. This, though, was deceptive, for his weight couldn't have changed.

"How do you feel?" was my first question.

"Fine. When I was going through, I had a kind of puffy sensation, such as you have when you fill your lungs with a deep breath; but that's gone now, and I feel perfectly normal, except that it seems much easier to move." To illustrate this, he ran out on the tennis court, which was close by, propelling himself with enormous bounds, and jumped over the net. He cleared it by fully three feet! He could have easily broken the world's record for the high jump.

"I've always wanted to be a big man," he cried, "and now I can be as big as I wish. I believe I'll go through once more."

Again I begged him to wait, but with as little success as before. He gave the micrometer wheel an almost imperceptible twist, and stretched himself out on the platform. I turned on the current and the rollers began to revolve. So intent was I watching Sidelburg as his head slowly entered the jaws of the marvelous machine, that I had not noticed the return of Jocko.

My first warning of danger was a harsh grating, gripping sound, exactly like that emitted by the machine the last time the steel rod went through it. I turned to the switchboard, and was horrified to see Jocko clinging to the handle of the controller, which—doubtless in imitation of his master—he had just pulled down.

Sidelburg's shoulders and chest were just emerging from between the rollers. They were swollen to enormous proportion. From his mouth escaped a shrill cry like that of a wounded fowl; and words, thin, quivering, and very far away pierced my terror-stricken brain. "Turn off the power — for God's sa—"

I dashed to the switch-board. Jocko evidently mistook my sudden action as directed against him, for he bared his teeth and leaped upon me. It was not difficult to move him from side to side, for he was very light, but his strength was enormous. He wrapped his long arms and legs around me and held me powerless. But desperation gave me the strength of a madman, and I finally wrenched an arm free, grasped a block of wood, and gave the ape a stunning blow on the head. He broke away from me, and with stupendous bounds leaped out of sight.

By this time, the rollers had passed over Sidelburg's torso and thighs, and were about even with his knees. His body was bloated to the size of a large balloon; and it seemed almost about to lift the machine, which was already rocking on its foundations.

Just as I pulled out the switch which stopped the motion of the rollers, a sudden gust of wind caught the swollen body, and added just enough force to wrench the press clear of the ground, Sidelburg's feet and ankles were clamped firmly between the rollers; and as he slowly rose in the air, like an enormous dirigible, he took the machine along with him.

THE FOUR-DIMENSIONAL ROLLER-PRESS

The next day some fisherman off the coast of Newfoundland reported seeing a Zeppelin flying end up at a height of about a mile. As far as I know, that was the last that was seen of William James Sidelburg and his four dimensional roller-press.

Some of my friends to whom I have related this story have asked me if I could reconstruct Sidelburg's invention.

This I feel quite confident that I could do, with the aid of the blue-prints and formulas which he left behind; but the mere thought of making the attempt is horribly repugnant to me. I have noticed that Nature has a way of visiting dire punishment upon importunate mortals who seek to pry too deeply into her secrets.

The MACHINE MAN of ARDATHIA
by Francis Flagg

I was conscious of being scooped up and drawn forward with inconcievable speed. For one breathless moment I was hung suspended...

Introduction

HERE is an astounding fourth-dimensional story, every bit as good as any that we have read in years. What will humanity look like 30,000 years hence? If, since the Egyptians or Romans, we have traveled to our present stage of development in the space of some 2,000 years, how high will the human have ascended in 30,000 years? Our new author has written excellent science into a most unusual and interesting story that can not fail to grip you.

THE MACHINE MAN OF ARDATHIA
By Francis Flagg

I DO not know what to believe. Sometimes, I am positive I dreamed it all. But, then, there is the matter of the heavy rocking-chair. That, undeniably, did disappear. Perhaps someone played a trick on me; but who would stoop to a deception so bizarre, merely for the purpose of befuddling the wits of an old man? Perhaps someone stole the rocking-chair; but why should anyone want to steal it? It was, it is true, a sturdy piece of furniture, but hardly valuable enough to excite the cupidity of a thief. Besides, it was in its place when I sat down in the easy-chair.

Of course, I may be lying. Peters, to whom I was misguided enough to tell everything on the night of its occurrence, wrote the story for his paper, and the editor says as much in his editorial when he remarks: "Mr. Matthews seems to possess an imagination equal to that of an H. G. Wells." And, considering the nature of my story I am quite ready to forgive him for doubting my veracity.

However, the few friends who know me better think that I had dined a little too wisely or too well, and was visited with a nightmare. Hodge suggested that the Jap who cleans my rooms had, for some reason, removed the rocking chair from its place, and that I merely took its presence for granted when I sat down in the other; but the Jap strenuously denies having done so.

I must explain that I have two rooms and a bath on the third floor of a modern apartment house fronting the Lake. Since my wife's death three years ago, I have lived thus, taking my breakfast and lunch at a restaurant, and my dinners, generally, at the club. I also have a room in a down-town office building where I spend a few hours every day working on my book, which is intended to be a critical analysis of the fallacies inherent in the Marxian theory of economics, embracing at the same time a thorough refutation of Lewis Morgan's *Ancient Society*. A rather ambitious undertaking, you will admit, and one not apt to engage the interest of a person given to inventing wild yards for the purpose of amazing his friends.

No; I emphatically deny having invented the story. However, the future will speak for itself. I will merely proceed to put the details of my strange experience on paper—justice to myself demands that I should do so, so many garbled accounts have appeared in the press—and leave the reader to draw his own conclusions.

Contrary to my usual custom, I had dined that evening with Hodge at the Hotel Oaks. Let me emphatically state that, while it is well-known among his intimates that Hodge has a decided taste for liquor, I had absolutely nothing of an intoxicating nature to drink, and Hodge will verify this. About eight-thirty, I refused an invitation to attend the theatre with him, and went to my rooms. There I changed into smoking-jacket and slippers, and lit a mild Havana.

The rocking-chair was occupying its accustomed place near

THE MACHINE MAN OF ARDATHIA 175

the centre of the sitting-room floor. I remember that clearly because, as usual, I had either to push it aside or step around it, wondering for the thousandth time, as I did so, why that idiotic Jap persisted in placing it in such an inconvenient spot, and resolving, also for the thousandth time to speak to him about it. With a note-book and pencil placed on the stand beside me, and a copy of Frederick Engel's *Origin of The Family, Private Property and The State,* I turned on the light in my green-shaded reading lamp, switched off all the others, and sank with a sigh of relief into the easy-chair.

It was my intention to make a few notes from Engels' work relative to plural marriages, showing that he contradicted certain conclusions of Morgan's, but after a few minutes' work, I leaned back in my chair and closed my eyes. I did not doze; I am positive of that. My mind was actively engaged in trying to piece together a sentence that would clearly express my thoughts.

I CAN best describe what happened, then, by saying there was an explosion. It wasn't that, exactly; but, at the time, it seemed to me there must have been an explosion. A blinding flash of light registered with appalling vividness, through the closed lids, on the retina of my eyes. My first thought was that someone had dynamited the building; my second, that the electric fuses had blown out. It was some time before I could see clearly. When I could:

"Good Lord!" I whispered weakly. "What's that?"

Occupying the space where the rocking-chair had stood (though I did not notice its absence at the time) was a cylinder of what appeared to be glass, standing, I should judge, above five feet high. Encased in this cylinder was what seemed to be a caricature of a man—or a child. I say caricature because, while the cylinder was all of five feet in height, the being inside of it was hardly three; and you can imagine my amazement while I stared at this apparition. After a while, I got up and switched on all the lights, to better observe it.

You may wonder why I did not try to call someone in, but that never occurred to me. In spite of my age—I am sixty—my nerves are steady, and I am not easily frightened. I walked very carefully around the cylinder, and viewed the creature inside from all angles. It was sustained in the centre, midway between top and bottom, by what appeared to be an intricate arrangement of glass and metal tubes. These tubes seemed to run at places into the body; and I noticed some sort of dark fluid circulating through the glass tubes.

The head was very large and hairless; it had bulging brows, and no ears. The eyes were large and winkless, the nose well defined; but the lower part of the face and mouth ran into the small, round body with no sign of a chin. Its legs hung down, skinny, flabby; and the arms were more like short tentacles reaching down from where the head and body joined. The thing was, of course, naked.

I drew the easy-chair up to the cylinder, and sat down facing it Several times I stretched out my hand in an effort to touch its surface, but some force prevented my fingers from making contact, which was very curious. Also, I could detect no movement of the body or limbs of the weird thing inside the glass.

"What I would like to know," I muttered, "is what you are and where you come from; are you alive, and am I dreaming or am I awake?"

Suddenly, the creature came to life. One of its tentacle-like hands, holding a metal tube, darted to its mouth. From the tube shot a white streak, which fastened itself to the cylinder.

"Ah!" came a clear, metallic voice. "English, Primitive; probably of the twentieth century." The words were uttered

THE MACHINE MAN OF ARDATHIA 177

with an indescribable intonation, much as if a foreigner were speaking our language. Yet, more than that, as if he were speaking a language long dead. I don't know why that thought should have occurred to me, then. Perhaps ...

"So you can talk!" I exclaimed.

The creature gave a metallic chuckle. "As you say, I can talk."

"Then tell me what you are."

"I am an Ardathian—a Machine-Man of Ardathia. And you...? Tell me, is that really hair on your head?"

"Yes," I replied.

"And those coverings you wear on your body, are they clothes?"

I answered in the affirmative.

"How odd! Then you really are a Primitive; a Prehistoric Man," The eyes behind the glass shield regarded me intently.

"A prehistoric man!" I exclaimed. "What do you mean?"

"I mean that you are one of that race of early men whose skeletons we have dug up, here and there, and reconstructed for our Schools of Biology. Marvellous how our scientists have copied you from some fragments of bone! The small head covered with hair, the beast-like jaw, the abnormally large body and legs, the artificial coverings made of cloth . . . even your language!"

FOR the first time, I began to suspect that I was the victim of a hoax. I got up again and walked carefully around the cylinder, but could detect no outside agency controlling the contraption. Besides, it was absurd to think that anyone would go to the trouble of constructing such a complicated apparatus as this appeared to be, merely for the sake of a practical joke. Nevertheless, I looked out on the landing. Seeing nobody, I came back and resumed my seat in front of the cylinder.

"Pardon me," I said, "but you referred to me as belonging to a period much more remote than yours."

"That is correct. If I am not mistaken in my calculations, you are thirty thousand years in the past. What date is this?"

"June 5th, 1939," I replied, feebly. The creature went through some contortions, sorted a few metal tubes with its hands, and then announced in its metallic voice:

"Computed in terms of your method of reckoning, I have travelled back through time exactly twenty-eight thousand years, nine months, three weeks, two days, seven hours, and a certain number of minutes and seconds which it is useless for me to enumerate exactly."

It was at this point that I endeavoured to make sure I was wide awake and in full possession of my faculties. I got up, selected a fresh cigar from the humidor, struck a light, and began puffing away. After a few puffs, I laid it beside the one I had been smoking earlier in the evening. I found it there, later. Incontestable proof.....

I said that I am a man of steady nerves. Once more I sat down in front of the cylinder, determined this time to find out what I could about the incredible creature within.

"You say you have travelled back through time thousands of years. How is that possible?" I demanded.

"By verifying time as a fourth dimension, and perfecting devices for travelling in it."

"In what manner?"

"I do not know whether I can explain it exactly, in your language, and you are too primitive and unevolved to understand mine. However, I shall try. Know, then, that space is as much a relative thing as time. In itself, aside from its relation to matter, it has no existence. You can neither see nor touch it, yet you move freely in space. Is that clear?"

"It sounds like Einstein's theory."

"Einstein?"

"One of our great scientists and mathematicians," I explained.

"So you have scientists and mathematicians? Wonderful! That bears out what Hoomi says. I must remember to tell. . . However, to resume my explanation. Time is apprehended in the same manner as is space—that is, in its relation to matter. When you measure space, you do so by letting your measuring rod leap from point to point of matter; or, in the case of spanning the void, let us say, from the Earth to Venus, you start and end with matter, remarking that between lies so many miles of space.

"But it is clear that you see and touch no space, merely spanning the distance between two points of matter with the vision or the measuring rod. You do the same when you compute time with the Sun, or by means of the clock which I see hanging on the wall there, Time, then, is no more of an abstraction than is space. If it is possible for man to move freely in space, it is possible for him to move freely in time, and we Ardathians are beginning to do so."

"But how?"

"I am afraid your limited intelligence could not grasp that. You must realise that compared with us, you are hardly as much as human. When I look at you, I perceive that your body is enormously larger than your head. This means that you are dominated by animal passions, and that your mental capacity is not very high."

That this weirdly humorous thing inside a glass cylinder should come to such a conclusion regarding me, made me smile.

"If any of my fellow citizens should see you," I replied, "they would consider you—well, absurd."

"That is because they would judge me by the only standard they know—themselves. In Ardathia, you would be regarded as bestial; in fact, that is exactly how your reconstructed skeletons are regarded. Tell me, is it true that you nourish your bodies by taking food through your mouths into your stomachs?"

"Yes."

"And are still at that stage of bodily evolution when you eliminate the waste products through the alimentary canal?"

I lowered my head.

"How revolting."

THE unwinking eyes regarded me intently. Then something happened which startled me greatly. The creature raised a glass tube to its face, and from the end of the tube leaped a purple ray which came through the glass casing and played over the room.

"There is no need to be alarmed," said the metallic voice. "I was merely viewing your habitat, and making some deductions. Correct me if I am wrong, please. You are an English-speaking man of the twentieth century. You and your kind live in cities and houses. You eat, digest, and reproduce your young, much as do the animals from which you have sprung. You use crude machines, and have an elementary understanding of physics and chemistry. Correct me if I am wrong, please."

"You are right, to a certain extent," I replied. "But I am not interested in having you tell me what I am; I know that. I wish to know what you are. You claim to have come from thirty thousand years in the future, but you advance no evidence to support the claim. How do I know you are not a trick, a fake, an hallucination of mine? You say you can move freely in time. Then how is it you have never come this way before? Tell me something about yourself; I am curious."

"Your questions are well put," replied the voice, "and I shall

THE MACHINE MAN OF ARDATHIA 181

seek to answer them. It is true that we Machine-Men of Ardathia are beginning to move in time as well as in space, but note that I say beginning. Our Time Machines are very crude, as yet, and I am the first Ardathian to penetrate the past beyond a period of six thousand years. You must realise that a time traveller runs certain hazards. At any place on the road, he may materialise inside of a solid of some sort. In that case, he is almost certain to be destroyed.

"Such was the constant danger until I perfected my enveloping ray. I cannot name or describe it in your tongue, but if you approach me too closely, you will feel its resistance. This ray has the effect of disintegrating and dispersing any body of matter inside which a time traveller may materialise. Perhaps you were aware of a great light when I appeared in your room? I probably took shape within a body of matter, and the ray destroyed it."

"The rocking-chair!" I exclaimed. "It was standing on the spot you now occupy."

"Then it has been reduced to its original atoms. This is a wonderful moment for me! My ray has proved an unqualified success, for the second time. It not only removes any hindering matter from about the time-traveller, but also creates a void within which he is perfectly safe from harm. But to resume ...

"It is hard to believe that we Ardathians evolved from such creatures as you. Our written history does not go back to a time when men nourished themselves by taking food into their stomachs through their mouths, or reproduced their young in the animal-like fashion in which you do. The earliest men of whom we have any records were the Bi-Chanics. They lived about fifteen thousand years before our era, and were already well along the road of mechanical evolution when their civilisation fell.

"The Bi-Chanics vaporised their food substances and breathed them through the nostril, excreting the waste products of the body through the pores of the skin. Their children were brought to the point of birth in ecto-genetic incubators. There is enough authentic evidence to prove that the Bi-Chanics had perfected the use of mechanical hearts, and were crudely able to make...

"I cannot find the words to explain what they made, but it does not matter. The point is that, while they had only partly subordinated machinery to their use, they are the earliest race of human beings of whom we possess any real knowledge, and it was their period of time that I was seeking when I inadvertently came too far and landed in yours."

The metallic voice ceased for a moment, and I took advantage of the pause to speak. "I do not know a thing about the Bi-Chanics, or whatever it is you call them," I remarked, "but they were certainly not the first to make mechanical hearts. I remember reading about a Russian scientist who kept a dog alive four hours by means of a motor which pumped the blood through the dog's body."

"You mean the motor was used as a heart?"

"Exactly."

The Ardathian made a quick motion with one of its hands.

"I have made a note of your information; it is very interesting."

"Furthermore," I pursued, "I recall reading of how, some years ago, one of our surgeons was hatching out rabbits and guinea pigs in ecto-genetic incubators."

The Ardathian made another quick gesture with its hand. I could see that my remarks excited it.

"Perhaps," I said, not without a feeling of satisfaction (for the casual allusion to myself as hardly human had irked my pride), "perhaps you will find it as interesting to visit the people of five hundred years from now, let us say, as you would to visit the Bi-Chanics."

THE MACHINE MAN OF ARDATHIA

"I assure you," replied the metallic voice, "that if I succeed in returning to my native Ardathia, those periods will be thoroughly explored. I can only express surprise at your having advanced as far as you have, and wonder why it is you have made no practical use of your knowledge."

"Sometimes I wonder myself," I returned. "But I am very much interested in learning more about yourself and your times. If you would resume your story ... ?"

"With pleasure," replied the Ardathian. "In Ardathia, we do not live in houses or in cities; neither do we nourish ourselves as do you, or as did the Bi-Chanics. The chemical fluid you see circulating through these tubes which ran into and through my body, has taken the place of blood. The fluid is produced by the action of a light-ray on certain life-giving elements in the air. It is constantly being produced in those tubes under my feet, and driven through my body be a mechanism too intricate for me to describe.

"The same fluid circulates through my body only once, nourishing it and gathering all impurities as it goes. Having completed its revolution, it is dissipated by means of another ray which carries it back into the surrounding air. Have you noticed the transparent substance enclosing me?"

"The cylinder of glass, you mean?"

"Glass! What do you mean by glass?"

"Why, that there," I said, pointing to the window. The Ardathian directed a metal tube at the spot indicated. A purple streak flashed out, hovered a moment on a pane, and then withdrew.

"No," came the metallic voice; "not that. The cylinder, as you call it, is made of a transparent substance, very strong and practically unbreakable. Nothing can penetrate it but the rays which you see, and the two whose action I have just described, which are invisible.

"We Ardathians, you must understand, are not delivered of the flesh; nor are we introduced into incubators as ova taken from female bodies, as were the Bi-Chanics. Among the Ardathians, there are no males or females. The cell from which we are to develop is created synthetically. It is fertilised by means of a ray, and then put into a cylinder such as you observe surrounding me. As the embryo develops, the various tubes and mechanical devices are introduced into the body by our mechanics, and become an integral part of it.

"When the young Ardathian is born, he does not leave the case in which he has developed. That case—or cylinder, as you call it—protects him from the action of a hostile environment. If it were to break and expose him to the elements, he would perish miserably. Do you follow me?"

NOT quite," I confessed. "You say that you have evolved from men like us, and then go on to state that you are synthetically conceived and machine made. I do not see how this evolution was possible."

"And you may never understand! Nevertheless, I shall try to explain. Did you not tell me you had wise ones among you who experiment with mechanical hearts and ecto-genetic incubators? Tell me, have you not others engaged in tests tending to show that it is the action of environment, and not the passing of time, which accounts for the ageing of organisms?"

"Well," I said, hesitatingly, "I have heard tell of chicken's hearts being kept alive in special containers which protect them from their normal environment."

"Ah!" exclaimed the metallic voice. "But Hoomi will be astounded when he learns that such experiments were carried on by prehistoric men fifteen thousand years before the Bi-Chanics! Listen closely, for what you have told me provides a starting-point from which you may be able to follow my explanation of man's evolution from your time to mine.

"Of the thousands of years separating your day from that of the Bi-Chanics, I have no authentic knowledge. My exact knowledge begins with the Bi-Chanics. They were the first to realise that man's bodily advancement lay in, and through, the machine. They perceived that man only became human when he fashioned tools; that the tools increased the length of his arms, the grip of his hands, the strength of his muscles. They observed that, with the aid of the machine, man could circle the Earth, speak to the planets, gaze intimately at the stars. We will increase our span of life on Earth, said the Bi-Chanics, by throwing the protection of the machine, the thing that the machine produces, around and into our bodies.

"This they did, to the best of their ability, and increased their longevity to an average of about two hundred years. Then came the Tri-Namics. More advanced than the Bi-Chanics, they reasoned that old age was caused, not by the passage of time, but by the action of environment on the matter of which men were composed. It is this reasoning which causes the men of your time to experiment with chicken's hearts. The Tri-Namics sought to perfect devices for safeguarding the flesh against the wear and tear of its environment. They made envelopes—cylinders—in which they attempted to bring embryos to birth, and to rear children; but they met with only partial success."

"You speak of the Bi-Chanics and of the Tri-Namics," I said, "as if they were two distinct races of people. Yet you imply that the latter evolved from the former. If the Bi-Chanics' civilisation fell, did any period of time elapse between that fall and the rise of the Tri-Namics? And how did the latter inherit from their predecessors?"

"It is because of your language, which I find very crude and inadequate, that I have not already made that clear," answered the Ardathian. "The Tri-Namics were really a more progressive part of the Bi-Chanics. When I said the civilisation of the latter fell, I did not mean what that implies in your language.

"You must realise that, fifteen thousand years in your future, the race of man was, scientifically speaking, making rapid strides. But it was not always possible for backward or conservative minds to adjust themselves to new discoveries. Minority groups, composed mostly of the young, forged ahead, proposed radical changes, entertained new ideas, and finally culminated in what I have alluded to as the Tri-Namics. Inevitably, in the course of time, the Bi-Chanics died off, and conservative methods with them. That is what I meant when I said their civilisation fell.

"In the same fashion did we follow the Tri-Namics. When the latter succeeded in raising children inside the cylinder, they destroyed themselves. Soon, all children were born in this manner; and in time, the fate of the Bi-Chanics became that of the Tri-Namics leaving behind them the Machine-Men of Ardathia, who differed radically from them in bodily structure, yet were none the less their direct descendants."

AT last, I began to get an inkling of what the Ardathian meant when it alluded to itself as a Machine-Man. The appalling story of man's final evolution into a controlling centre that directed a mechanical body, awoke something akin to fear in my heart. If it were true, what of the soul, the spirit. . . ? The metallic voice went on.

"You must not imagine that the early Ardathians possessed a cylinder as invulnerable as the one which protects me. The first envelopes of this nature were made of a pliable substance, which wore out within three centuries. But the substance composing the envelope has gradually been improved, perfected, until now it is immune for fifteen hundred years to anything save a powerful explosion or some other major catastrophe."

"Fifteen hundred years!" I exclaimed.

"Barring accident, that is the length of time an Ardathian lives. But to us, fifteen hundred years is no longer than a hundred would be to you. Remember, please, that time is relative: twelve hours of your time is a second of ours, and a year... But suffice it to say that very few Ardathians live out their allotted span. Since we are constantly engaged in hazardous experiments and dangerous expeditions, accidents are many. Thousands of our brave explorers have plunged into the past and never returned. They probably materialised inside solids, and were annihilated; but I believe I have finally overcome this danger with my disintegrating ray."

"And how old are you?"

"As you count time, five hundred and seventy years. You must understand that there has been no change in my body since birth. If the cylinder were everlasting, or proof against accident, I should live for ever. It is the wearing out, or breaking up, of the envelope, which exposes us to the dangerous forces of nature and causes death. Some of our scientists are trying to perfect means for building up the cylinder as fast as the wear and tear of environment breaks it down; others are seeking to rear embryos to birth with nothing but rays for covering—rays incapable of harming the organism, yet immune to dissipation by environment and incapable of destruction by explosion. So far, they have been unsuccessful; but I have every confidence in their ultimate triumph. Then we shall be as immortal as the planet on which we live."

I stared at the cylinder, at the creature inside the cylinder, at the ceiling, the four walls of the room, and then back again at the cylinder, I pinched the soft flesh of my thigh with my fingers. I was awake, all right; there could be no doubt about that.

"Are there any questions you would like to ask?" came the metallic voice.

"Yes," I said at last, half-fearfully. "What joy can there be in existence for you? You have no sex; you cannot mate. It seems to me—" I hesitated. "It seems to me that no hell could be worse than centuries of being caged alive inside that thing you call an envelope. Now, I have full command of my limbs and can go where I please. I can—"

I came to a breathless stop, awed by the lurid light which suddenly gleamed in the winkless eyes.

"Poor prehistoric mammal," came the answer, "how could you, groping in the dawn of human existence, comprehend what is beyond your lowly environment! Compared to you, we are as gods. No longer are our loves and hates the reactions of viscera. Our thoughts, out thinking, our emotions, are conditioned, moulded to the extent that we control our immediate environment. There is no such thing as—

"But it is impossible to continue. Your mentality—it is not the word I like to use but, as I have repeatedly said, your language is woefully inadequate—has a restricted range of but a few thousand words: therefore, I cannot explain further. Only the same lack—in a different fashion, of course, and with objects instead of words—hinders the free movement of your limbs. You have command of them, you say. Poor primitive, do you realise how shackled you are with nothing but your hands and feet? You augment them, of course, with a few machines, but they are crude and cumbersome. It is you who are caged alive, and not I. I have broken through the walls of your cage, have shaken off its shackles—have gone free. Behold the command I have of my limbs!"

FROM an extended tube shot a streak of white, like a funnel, whose radius was great enough to encircle my seated body. I was conscious of being scooped up, and drawn forward, with inconceivable speed. For one breathless

THE MACHINE MAN OF ARDATHIA 189

moment, I hung suspended against the cylinder itself, the winkless eyes not an inch from my own. In that moment, I had the sensation of being probed, handled. Several times I was revolved, as a man might twirl a stick. Then I was back in the easy-chair again, white and shaken.

"It is true that I never leave the envelope in which I am encased," continued the metallic voice, "but I have at my command rays which can bring me anything I desire. In Ardathia are machines—it would be useless for me to describe them to you—with which I can walk, fly, move mountains, delve in the earth, investigate the stars, and loose forces of which you have no conception. Those machines are mechanical parts of my body, extensions of my limbs. I take them off and put them on at will. With their help, I can view one continent while busily employed in another, I can make time machines, harness rays, and plunge for thirty thousand years into the past. Let me again illustrate."

The tentacle-like hand of the Ardathian waved a tube. The five-foot cylinder glowed with an intense light, spun like a top, and so spinning, dissolved into space. Even as I gaped, like one petrified, the cylinder reappeared with the same rapidity. The metallic voice announced:

"I have just been five years into your future."

"My future!" I exclaimed. "How can that be when I have not lived it yet?"

"But of course you have lived it!"

I stared, bewildered.

"Could I visit my past if you had not lived your future?" the creature persisted.

"I do not understand," I said, feebly. "It doesn't seem possible that while I am here, actually in this room, you should be able to travel ahead in time and find out what I shall be doing in a future I haven't reached yet."

"That is because you are unable to grasp intelligently what time is. Think of it as a dimension—a fourth dimension—which stretches like a road ahead and behind you."

"But even then," I protested, "I could only be at one place at a given time, on that road, and not where I am and somewhere else in the same second."

"You are never anywhere at any time," replied the metallic voice, "save always in the past or the future. But it is useless trying to acquaint you with a simple truth, thirty thousand years ahead of your ability to understand it. As I said, I travelled five years into your future. Men were wrecking this building."

"Tearing down this place? Nonsense! It was only erected two years ago."

"Nevertheless, they were tearing it down. I sent forth my visual-ray to locate you. You were in a great room with numerous other men. They were all doing a variety of odd things. There was—"

At that moment came a heavy knock on the door of my room.

"What's the matter, Matthews?" called a loud voice. "What are you talking about, all this time? Are you sick?"

I uttered an exclamation of annoyance, because I recognised the voice of John Peters, a newspaperman who occupied the apartment next to mine. My first impulse was to tell him I was busy, but the next moment I had a better idea. Here was someone to whom I could show the cylinder, and the creature inside it; someone to bear witness to having seen it, besides myself! I hurried to the door and threw it open.

"Quick!" I said, grasping Peters by the arm and hauling him into the room. "What do you think of that?"

"Think of what?" he demanded.

"Why of that, there," I began, pointing with my finger, and then stopping short with my mouth wide open; for on the spot where, a few seconds before, the cylinder had stood, there was nothing. The envelope and the Ardathian had disappeared.

THE MACHINE MAN OF ARDATHIA

AUTHOR'S NOTE

THE material for this manuscript came into my hands in an odd fashion. About a year after the Press had ceased to print garbled versions of Matthews' experience, I made the acquaintance of his friend, Hodge, with whom he had dined on that evening. I asked him about Matthews, He said:

"Did you know they've put him in an asylum? You didn't? Well, they have. He's crazy enough now, poor devil; though he was always a little queer, I thought I went to visit him the other day, and it gave me quite a shock to see him in a ward with a lot of other men, all doing something queer.

"By the way, Peters told me the other day that the apartment house where Matthews lived is to be torn down. They are going to demolish several houses along the Lake Shore, to widen the boulevard; but he says they won't wreck them for three or four years yet. Funny, eh? Would you like to see what Matthews wrote about the affair himself?"

The TISSUE-CULTURE KING
By Julian Huxley
Reprinted from the Yale Review

"I thought I would see whether art could not improve upon nature, and set myself to recall exprimental embryology...I utilize the plasticity of the earliest stages to give double-headed and cyclopean monsters... But my specialities are three-headed snakes, and toads with an extra heaven-pointed head." Hanscombe called it "Home of the Living Fetishes."

Introduction

THAT a darkest Africa story could contain a wondrous assortment of science and adventure all rolled into one, you would scarcely believe possible, yet that is exactly what Julian Huxley, grandson of Thomas Henry Huxley famous English scientist, and himself Professor of Zoology in King's College, London, gives us here. While so far science does not countenance telepathy, no real thought transference having ever been proved, that does not mean to say that it never will be achieved. *Amazing Stories'* sister magazine, *Science and Invention*, has a standing prize of $1,000 for an actual proof of telepathy, which so far has never been claimed. Just the same, maybe 10,000 years hence the human race may have progressed far enough to make telepathy a reality.

THE TISSUE-CULTURE KING

By Julian Huxley

WE had been for three days engaged in crossing a swamp. At last we were out on dry ground, winding up a gentle slope. Near the top the brush grew thicker. The look of a rampart grew as we approached; it had the air of having been deliberately planted by men. We did not wish to have to hack our way through the spiky barricade, so turned to the right along the front of the green wall. After three or four hundred yards we came on a clearing which led into the bush, narrowing down to what seemed a regular passage or track-way. This made us a little suspicious. However, I thought we had better make all the progress we could, and so ordered the caravan to turn into the opening, myself taking second place behind the guide.

Suddenly the tracker stopped with a guttural exclamation. I

looked, and there was one of the great African toads, hopping with a certain ponderosity across the path. But it had a second head growing upwards from its shoulders! I had never seen anything like this before, and wanted to secure such a remarkable monstrosity for our collections; but as I moved forward, the creature took a couple of hops into the shelter of the prickly scrub.

We pushed on, and I became convinced that the gap we were following was artificial. After a little, a droning sound came to our ears, which we very soon set down as that of a human voice. The party was halted, and I crept forward with the guide. Peeping through the last screen of brush we looked down into a hollow and were immeasurably startled at what we saw there. The voice proceeded from an enormous negro man at least eight feet high, the biggest man I had ever seen outside a circus.

He was squatting, from time to time prostrating the forepart of his body, and reciting some prayer or incantation. The object of his devotion was before him on the ground; it was a small flat piece of glass held on a little carved ebony stand. By his side was a huge spear, together with a painted basket with a lid.

After a minute or so, the giant bowed down in silence, then took up the ebony-and-glass object and placed it in the basket. Then to my utter amazement he drew out a two-headed toad like the first I had seen, but in a cage of woven grass, placed it on the ground, and proceeded to more genuflection and ritual murmurings. As soon as this was over, the toad was replaced, and the squatting giant tranquilly regarded the landscape.

Beyond the hollow or dell lay an undulating country, with clumps of bush. A sound in the middle distance attracted attention; glimpses of color moved through the scrub; and a party of three or four dozen men were seen approaching, most of them as gigantit as our first acquaintance. All marched in order, armed with great spears, and wearing colored loin straps with a sort of sporran, it seemed, in front. They were preceded

THE TISSUE-CULTURE KING

by an intelligent-looking negro of ordinary stature armed with a club, and accompanied by two figures more remarkable than the giants. They were under-sized, almost dwarfish, with huge heads, and enormously fat and brawny both in face and body. They wore bright yellow cloaks over their black shoulders.

At sight of them, our giant rose and stood stiffly by the side of his basket. The party approached and halted. Some order was given, a giant stepped out from the ranks towards ours, picked up the basket, handed it stiffly to the newcomer, and fell into place in the little company. We were clearly witnessing some regular routine of relieving guard, and I was racking my brains to think what the whole thing might signify—guards, giants, dwarfs, toads—when to my dismay I heard an exclamation at my shoulder.

It was one of those damned porters, a confounded fellow who always liked to show his independence. Bored with waiting, I suppose, he had self-importantly crept up to see what it was all about, and the sudden sight of the company of giants had been too much for his nerves. I made a signal to lie quiet, but it was too late. The exclamation had been heard; the leader gave a quick command, and the giants rushed up and out in two groups to surround us.

Violence and resistance were clearly out of the question. With my heart in my mouth, but with as much dignity as I could muster, I jumped up and threw out my empty hands, at the same time telling the tracker not to shoot. A dozen spears seemed towering over me, but none were launched; the leader ran up the slope and gave a command. Two giants came up and put my hands through their arms. The tracker and the porter were herded in front at the spear point. The other porters now discovered there was something amiss, and began to shout and run away, with half the spearmen after them. We three were gently but firmly marched down and across the hollow.

I understood nothing of the language, and called to my tracker to try his hand. It turned out that there was some dialect of which he had a little understanding, and we could learn nothing save the fact that we were being taken to some superior authority.

For two days we were marched through pleasant park-like country, with villages at intervals. Every now and then some new monstrosity in the shape of a dwarf or an incredibly fat woman or a two-headed animal would be visible, until I thought I had stumbled on the original source of supply of circus freaks.

The country at last began to slope gently down to a pleasant river-valley; and presently we neared the capital. It turned out to be a really large town for Africa, its mud walls of strangely impressive architectural form, with their heavy, slabby buttresses, and giants standing guard upon them. Seeing us approach, they shouted, and a crowd poured out of the nearest gate. My God, what a crowd! I was getting used to giants by this time, but here was a regular Barnum and Bailey show; more semi-dwarfs; others like them but more so—one could not tell whether the creatures were precociously mature children or horribly stunted adults; others portentously fat, with arms like sooty legs of mutton, and rolls and volutes of fat crisping out of their steatopygous posteriors; still others precociously senile and wizened, others hateful and imbecile in looks. Of course, there were plenty of ordinary negroes too, but enough of the extraordinary to make one feel pretty queer. Soon after we got inside, I suddenly noted something else which appeared inexplicable—a telephone wire, with perfectly good insulators, running across from tree to tree. A telephone—in an unknown African town. I gave it up.

But another surprise was in store for me. I saw a figure pass across from one large building to another—a figure unmistakably that of a white man. In the first place, it was wearing white ducks and sun helmet; in the second, it had a pale face.

He turned at the sound of our cavalcade and stood looking a

THE TISSUE-CULTURE KING

moment; then walked towards us.

"Halloa!" I shouted. "Do you speak English?"

"Yes," he answered, "but keep quiet a moment," and began talking quickly to our leaders, who treated him with the greatest deference. He dropped back to me and spoke rapidly: "You are to be taken into the council hall to be examined: but I will see to it that no harm comes to you. This is a forbidden land to strangers, and you must be prepared to be held up for a time. You will be sent down to see me in the temple buildings as soon as the formalities are over, and I'll explain things. They want a bit of explaining," he added with a dry laugh. "By the way, my name is Hascombe, lately research worker at Middlesex Hospital, now religious adviser to His Majesty King Mgobe." He laughed again and pushed ahead. He was an interesting figure—perhaps fifty years old, spare body, thin face, with a small beard, and rather sunken, hazel eyes. As for his expression, he looked cynical, but also as if he were interested in life.

By this time we were at the entrance to the hall. Our giants formed up outside, with my men behind them, and only I and the leader passed in. The examination was purely formal, and remarkable chiefly for the ritual and solemnity which characterized all the actions of the couple of dozen fine-looking men in long robes who were our examiners. My men were herded off to some compound. I was escorted down to a little hut, furnished with some attempt at European style, where I found Hascombe.

As soon as we were alone I was after him with my questions. "Now you can tell me. Where are we? What is the meaning of all this circus business and this menagerie of monstrosities? And how do you come here?" He cut me short. "It's a long story, so let me save time by telling it my own way."

I am not going to tell it as he told it; but will try to give a more connected account, the result of many later talks with him, and of my own observations.

Hascombe had been a medical student of great promise; and after his degree had launched out into research. He had first started on parasitic protozoa, but had given that up in favor of tissue culture; from these he had gone off to cancer research, and from that to a study of developmental physiology. Later a big Commission on sleeping sickness had been organized, and Hascombe, restless and eager for travel, had pulled wires and got himself appointed as one of the scientific staff sent to Africa. He was much impressed with the view that wild game acted as a reservoir for the *Trypanosoma gambiense*. When he learned of the extensive migrations of game, he saw here an important possible means of spreading the disease and asked leave to go up country to investigate the whole problem. When the Commission as a whole had finished its work, he was allowed to stay in Africa with one other white man and a company of porters to see what he could discover. His white companion was a laboratory technician, a taciturn non-commissioned officer of science called Aggers.

There is no object in telling of their experiences here. Suffice it that they lost their way and fell into the hands of this same tribe. That was fifteen years ago: and Aggers was now long dead—as the result of a wound inflicted when he was caught, after a couple of years, trying to escape.

On their capture, they too had been examined in the council chamber, and Hascombe (who had interested himself in a dilettante way in anthropology as in most other subjects of scientific inquiry) was much impressed by what he described as the exceedingly religious atmosphere. Everything was done with an elaboration of ceremony; the chief seemed more priest than king, and performed various rites at intervals, and priests were busy at some sort of altar the whole time. Among other things, he noticed that one of their rites was connected with blood. First the chief and then the councillors were in turn requisitioned for a drop of vital fluid pricked from their finger-tips, and the mixture, held in a little vessel, was slowly evaporated over a flame.

Some of Hascombe's men spoke a dialect not unlike that of their captors, and one was acting as interpreter. Things did not look too favorable. The country was a "holy place," it seemed, and the tribe a "holy race." Other Africans who trespassed there, if not killed, were enslaved, but for the most part they let well alone, and did not trespass. White men they had heard of, but never seen till now, and the debate was what to do—to kill, let go, or enslave? To let them go was contrary to all their principles: the holy place would be defiled if the news of it were spread abroad. To enslave them—yes; but what were they good for? and the Council seemed to feel an instinctive dislike for these other-colored creatures. Hascombe had an idea. He turned to the interpreter. "Say this: 'You revere the Blood. So do we white men; but we do more—we can render visible the blood's hidden nature and reality, and with permission I will show this great magic.' " He beckoned to the bearer who carried his precious microscope, set it up, drew a drop of blood from the tip of his finger with his knife, and mounted it on a slide under a coverslip. The bigwigs were obviously interested. They whispered to each other. At length, "Show us," commanded the chief.

Hascombe demonstrated his preparation with greater interest than he had ever done to first-year medical students in the old days. He explained that the blood was composed of little people of various sorts, each with their own lives, and that to spy upon them thus gave us new powers over them. The elders were more or less impressed. At any rate the sight of these thousands of corpuscles where they could see nothing before made them think, made them realize that the white man had power which might make him a desirable servant.

They would not ask to see their own blood for fear that the sight would put them into the power of those who saw it. But they had blood drawn from a slave. Hascombe asked too for a bird, and was able to create a certain interest by allowing how different were the little people of its blood.

"Tell them," he said to the interpreter, "that I have many other powers and magics which I will show them if they will give me time."

The long and short of it was that he and his party were spared—He said he knew then what one felt when the magistrate said: "remanded for a week."

He had been attracted by one of the elder statesmen of the tribe—a tall, powerful-looking man of middle-age; and was agreeably surprised when this man came round next day to see him. Hascombe later nicknamed him the Prince-Bishop, for his combination of the qualities of the statesman and the ecclesiastic: his real name was Bugala. He was as anxious to discover more about Hascombe's mysterious powers and resources as Hascombe was to learn what he could of the people into whose hands he had fallen, and they met almost every evening and talked far into the night.

Bugala's inquiries were as little prompted as Hascombe's by a purely academic curiosity. Impressed himself by the microscope, and still more by the effect which it had had on his colleagues, he was anxious to find out whether by utilizing the powers of the white man he could not secure his own advancement. At length, they struck a bargain. Bugala would see to it that no harm befell Hascombe. But Hascombe must put his resources and powers at the disposal of the Council; and Bugala would take good care to arrange matters so that he himself benefited. So far as Hascombe could make out, Bugala imagined a radical change in the national religion, a sort of reformation based on Hascombe's conjuring tricks; and that he would emerge as the High Priest of this changed system.

Hascombe had a sense of humor, and it was tickled. It seemed

THE TISSUE-CULTURE KING 201

pretty clear that they could not escape, at least for the present. That being so, why not take the opportunity of doing a little research work at state expense—an opportunity which he and his like were always clamoring for at home? His thoughts began to run away with him. He would find out all he could of the rites and superstitions of the tribe. He would, by the aid of his knowledge and his scientific skill, exalt the details of these rites, the expression of those superstitions, the whole physical side of their religiosity, on to a new level which should to them appear truly miraculous.

It would not be worth my troubling to tell all the negotiations, the false starts, the misunderstandings. In the end he secured what he wanted—a building which could be used as a laboratory; an unlimited supply of slaves for the lower and priests for the higher duties of laboratory assistants, and the promise that when his scientific stores were exhausted they would do their best to secure others from the coast—a promise which was scrupulously kept, so that he never went short for lack of what money could buy.

He next applied himself diligently to a study of their religion and found that it was built round various main motifs. Of these, the central one was the belief in the divinity and tremendous importance of the Priest-King. The second was a form of ancestor-worship. The third was an animal cult, in particular of the more grotesque species of the African fauna. The fourth was sex, *con variazioni*. Hascombe reflected on these facts. Tissue culture; experimental embryology; endocrine treatment; artificial parthenogenesis. He laughed and said to himself: "Well, at least I can try, and it ought to be amusing."

That was how it all started. Perhaps the best way of giving some idea of how it had developed will be for me to tell my own impressions when Hascombe took me round his laboratories. One whole quarter of the town was devoted entirely to religion—it struck me as excessive, but Hascombe reminded me that Tibet spends one-fifth of its revenues on melted butter to burn before its shrines. Facing the main square was the chief temple, built impressively enough of solid mud. On either side were the apartments where dwelt the servants of the gods and administrators of the sacred rites. Behind were Hascombe's laboratories, some built of mud, others, under his later guidance, of wood. They were guarded night and day by patrols of giants, and were arranged in a series of quadrangles. Within one quadrangle 'was a pool which served as an aquarium; in another, aviaries and great hen-houses; in yet another, cages with various animals; in the fourth a little botanic garden. Behind were stables with dozens of cattle and sheep, and a sort of experimental ward for human beings.

He took me into the nearest of the buildings. "This," he said, "is known to the people as the Factory (it is difficult to give the exact sense of the word, but it literally means producing-place), the Factory of Kingship or Majesty, and the Wellspring of Ancestral Immortality." I looked round, and saw platoons of buxom and shining African women, becomingly but unusually dressed in tight-fitting white dresses and caps, and wearing rubber gloves. Microscopes were much in evidence, as also various receptacles from which steam was emerging. The back of the room was screened off by a wooden screen in which were a series of glass doors; and these doors opened into partitions, each labelled with a name in that unknown tongue, and each containing a number of objects like the one I had seen taken out of the basket by the giant before we were captured. Pipes surrounded this chamber, and appeared to be distributing heat from a fire in one corner.

"Factory of Majesty!" I exclaimed. "Wellspring of Immortality! What the dickens do you mean?"

"If you prefer a more prosaic name," said Hascombe, "I should call this the Institute of, Religious Tissue Culture." My mind went back to a day in 1918 when I had been taken by a

THE TISSUE-CULTURE KING 203

biological friend in New York to see the famous Rockefeller Institute; and at the word tissue culture I saw again before me Dr. Alexis Carrell and troops of white-garbed American girls making cultures, sterilizing, microscopizing, incubating and the rest of it. The Hascombe Institute was, it is true, not so well equipped, but it had an even larger, if differently colored, personnel.

Hascombe began his explanations. "As you probably know, Frazer's 'Golden Bough' (Ed. Note: *Golden Bough*—A very elaborate treatise on a division of Roman mythology, especially on the cult of Diana, which they would continue to worship after the old folks were gone, and so left their parents and grandparents much freer than before from the irksome restrictions which in all ages have beset the officially holy.) introduced us to the idea of a sacred priest-king, and showed how fundamental it was in primitive societies. The welfare of the tribe is regarded as inextricably bound up with that of the King, and extraordinary precautions are taken to preserve him from harm. In this kingdom, in the old days, the King was hardly allowed to set his foot to the ground in case he should lose divinity; his cut hair and nail-parings were entrusted to one of the most important officials of state, whose duty it was to bury them secretly, in case some enemy should compass the King's illness or death by using them in black magic rites. If anyone of base blood trod on the King's shadow, he paid the penalty with his life. Each year a slave was made mock-king for a week, allowed to enjoy all the king's privileges, and was decapitated at the close of his brief glory; and by this means it was supposed that the illnesses and misfortunes that might befall the King were vicariously got rid of.

"I first of all rigged up my apparatus, and with the aid of Aggers, succeeded in getting good cultures, first of chick tissues and later, by the aid of embryo-extract, of various adult mammalian tissues. I then went to Bugala, and told him that I could increase the safety, if not of the King as an individual, at least of the life which was in him, and that I presumed that this would be equally satisfactory from a theological point of view. I pointed out that if he chose to be made guardian of the King's subsidiary lives, he would be in a much more important position than the chamberlain or the burier of the sacred nail-parings, and might make the post the most influential in the realm.

"Eventually I was allowed (under threats of death if anything untoward occurred) to remove small portions of His Majesty's subcutaneous connective tissue under a local anaesthetic. In the presence of the assembled nobility I put fragments of this into culture medium, and showed it them under the microscope. The cultures were then put away in the incubator, under a guard—relieved every eight hours—of half a dozen warriors. After three days, to my joy they had all taken and showed abundant growth. I could see that the Council was impressed, and reeled off a magnificent speech, pointing out that this growth constituted an actual increase in the quantity of the divine principle inherent in royalty; and, what was more, that I could increase it indefinitely. With that I cut each of my cultures into eight, and sub-cultured all the pieces. They were again put under guard, and again examined after three days. Not all of them had taken this time, and there were some murmurings and angry looks, on the ground that I had killed some of the King; but I pointed out that the *King* was still the King, that his little wound had completely healed, and that any successful cultures represented so much extra sacredness and protection to the state. I must say that they were very reasonable, and had good theological acumen, for they at once took the hint.

"I pointed out to Bugala, and he persuaded the rest without much difficulty, that they could now disregard some of the older implications of the doctrines of kingship. The most important new idea which I was able to introduce was *mass-production*. Our aim was to multiply the King's tissues indefinitely, to ensure that

THE TISSUE-CULTURE KING 205

some of their protecting power should reside everywhere in the country. Thus by concentrating upon quantity, we could afford to remove some of the restrictions upon the King's mode of life. This was of course agreeable to the King; and also to Bugala, who saw himself wielding undreamt-of power. One might have supposed that such an innovation would have met with great resistance simply on account of its being an innovation; but I must admit that these people compared very favorably with the average business man in their lack of prejudice.

"Having thus settled the principle, I had many debates with Bugala as to the best methods for enlisting the mass of the population in our scheme. What an opportunity for scientific advertising! But, unfortunately, the population could not read. However, war propaganda worked very well in more or less illiterate countries—why not here?"

Hascombe organized a series of public lectures in the capital, at which he demonstrated his regal tissues to the multitude, who were bidden to the place by royal heralds. An impressive platform group was always supplied from the ranks of the nobles. The lecturer explained how important it was for the community to become possessed of greater and greater stores of the sacred tissues. Unfortunately, the preparation was laborious and expensive, and it behooved them all to lend a hand. It had accordingly been arranged that to everyone subscribing a cow or buffalo, or its equivalent—three goats, pigs, or sheep—a portion of the royal anatomy should be given, handsomely mounted in an ebony holder. Sub-culturing would be done at certain hours and days, and it would be obligatory to send the cultures for renewal. If through any negligence the tissue died, no renewal would be made. The subscription entitled the receiver to sub-culturing rights for a year, but was of course renewable. By this means not only would the totality of the King be much increased, to the benefit of all, but each cultureholder would possess an actual part of His Majesty, and would have the infinite joy and privilege of aiding by his own efforts the multiplication of divinity.

Then they could also serve their country by dedicating a daughter to the state. These young women would be housed and fed by the state, and taught the technique of the sacred culture. Candidates would be selected according to general fitness, but would of course, in addition, be required to attain distinction in an examination on the principles of religion. They would be appointed for a probationary period of six months. After this they would receive a permanent status, with the title of Sisters of the Sacred Tissue. From this, with age, experience, and merit, they could expect promotion to the rank of mothers, grandmothers, great-grandmothers, and grand ancestresses of the same. The merit and benefit they would receive from their close contact with the source of all benefits would overflow on to their families.

The scheme worked like wildfire. Pigs, goats, cattle, buffaloes, and negro maidens poured in. Next year the scheme was extended to the whole country, a peripatetic laboratory making the rounds weekly.

By the close of the third year there was hardly a family in the Country which did not possess at least one sacred culture. To be without one would have been like being without one's trousers—or at least without one's hat (Ed. note: This was written before the year 1927.)—on Fifth Avenue. Thus did Bugala effect a reformation in the national religion, enthrone himself as the most important personage in the country, and entrench applied science and Hascombe firmly in the organization of the state.

Encouraged by his success, Hascombe soon set out to capture the ancestry-worship branch of the religion as well. A public proclamation was made pointing out how much more satisfactory it would be if worship could be made not merely to the charred bones of one's forbears, but to bits of them still actually living

THE TISSUE-CULTURE KING 207

and growing. All who were desirous of profiting by the enterprise of Bugala's Department of State should therefore bring their older relatives to the laboratory at certain specified hours, and fragments would be painlessly extracted for culture.

This, too, proved very attractive to the average citizen. Occasionally, it is true, grandfathers or aged mothers arrived in a state of indignation and protest. However, this did not matter, since, according to the law, once children were twenty-five years of age, they were not only assigned the duty of worshipping their ancestors, alive or dead, but were also given complete control over them, in order that all rites might be duly performed to the greater safety of the commonweal. Further, the ancestors soon found that the operation itself was trifling, and, what was more, that once accomplished, it had the most desirable results. For their descendants preferred to concentrate at once upon the culture.

Thus, by almost every hearth in the kingdom, instead of the old-fashioned rows of red jars containing the incinerated remains of one or other of the family forbears, the new generation saw growing up a collection of family slides. Each would be taken out and reverently examined at the hour of prayer. "Grandpapa is not growing well this week," you would perhaps hear the young black devotee say; the father of the family would pray over the speck of tissue; and if that failed, it would be taken back to the factory for rejuvenation. On the other hand, what rejoicing when a rhythm of activity stirred in the cultures! A spurt on the part of great-grandmother's tissues would bring her wrinkled old smile to mind again; and sometimes it seemed as if one particular generation were all stirred simultaneously by a pulse of growth, as if combining to bless their devout descendants.

To deal with the possibility of cultures dying out, Hascombe started a central storehouse, where duplicates of every strain were kept, and it was this repository of the national tissues which had attracted my attention at the back of the laboratory. No such collection had ever existed before, he assured me. Not a necropolis, but a histopolis, if I may coin a word: not a cemetery, but a place of eternal growth.

THE second building was devoted to endocrine products—an African Armour's—and was called by the people the "Factory of Ministers to the Shrines."

"Here," he said, "you will not find much new. You know the craze for 'glands' that was going on at home years ago, and its results, in the shape of pluriglandular preparations, a new genre of patent medicines, and a popular literature that threatened to outdo the Freudians, and explain human beings entirely on the basis of glandular make-up, without reference to the mind at all.

"I had only to apply my knowledge in a comparatively simple manner. The first thing was to show Bugala how, by repeated injections of pre-pituitary, I could make an ordinary baby grow up into a giant. This pleased him, and he introduced the idea of a sacred bodyguard, all of really gigantic stature, quite overshadowing Frederick's Grenadiers.

"I did, however, extend knowledge in several directions. I took advantage of the fact that their religion holds in reverence monstrous and imbecile forms of human beings. That is, of course, a common phenomenon in many countries, where halfwits are supposed to be inspired, and dwarfs the object of superstitious awe. So I went to work to create various new types. By employing a particular extract of adrenal cortex, I produced children who would have been a match for the Infant Hercules, and, indeed, looked rather like a cross between him and a brewer's drayman. By injecting the same extract into adolescent girls I was able to provide them with the most copious mustaches, after which they found ready employment as prophetesses.

"Tampering with the post-pituitary gave remarkable cases

of obesity. This, together with the passion of the men for fatness in their women, Bugala took advantage of, and I believe made quite a fortune by selling as concubines female slaves treated in this way. Finally, by another pituitary treatment, I at last mastered the secret of true dwarfism, in which perfect proportions are retained.

"Of these productions, the dwarfs are retained as acolytes in the temple; a band of the obese young ladies form a sort of Society of Vestal Virgins, with special religious duties, which, as the embodiment of the national ideal of beauty, they are supposed to discharge with peculiarly propitious effect; and the giants form our Regular Army.

"The Obese Virgins have set me a problem which I confess I have not yet solved. Like all races who set great store by sexual enjoyment, these people have a correspondingly exaggerated reverence for virginity. It therefore occurred to me that if I could apply Jacques Loeb's great discovery of artificial parthenogenesis to man, or, to be precise, to these young ladies, I should be able to grow a race of vestals, self-reproducing yet ever virgin, to whom in concentrated form should attach that reverence of which I have just spoken. You see, I must always remember that it is no good proposing any line of work that will not benefit the national religion. I suppose state-aided research would have much the same kinds of difficulties in a really democratic state. Well this, as I say, has so far beaten me. I have taken the matter a step further than Bataillon with his fatherless frogs, and have induced parthenogenesis in the *eggs* of reptiles and birds; but so far I have failed with mammals. However, I've not given up yet!"

Then we passed to the next laboratory, which was full of the most incredible animal monstrosities. "This laboratory is the most amusing," said Hascombe. "Its official title is 'Home of the Living Fetishes.' Here again I have simply taken a prevalent trait of the populace, and used it as a peg on which to hang research. I told you that they always had a fancy for the grotesque in animals, and used the most bizarre forms, in the shape of little clay or ivory statuettes, for fetishes.

"I thought I would see whether art could not improve upon nature, and set myself to recall my experimental embryology. I use only the simplest methods. I utilize the plasticity of the earliest stages to give double-headed and cyclopean monsters. That was, of course, done years ago in newts by Spemann and fish by Stockard; and I have merely applied the mass-production methods of Mr. Ford to their results. But my specialties are three-headed snakes, and toads with an extra heaven-pointing head. The former are a little difficult, but there is a great demand for them, and they fetch a good price. The frogs are easier: I simply apply Harrison's methods to embryo tadpoles."

He then showed me into the last building. Unlike the others, this contained no signs of research in progress, but was empty. It was draped with black hangings, and lit only from the top. In the centre were rows of ebony benches, and in front of them a glittering golden ball on a stand.

"Here I am beginning my work on reinforced telepathy," he told me. "Some day you must come and see what it's all about, for it really is interesting."

YOU may imagine that I was pretty well flabbergasted by this catalogue of miracles. Every day I got a talk with Hascombe, and gradually the talks became recognized events of our daily routine. One day I asked if he had given up hope of escaping. He showed a queer hesitation in replying. Eventually he said, "To tell you the truth, my dear Jones, I have really hardly thought of it these last few years. It seemed so impossible at first that I deliberately put it out of my head and turned with more and more energy, I might almost say fury, to my work. And now, upon my soul, I am not quite sure whether I

THE TISSUE-CULTURE KING 211

want to escape or not."

"Not *want* to!" I exclaimed; "surely you can't mean that!"

"I am not so sure," he rejoined. "What I most want is to get ahead with this work of mine. Why, man, you don't realize what a chance I've got! And it is all growing so fast—I can see every kind of possibility ahead"; and he broke off into silence. However, although I was interested enough in his past achievements, I did not feel willing to sacrifice my future to his perverted intellectual ambitions. But he would not leave his work.

The experiments which most excited his imagination were those he was conducting into mass telepathy. He had received his medical training at a time when abnormal psychology was still very unfashionable in England, but had luckily been thrown in contact with a young doctor who was a keen student of hypnotism, through whom he had been introduced to some of the great pioneers, like Bramwell and Wingfield. As a result, he had become a passable hypnotist himself, with a fair knowledge of the literature.

In the early days of his captivity he became interested in the sacred dances which took place every night of full moon, and were regarded as propitiations of the celestial powers. The dancers all belong to a special sect. After a series of exciting figures, symbolizing various activities of the chase, war, and love, the leader conducts his band to a ceremonial bench. He then begins to make passes at them; and what impressed Hascombe was this, that a few seconds sufficed for them to fall back in deep hypnosis against the ebony rail. It recalled, he said, the most startling cases of collective hypnosis recorded by the French scientists. The leader next passed from one end of the bench to the other, whispering a brief sentence into each ear. He then, according to immemorial rite, approached the Priest-King, and, after having exclaimed aloud "Lord of Majesty, command what thou wilt for thy dancers to perform," the King would thereupon command some action which had previously been kept secret. The command was often to fetch some object and deposit at the moon-shrine; or to fight the enemies of the state; or (and this was what the company most liked) to be some animal, or bird. Whatever the command, the hypnotized men would obey it, for the leader's whispered words had been an order to hear and carry out only what the King said; and the strangest scenes would be witnessed as they ran, completely oblivious of all in their path, in search of the gourds or sheep they had been called on to procure, or lunged in a symbolic way at invisible enemies, or threw themselves on all fours and roared as lions, or galloped as zebras, or danced as cranes. The command executed, they stood like stocks or stones, until their leader, running from one to the other, touched each with a finger and shouted "Wake." They woke, and limp, but conscious of having been the vessels of the unknown spirit, danced back to their special but or clubhouse.

This susceptibility to hypnotic suggestion struck Hascombe, and he obtained permission to test the performers more closely. He soon established that the people were, as a race, extremely prone to dissociation, and could be made to lapse into deep hypnosis with great ease, but a hypnosis in which the subconscious, though completely cut off from the waking self, comprised portions of the personality not retained in the hypnotic selves of Europeans.

Like most who have fluttered round the psychological candle, he had been interested in the notion of telepathy; and now, with this supply of hypnotic subjects under his hands, began some real investigation of the problem.

By picking his subjects, he was soon able to demonstrate the existence of telepathy, by making suggestions to one hypnotized man who transferred them without physical intermediation to another at a distance. Later—and this was the culmination of his work—he found that when he made a suggestion to several

THE TISSUE-CULTURE KING   213

subjects at once, the telepathic effect was much stronger than if he had done it to one at a time—the hypnotized minds were reinforcing each other. "I'm after the super-consciousness," Hascombe said, "and I've already got the rudiments of it."

I must confess that I got almost as excited as Hascombe over the possibilities thus opened up. It certainly seemed as if he were right in principle.

If all the subjects were in practically the same psychological state, extraordinary reinforcing effects were observed. At first the attainment of this similarity of condition was very difficult; gradually, however, we discovered that it was possible to tune hypnotic subjects to the same pitch, if I may use the metaphor, and then the fun really began.

First of all we found that with increasing reinforcement, we could get telepathy conducted to greater and greater distances, until finally we could transmit commands from the capital to the national boundary, nearly a hundred miles. We next found that it was not necessary for the subject to be in hypnosis to receive the telepathic command. Almost everybody, but especially those of equable temperament, could thus be influenced. Most extraordinary of all, however, were what we at first christened "near effects," since their transmission to a distance was not found possible until later. If, after Hascombe had suggested some simple command to a largish group of hypnotized subjects, he or I went right up among them, we would experience the most extraordinary sensation, as of some superhuman personality repeating the command in a menacing and overwhelming way and, whereas with one part of ourselves we felt that we must carry out the command, with another we felt, if I may say so, as if we were only a part of the command, or of something much bigger than ourselves which was commanding. And this, Hascombe claimed, was the first real beginning of the super-consciousness.

BUGALA, of course, had to be considered. Hascombe, with the old Tibetan prayer-wheel at the back of his mind, suggested that eventually he would be able to induce hypnosis in the whole population, and then transmit a prayer. This would ensure that the daily prayer, for instance, was really said by the whole population, and, what is more, simultaneously, which would undoubtedly much enhance its efficacy. And it would make it possible in times of calamity or battle to keep the whole praying force of the nation at work for long spells together.

Bugala was deeply interested. He saw himself, through this mental machinery, planting such ideas as he wished in the brain-cases of his people. He saw himself willing an order; and the whole population rousing itself out of trance to execute it. He dreamt dreams before which those of the proprietor of a newspaper syndicate, even those of a director of propaganda in wartime, would be pale and timid. Naturally, he wished to receive personal instruction in the methods himself; and, equally naturally, we could not refuse him, though I must say that I often felt a little uneasy as to what he might choose to do if he ever decided to override Hascombe and to start experimenting on his own. This, combined with my constant longing to get away from the place, led me to cast about again for means of escape. Then it occurred to me that this very method about which I had such gloomy presentiments, might itself be made the key to our prison.

So one day, after getting Hascombe worked up about the loss to humanity it would be to let this great discovery die with him in Africa, I set to in earnest. "My dear Hascombe," I said, " you must get home out of this. What is there to prevent you saying to Bugala that your experiments are nearly crowned with success, but that for certain tests you must have a much greater number of subjects at your disposal? You can then get a battery of two

THE TISSUE-CULTURE KING   215

hundred men, and after you have tuned them, the reinforcement will be so great that you will have at your disposal a mental force big enough to affect the whole population. Then, of course, one fine day we should raise the potential of our mind-battery to the highest possible level, and send out through it a general hypnotic influence. The whole country, men, women, and children, would sink into stupor. Next we should give our experimental squad the suggestion to broadcast 'sleep for a week.' The telepathic message would be relayed to each of the thousands of minds waiting receptively for it, and would take root in them, until the whole nation became a single super-consciousness, conscious only of the one thought 'sleep' which we had thrown into it."

The reader will perhaps ask how we ourselves expected to escape from the clutches of the super-consciousness we had created. Well, we had discovered that metal was relatively impervious to the telepathic effect, and had prepared for ourselves a sort of tin pulpit, behind which we could stand while conducting experiments. This, combined with caps of metal foil, enormously reduced the effects on ourselves. We had not informed Bugala of this property of metal.

Hascombe was silent. At length he spoke. "I like the idea, he said; "I like to think that if I ever do get back to England and to scientific recognition, my discovery will have given me the means of escape."

FROM that moment we worked assiduously to perfect our method and our plans. After about five months everything seemed propitious. We had provisions packed away, and compasses. I had been allowed to keep my rifle, on promise that I would never discharge it. We had made friends with some of the men who went trading to the coast, and had got from them all the information we could about the route, without arousing their suspicions.

At last, the night arrived. We assembled our men as if for an ordinary practice, and after hypnosis had been induced, started to tune them. At this moment Bugala came in, unannounced. This was what we had been afraid of; but there had been no means of preventing it. "What shall we do?" I whispered to Hascombe, in English. "Go right ahead and be damned to it," was his answer; "we can put him to sleep with the rest."

So we welcomed him, and gave him a seat as near as possible to the tightly-packed ranks of the performers. At length the preparations were finished. Hascombe went into the pulpit and said, "Attention to the words which are to be suggested." There was a slight stiffening of the bodies. "Sleep!" said Hascombe. "*Sleep* is the command: I command all in this land to sleep unbrokenly." Bugala leapt up with an exclamation; but the induction had already begun.

We with our metal coverings were immune. But Bugala was struck by the full force of the mental current. He sank back on his chair, helpless. For a few minutes his extraordinary will resisted the suggestion. Although he could not move, his angry eyes were open. But at length he succumbed, and he too slept.

We lost no time in starting, and made good progress through the silent country. The people were sitting about like wax figures. Women sat asleep by their milk-pails, the cow by this time far away. Fat-bellied naked children slept at their games. The houses were full of sleepers sleeping upright round their food, recalling Wordsworth's famous "party in a parlor."

So we went on, feeling pretty queer and scarcely believing in this morphic state into which we had plunged a nation. Finally the frontier was reached, where with extreme elation, we passed an immobile and gigantic frontier guard. A few miles further we had a good solid meal, and a doze. Our kit was rather heavy, and we decided to jettison some superfluous weight, in the shape of some food, specimens, and our metal headgear, or mind-

THE TISSUE-CULTURE KING 217

protectors, which at this distance, and with the hypnosis wearing a little thin, were, we thought, no longer necessary.

ABOUT nightfall on the third day, Hascombe suddenly stopped and turned his head.

"What's the matter?" I said, "Have you seen a lion?" His reply was completely unexpected. "No. I was just wondering whether really I ought not to go back again."

"Go back again," I cried. "What in the name of God Almighty do you want to do that for?"

"It suddenly struck me that I ought to," he said, "about five minutes ago. And really, when one comes to think of it, I don't suppose I shall ever get such a chance at research again. What's more, this is a dangerous journey to the coast, and I don't expect we shall get through alive."

I was thoroughly upset and put out, and told him so. And suddenly, for a few moments, I felt I must go back too. It was like that old friend of our boyhood, the voice of conscience.

"Yes, to be sure, we ought to go back," I thought with fervor. But suddenly checking myself as the thought came under the play of reason—"Why should we go back?" All sorts of reasons were proffered, as it were by unseen hands reaching up out of the hidden parts of me.

And then I realized what had happened. Bugala had waked up; he had wiped out the suggestion we had given to the superconsciousness, and in its place put in another. I could see him thinking it out, the cunning devil (one must give him credit for brains!), and hear him, after making his passes, whisper to the nation in prescribed form his new suggestion: "Will to return!" "Return!" For most of the inhabitants the command would have no meaning, for they would have been already at home. Doubtless some young men out on the hills, or truant children, or girls run off in secret to meet their lovers, were even now returning, stiffly and in somnambulistic trance, to their homes. It was only for them that the new command of the super-consciousness had any meaning—and for us.

I am putting it in a long and discursive way; at the moment I simply *saw* what had happened in a flash. I told Hascombe, I showed him it *must* be so, that nothing else would account for the sudden change, I begged and implored him to use his reason, to stick to his decision and to come on. How I regretted that, in our desire to discard all useless weight, we had left behind our metal telepathy-proof head coverings!

But Hascombe would not, or could not, see my point. I suppose he was much more imbued with all the feelings and spirit of the country, and so more susceptible. However that may be, he *was* immovable. He must go back; he knew it; he saw it clearly; it was his sacred duty; and much other similar rubbish. All this time the suggestion was attacking me too; and finally I felt that if I did not put more distance between me and that unisonic battery of will, I should succumb as well as he.

"Hascombe," I said, "I am going on. For God's sake, come with me." And I shouldered my pack, and *set* off. He was shaken, I saw, and came a few steps after me. But finally he turned, and, in spite of my frequent pauses and shouts to him to follow made off in the direction we had come. I can assure you that it was with a gloomy soul that I continued my solitary way. I shall not bore you with my adventures. Suffice it to say that at last I got to a white outpost, weak with fatigue and poor food and fever.

I kept very quiet about my adventures, only giving out that our expedition had lost its way and that my men had run away or been killed by the local tribes. At last I reached England. But I was a broken man, and a profound gloom had invaded my mind at the thought of Hascombe and the way he had been caught in his own net. I never found out what happened to him, and I do not suppose that I am likely to find out now. You may ask why I did not try to organize a rescue expedition; or why, at least, I did not bring Hascombe's discoveries before the Royal Society or the Metaphysical Institute. I can only repeat that I was a broken man. I did not expect to be believed; I was not at all sure that I could repeat our results, even on the same human material, much less with men of another race; I dreaded ridicule; and finally I was tormented by doubts as to whether the knowledge of mass-telepathy would not be a curse rather than a blessing to mankind.

However, I am an oldish man now and, what is more, old for my years. I want to get the story off my chest. Besides, old men like sermonizing and you must forgive, gentle reader, the sermonical turn which I now feel I must take. The question I want to raise is this: Dr. Hascombe attained to an unsurpassed power in a number of the applications of science—but *to what end did all this power serve?*

It is the merest cant and twaddle to go on asserting, as most of our press and people continue to do, that increase of scientific knowledge and power must in itself be good. I commend to the great public the obvious moral of my story and ask them to think what they propose to do with the power which is gradually being accumulated for them by the labors of those who labor because they like power, or because they want to find the truth about how things work.

The COLOUR OUT OF SPACE
By H. P. Lovecraft

...and in the fearsome instant of deeper darkness, the watchers saw wriggling at that treetop height, a thousand tiny points of faint and unhallowed radiance, tipping each bough like the fire of St. Elmo...and all the while the shaft of phosphorescence from the well was getting brighter and brighter and bringing to the minds of the huddled men, a sense of doom and abnormality... It was no longer shining out; it was pouring out; and as the shapeless steam of unplaceable colour left the well, it seemed to flow directly into the sky.

Introduction

HERE is a totally different story that we can highly recommend to you. We could wax rhapsodical in our praise, as the story is one of the finest pieces of literature it has been our good fortune to read. The theme is original, and yet fantastic enough to make it rise head and shoulders above many contemporary scientifiction stories. You will not regret having read this marvellous tale.

THE COLOUR OUT OF SPACE
By H. P. Lovecraft

WEST of Arkham the hills rise wild, and there are valleys with deep woods that no axe has ever cut. There are dark narrow glens where the trees slope fantastically, and where thin brooklets trickle without ever having caught the glint of sunlight. On the gentler slopes there are farms, ancient and rocky, with squat, moss-coated cottages brooding eternally over old New England secrets in the lee of great ledges; but these are all vacant now, the wide chimneys crumbling and the shingled sides bulging perilously beneath low gambrel roofs.

The old folk have gone away, and foreigners do not like to live there. French-Canadians have tried it, Italians have tried it, and the Poles have come and departed. It is not because of anything that can be seen or heard or handled, but because of something that is imagined. The place is not good for the imagination, and does not bring restful dreams at night. It must be this which keeps the foreigners away, for old Ammi Pierce has never told them of anything he recalls from the strange days. Ammi, whose head has been a little queer for years, is the only one who still remains, or who ever talks of the strange days; and he dares to do this because his house is so near the open fields and the travelled roads around Arkham.

There was once a road over the hills and through the valleys, that ran straight where the blasted heath is now; but people ceased to use it and a new road was laid curving far toward the south. Traces of the old one can still be found amidst the weeds of a returning wilderness, and some of them will doubtless linger even when half the hollows are flooded for the new reservoir. Then the dark woods will be cut down and the blasted heath will slumber far below blue waters whose surface will mirror the sky and ripple in the sun. And the secrets of the strange days will be one with the deep's secrets; one with the hidden lore of old ocean, and all the mystery of primal earth.

When I went into the hills and vales to survey for the new reservoir they told me the place was evil. They told me this in Arkham, and because that is a very old town full of witch legends I thought the evil must be something which grandams had whispered to children through centuries. The name "blasted heath" seemed to me very odd and theatrical, and I wondered how it had come into the folklore of a Puritan people. Then I saw that dark westward tangle of glens and slopes for myself, and ceased to wonder at anything besides its own elder mystery. It was morning when I saw it, but shadow lurked always there. The trees grew too thickly, and their trunks were too big for any healthy New England wood. There was too much silence in the dim alleys between them, and the floor was too soft with the dank moss and mattings of infinite years of decay.

In the open spaces, mostly along the line of the old road, there were little hillside farms; sometimes with all the buildings standing, sometimes with only one or two, and sometimes with only a lone chimney or fast-filling cellar. Weeds and briers reigned, and furtive wild things rustled in the undergrowth.

THE COLOUR OUT OF SPACE 223

Upon everything was a haze of restlessness and oppression; a touch of the unreal and the grotesque, as if some vital element of perspective or chiaroscuro were awry. I did not wonder that the foreigners would not stay, for this was no region to sleep in. It was too much like a landscape of Salvator Rosa; too much like some forbidden woodcut in a tale of terror.

But even all this was not so bad as the blasted heath. I knew it the moment I came upon it at the bottom of a spacious valley; for no other name could fit such a thing, or any other thing fit such a name. It was as if the poet had coined the phrase from having seen this one particular region. It must, I thought as I viewed it, be the outcome of a fire; but why had nothing new ever grown over those five acres of grey desolation that sprawled open to the sky like a great spot eaten by acid in the woods and fields? It lay largely to the north of the ancient road line, but encroached a little on the other side. I felt an odd reluctance about approaching, and did so at last only because my business took me through and past it. There was no vegetation of any kind on that broad expanse, but only a fine grey dust or ash which no wind seemed ever to blow about. The trees near it were sickly and stunted, and many dead trunks stood or lay rotting at the rim. As I walked hurriedly by I saw the tumbled bricks and stones of an old chimney and cellar on my right, and the yawning black maw of an abandoned well whose stagnant vapours played strange tricks with the hues of the sunlight. Even the long, dark woodland climb beyond seemed welcome in contrast, and I marvelled no more at the frightened whispers of Arkham people. There had been no house or ruin near; even in the old days the place must have been lonely and remote. And at twilight, dreading to repass that ominous spot, I walked circuitously back to the town by the curving road on the south. I vaguely wished some clouds would gather, for an odd timidity about the deep skyey voids above had crept into my soul.

In the evening I asked old people in Arkham about the blasted heath, and what was meant by that phrase "strange days" which so many evasively muttered. I could not, however, get any good answers except that all the mystery was much more recent than I had dreamed. It was not a matter of old legendry at all, but something within the lifetime of those who spoke. It had happened in the 'eighties, and a family had disappeared or was killed. Speakers would not be exact; and because they all told me to pay no attention to old Ammi Pierce's crazy tales, I sought him out the next morning, having heard that he lived alone in the ancient tottering cottage where the trees first begin to get very thick. It was a fearsomely archaic place, and had begun to exude the faint miasmal odour which clings about houses that have stood too long. Only with persistent knocking could I rouse the aged man, and when he shuffled timidly to the door I could tell he was not glad to see me. He was not so feeble as I had expected; but his eyes drooped in a curious way, and his unkempt clothing and white beard made him seem very worn and dismal.

Not knowing just how he could best be launched on his tales, I feigned a matter of business; told him of my surveying, and asked vague questions about the district. He was far brighter and more educated than I had been led to think, and before I knew it had grasped quite as much of the subject as any man I had talked with in Arkham. He was not like other rustics I had known in the sections where reservoirs were to be. From him there were no protests at the miles of old wood and farmland to be blotted out, though perhaps there would have been had not his home lain outside the bounds of the future lake. Relief was all that he shewed; relief at the doom of the dark ancient valleys through which he had roamed all his life. They were better under water now—better under water since the strange days. And with this opening his husky voice sank low, while his

THE COLOUR OUT OF SPACE

body leaned forward and his right forefinger began to point shakily and impressively.

It was then that I heard the story, and as the rambling voice scraped and whispered on I shivered again and again despite the summer day. Often I had to recall the speaker from ramblings, piece out scientific points which he knew only by a fading parrot memory of professors' talk, or bridge over gaps, where his sense of logic and continuity broke down. When he was done I did not wonder that his mind had snapped a trifle, or that the folk of Arkham would not speak much of the blasted heath. I hurried back before sunset to my hotel, unwilling to have the stars come out above me in the open; and the next day returned to Boston to give up my position. I could not go into that dim chaos of old forest and slope again, or face another time that grey blasted heath where the black well yawned deep beside the tumbled bricks and stones. The reservoir will soon be built now, and all those elder secrets will be safe forever under watery fathoms. But even then I do not believe I would like to visit that country by night—at least not when the sinister stars are out; and nothing could bribe me to drink the new city water of Arkham.

It all began, old Ammi said, with the meteorite. Before that time there had been no wild legends at all since the witch trials, and even then these western woods were not feared half so much as the small island in the Miskatonic where the devil held court beside a curious stone altar older than the Indians. These were not haunted woods, and their fantastic dusk was never terrible till the strange days. Then there had come that white noontide cloud, that string of explosions in the air, and that pillar of smoke from the valley far in the wood. And by night all Arkham had heard of the great rock that fell out of the sky and bedded itself in the ground beside the well at the Nahum Gardner place. That was the house which had stood where the blasted heath was to come—the trim white Nahum Gardner house amidst its fertile gardens and orchards.

Nahum had come to town to tell people about the stone, and had dropped in at Ammi Pierce's on the way. Ammi was forty then, and all the queer things were fixed very strongly in his mind. He and his wife had gone with the three professors from Miskatonic University who hastened out the next morning to see the weird visitor from unknown stellar space, and had wondered why Nahum had called it so large the day before. It had shrunk, Nahum said as he pointed out the big brownish mound above the ripped earth and charred grass near the archaic well-sweep in his front yard; but the wise men answered that stones do not shrink. Its heat lingered persistently, and Nahum declared it had glowed faintly in the night. The professors tried it with a geologist's hammer and found it was oddly soft. It was, in truth, so soft as to be almost plastic; and they gouged rather than chipped a specimen to take back to the college for testing. They took it in an old pail borrowed from Nahum's kitchen, for even the small piece refused to grow cool. On the trip back they stopped at Ammi's to rest, and seemed thoughtful when Mrs. Pierce remarked that the fragment was growing smaller and burning the bottom of the pail. Truly, it was not large, but perhaps they had taken less than they thought.

The day after that—all this was in June of '82—the professors had trooped out again in a great excitement. As they passed Ammi's they told him what queer things the specimen had done, and how it had faded wholly away when they put it in a glass beaker. The beaker had gone, too, and the wise men talked of the strange stone's affinity for silicon. It had acted quite unbelievably in that well-ordered laboratory; doing nothing at all and shewing no occluded gases when heated on charcoal, being wholly negative in the borax bead, and soon proving itself absolutely non-volatile at any producible temperature, including that of the oxy-hydrogen blowpipe. On an anvil it appeared highly malleable, and in the dark its luminosity was very marked. Stubbornly refusing to grow cool, it soon had the college in a state of real excitement; and when upon heating before the spectroscope it displayed shining bands unlike any known colours of the normal spectrum there was much breathless talk of new elements, bizarre optical properties, and other things which puzzled men of science are wont to say when faced by the unknown.

Hot as it was, they tested it in a crucible with all the proper reagents. Water did nothing. Hydrochloric acid was the same. Nitric acid and even aqua regia merely hissed and spattered against its torrid invulnerability. Ammi had difficulty in recalling all these things, but recognized some solvents as I mentioned them in the usual order of use. There were ammonia and caustic soda, alcohol and ether, nauseous carbon disulphide and a dozen others; but although the weight grew steadily less as time passed, and the fragment seemed to be slightly cooling, there was no change in the solvents to shew that they had attacked the substance at all. It was a metal, though, beyond a doubt. It was magnetic, for one thing; and after its immersion in the acid solvents there seemed to be faint traces of the Widmanstätten figures found on meteoric iron. When the cooling had grown very considerable, the testing was carried on in glass; and it was in a glass beaker that they left all the chips made of the original fragment during the work. The next morning both chips and beaker were gone without trace, and only a charred spot marked the place on the wooden shelf where they had been.

All this the professors told Ammi as they paused at his door, and once more he went with them to see the stony messenger from the stars, though this time his wife did not accompany him. It had now most certainly shrunk, and even the sober professors could not doubt the truth of what they saw. All around the dwindling brown lump near the well was a vacant space, except where the earth had caved in; and whereas it had been a good seven feet across the day before, it was now scarcely five. It was still hot, and the sages studied its surface curiously as they detached another and larger piece with hammer and chisel. They gouged deeply this time, and as they pried away the smaller mass they saw that the core of the thing was not quite homogeneous.

They had uncovered what seemed to be the side of a large coloured globule imbedded in the substance. The colour, which resembled some of the bands in the meteor's strange spectrum, was almost impossible to describe; and it was only by analogy that they called it colour at all. Its texture was glossy, and upon tapping it appeared to promise both brittleness and hollowness. One of the professors gave it a smart blow with a hammer, and it burst with a nervous little pop. Nothing was emitted, and all trace of the thing vanished with the puncturing. It left behind a hollow spherical space about three inches across, and all thought it probable that others would be discovered as the enclosing substance wasted away.

Conjecture was vain; so after a futile attempt to find additional globules by drilling, the seekers left again with their new specimen—which proved, however, as baffling in the laboratory as its predecessor had been. Aside from being almost plastic, having heat, magnetism, and slight luminosity, cooling slightly in powerful acids, possessing an unknown spectrum, wasting away in air, and attacking silicon compounds with mutual destruction as a result, it presented no identifying features whatsoever; and at the end of the tests the college scientists were forced to own that they could not place it. It was nothing of this earth, but a piece of the great outside; and as such dowered with outside properties and obedient to outside laws.

That night there was a thunderstorm, and when the professors went out to Nahum's the next day they met with a

THE COLOUR OUT OF SPACE 229

bitter disappointment. The stone, magnetic as it had been, must have had some peculiar electrical property; for it had "drawn the lightning," as Nahum said, with a singular persistence. Six times within an hour the farmer saw the lightning strike the furrow in the front yard, and when the storm was over nothing remained but a ragged pit by the ancient well-sweep, half-choked with caved-in earth. Digging had borne no fruit, and the scientists verified the fact of the utter vanishment. The failure was total; so that nothing was left to do but go back to the laboratory and test again the disappearing fragment left carefully cased in lead. That fragment lasted a week, at the end of which nothing of value had been learned of it. When it had gone, no residue was left behind, and in time the professors felt scarcely sure they had indeed seen with waking eyes that cryptic vestige of the fathomless gulfs outside; that lone, weird message from other universes and other realms of matter, force, and entity.

As was natural, the Arkham papers made much of the incident with its collegiate sponsoring, and sent reporters to talk with Nahum Gardner and his family. At least one Boston daily also sent a scribe, and Nahum quickly became a kind of local celebrity. He was a lean, genial person of about fifty, living with his wife and three sons on the pleasant farmstead in the valley. He and Ammi exchanged visits frequently, as did their wives; and Ammi had nothing but praise for him after all these years. He seemed slightly proud of the notice his place had attracted, and talked often of the meteorite in the succeeding weeks. That July and August were hot; and Nahum worked hard at his haying in the ten-acre pasture across Chapman's Brook; his rattling wain wearing deep ruts in the shadowy lanes between. The labour tired him more than it had in other years, and he felt that age was beginning to tell on him.

Then fell the time of fruit and harvest. The pears and apples slowly ripened, and Nahum vowed that his orchards were prospering as never before. The fruit was growing to phenomenal size and unwonted gloss, and in such abundance that extra barrels were ordered to handle the future crop. But with the ripening came sore disappointment; for of all that gorgeous array of specious lusciousness not one single jot was fit to eat. Into the fine flavour of the pears and apples had crept a stealthy bitterness and sickishness, so that even the smallest of bites induced a lasting disgust. It was the same with the melons and tomatoes, and Nahum sadly saw that his entire crop was lost. Quick to connect events, he declared that the meteorite had poisoned the soil, and thanked Heaven that most of the other crops were in the upland lot along the road.

Winter came early, and was very cold. Ammi saw Nahum less often than usual, and observed that he had begun to look worried. The rest of his family, too, seemed to have grown taciturn; and were far from steady in their church-going or their attendance at the various social events of the countryside. For this reserve or melancholy no cause could be found, though all the household confessed now and then to poorer health and a feeling of vague disquiet. Nahum himself gave the most definite statement of anyone when he said he was disturbed about certain footprints in the snow. They were the usual winter prints of red squirrels, white rabbits, and foxes, but the brooding farmer professed to see something not quite right about their nature and arrangement. He was never specific, but appeared to think that they were not as characteristic of the anatomy and habits of squirrels and rabbits and foxes as they ought to be. Ammi listened without interest to this talk until one night when he drove past Nahum's house in his sleigh on the way back from Clark's Corners. There had been a moon, and a rabbit had run across the road, and the leaps of that rabbit were longer than either Ammi or his horse liked. The latter, indeed, had almost run away when brought up by a firm rein. Thereafter

Ammi gave Nahum's tales more respect, and wondered why the Gardner dogs seemed so cowed and quivering every morning. They had, it developed, nearly lost the spirit to bark.

In February the McGregor boys from Meadow Hill were out shooting woodchucks, and not far from the Gardner place bagged a very peculiar specimen. The proportions of its body seemed slightly altered in a queer way impossible to describe, while its face had taken on an expression which no one ever saw in a woodchuck before. The boys were genuinely frightened, and threw the thing away at once, so that only their grotesque tales of it ever reached the people of the countryside. But the shying of the horses near Nahum's house had now become an acknowledged thing, and all the basis for a cycle of whispered legend was fast taking form.

People vowed that the snow melted faster around Nahum's than it did anywhere else, and early in March there was an awed discussion in Potter's general store at Clark's Corners. Stephen Rice had driven past Gardner's in the morning, and had noticed the skunk-cabbages coming up through the mud by the woods across the road. Never were things of such size seen before, and they held strange colours that could not be put into any words. Their shapes were monstrous, and the horse had snorted at an odour which struck Stephen as wholly unprecedented. That afternoon several persons drove past to see the abnormal growth, and all agreed that plants of that kind ought never to sprout in a healthy world. The bad fruit of the fall before was freely mentioned, and it went from mouth to mouth that there was poison in Nahum's ground. Of course it was the meteorite; and remembering how strange the men from the college had found that stone to be, several farmers spoke about the matter to them.

One day they paid Nahum a visit; but having no love of wild tales and folklore were very conservative in what they inferred. The plants were certainly odd, but all skunk-cabbages are more or less odd in shape and odour and hue. Perhaps some mineral element from the stone had entered the soil, but it would soon be washed away. And as for the footprints and frightened horses—of course this was mere country talk which such a phenomenon as the aërolite would be certain to start. There was really nothing for serious men to do in cases of wild gossip, for superstitious rustics will say and believe anything. And so all through the strange days the professors stayed away in contempt. Only one of them, when given two phials of dust for analysis in a police job over a year and a half later, recalled that the queer colour of that skunk-cabbage had been very like one of the anomalous bands of light shewn by the meteor fragment in the college spectroscope, and like the brittle globule found imbedded in the stone from the abyss. The samples in this analysis case gave the same odd bands at first, though later they lost the property.

The trees budded prematurely around Nahum's, and at night they swayed ominously in the wind. Nahum's second son Thaddeus, a lad of fifteen, swore that they swayed also when there was no wind; but even the gossips would not credit this. Certainly, however, restlessness was in the air. The entire Gardner family developed the habit of stealthy listening, though not for any sound which they could consciously name. The listening was, indeed, rather a product of moments when consciousness seemed half to slip away. Unfortunately such moments increased week by week, till it became common speech that "something was wrong with all Nahum's folks." When the early saxifrage came out it had another strange colour; not quite like that of the skunk-cabbage, but plainly related and equally unknown to anyone who saw it. Nahum took some blossoms to Arkham and shewed them to the editor of the Gazette, but that dignitary did no more than write a humorous article about them, in which the dark fears of rustics were held up to polite

THE COLOUR OUT OF SPACE 233

ridicule. It was a mistake of Nahum's to tell a stolid city man about the way the great, overgrown mourning-cloak butterflies behaved in connection with these saxifrages.

April brought a kind of madness to the country folk, and began that disuse of the road past Nahum's which led to its ultimate abandonment. It was the vegetation. All the orchard trees blossomed forth in strange colours, and through the stony soil of the yard and adjacent pasturage there sprang up a bizarre growth which only a botanist could connect with the proper flora of the region. No sane wholesome colours were anywhere to be seen except in the green grass and leafage; but everywhere those hectic and prismatic variants of some diseased, underlying primary tone without a place among the known tints of earth. The "Dutchman's breeches" became a thing of sinister menace, and the bloodroots grew insolent in their chromatic perversion. Ammi and the Gardners thought that most of the colours had a sort of haunting familiarity, and decided that they reminded one of the brittle globule in the meteor. Nahum ploughed and sowed the ten-acre pasture and the upland lot, but did nothing with the land around the house. He knew it would be of no use, and hoped that the summer's strange growths would draw all the poison from the soil. He was prepared for almost anything now, and had grown used to the sense of something near him waiting to be heard. The shunning of his house by neighbors told on him, of course; but it told on his wife more. The boys were better off, being at school each day; but they could not help being frightened by the gossip. Thaddeus, an especially sensitive youth, suffered the most.

In May the insects came, and Nahum's place became a nightmare of buzzing and crawling. Most of the creatures seemed not quite usual in their aspects and motions, and their nocturnal habits contradicted all former experience. The Gardners took to watching at night—watching in all directions at random for something . . . they could not tell what. It was then that they all owned that Thaddeus had been right about the trees. Mrs. Gardner was the next to see it from the window as she watched the swollen boughs of a maple against a moonlit sky. The boughs surely moved, and there was no wind. It must be the sap. Strangeness had come into everything growing now. Yet it was none of Nahum's family at all who made the next discovery. Familiarity had dulled them, and what they could not see was glimpsed by a timid windmill salesman from Bolton who drove by one night in ignorance of the country legends. What he told in Arkham was given a short paragraph in the Gazette; and it was there that all the farmers, Nahum included, saw it first. The night had been dark and the buggy-lamps faint, but around a farm in the valley which everyone knew from the account must be Nahum's, the darkness had been less thick. A dim though distinct luminosity seemed to inhere in all the vegetation, grass, leaves, and blossoms alike, while at one moment a detached piece of the phosphorescence appeared to stir furtively in the yard near the barn.

The grass had so far seemed untouched, and the cows were freely pastured in the lot near the house, but toward the end of May the milk began to be bad. Then Nahum had the cows driven to the uplands, after which the trouble ceased. Not long after this the change in grass and leaves became apparent to the eye. All the verdure was going grey, and was developing a highly singular quality of brittleness. Ammi was now the only person who ever visited the place, and his visits were becoming fewer and fewer. When school closed the Gardners were virtually cut off from the world, and sometimes let Ammi do their errands in town. They were failing curiously both physically and mentally, and no one was surprised when the news of Mrs. Gardner's madness stole around.

It happened in June, about the anniversary of the meteor's

THE COLOUR OUT OF SPACE

fall, and the poor woman screamed about things in the air which she could not describe. In her raving there was not a single specific noun, but only verbs and pronouns. Things moved and changed and fluttered, and ears tingled to impulses which were not wholly sounds. Something was taken away—she was being drained of something—something was fastening itself on her that ought not to be—someone must make it keep off—nothing was ever still in the night—the walls and windows shifted. Nahum did not send her to the county asylum, but let her wander about the house as long as she was harmless to herself and others. Even when her expression changed he did nothing. But when the boys grew afraid of her, and Thaddeus nearly fainted at the way she made faces at him, he decided to keep her locked in the attic. By July she had ceased to speak and crawled on all fours, and before that month was over Nahum got the mad notion that she was slightly luminous in the dark, as he now clearly saw was the case with the nearby vegetation.

It was a little before this that the horses had stampeded. Something had aroused them in the night, and their neighing and kicking in their stalls had been terrible. There seemed virtually nothing to do to calm them, and when Nahum opened the stable door they all bolted out like frightened woodland deer. It took a week to track all four, and when found they were seen to be quite useless and unmanageable. Something had snapped in their brains, and each one had to be shot for its own good. Nahum borrowed a horse from Ammi for his haying, but found it would not approach the barn. It shied, balked, and whinnied, and in the end he could do nothing but drive it into the yard while the men used their own strength to get the heavy wagon near enough the hayloft for convenient pitching. And all the while the vegetation was turning grey and brittle. Even the flowers whose hues had been so strange were greying now, and the fruit was coming out grey and dwarfed and tasteless.

The asters and golden-rod bloomed grey and distorted, and the roses and zinneas and hollyhocks in the front yard were such blasphemous-looking things that Nahum's oldest boy Zenas cut them down. The strangely puffed insects died about that time, even the bees that had left their hives and taken to the woods.

By September all the vegetation was fast crumbling to a greyish powder, and Nahum feared that the trees would die before the poison was out of the soil. His wife now had spells of terrific screaming, and he and the boys were in a constant state of nervous tension. They shunned people now, and when school opened the boys did not go. But it was Ammi, on one of his rare visits, who first realised that the well water was no longer good. It had an evil taste that was not exactly fetid nor exactly salty, and Ammi advised his friend to dig another well on higher ground to use till the soil was good again. Nahum, however, ignored the warning, for he had by that time become calloused to strange and unpleasant things. He and the boys continued to use the tainted supply, drinking it as listlessly and mechanically as they ate their meagre and ill-cooked meals and did their thankless and monotonous chores through the aimless days. There was something of stolid resignation about them all, as if they walked half in another world between lines of nameless guards to a certain and familiar doom.

Thaddeus went mad in September after a visit to the well. He had gone with a pail and had come back empty-handed, shrieking and waving his arms, and sometimes lapsing into an inane titter or a whisper about "the moving colours down there." Two in one family was pretty bad, but Nahum was very brave about it. He let the boy run about for a week until he began stumbling and hurting himself, and then he shut him in an attic room across the hall from his mother's. The way they screamed at each other from behind their locked doors was very terrible, especially to little Merwin, who fancied they talked in some terrible language that was not of earth. Merwin was getting frightfully imaginative, and his restlessness was worse after the shutting away of the brother who had been his greatest playmate.

Almost at the same time the mortality among the livestock commenced. Poultry turned greyish and died very quickly, their meat being found dry and noisome upon cutting. Hogs grew inordinately fat, then suddenly began to undergo loathsome changes which no one could explain. Their meat was of course useless, and Nahum was at his wit's end. No rural veterinary would approach his place, and the city veterinary from Arkham was openly baffled. The swine began growing grey and brittle and falling to pieces before they died, and their eyes and muzzles developed singular alterations. It was very inexplicable, for they had never been fed from the tainted vegetation. Then something struck the cows. Certain areas or sometimes the whole body would be uncannily shrivelled or compressed, and atrocious collapses or disintegrations were common. In the last stages—and death was always the result—there would be a greying and turning brittle like that which beset the hogs. There could be no question of poison, for all the cases occurred in a locked and undisturbed barn. No bites of prowling things could have brought the virus, for what live beast of earth can pass through solid obstacles? It must be only natural disease—yet what disease could wreak such results was beyond any mind's guessing. When the harvest came there was not an animal surviving on the place, for the stock and poultry were dead and the dogs had run away. These dogs, three in number, had all vanished one night and were never heard of again. The five cats had left some time before, but their going was scarcely noticed since there now seemed to be no mice, and only Mrs. Gardner had made pets of the graceful felines.

On the nineteenth of October Nahum staggered into

Ammi's house with hideous news. The death had come to poor Thaddeus in his attic room, and it had come in a way which could not be told. Nahum had dug a grave in the railed family plot behind the farm, and had put therein what he found. There could have been nothing from outside, for the small barred window and locked door were intact; but it was much as it had been in the barn. Ammi and his wife consoled the stricken man as best they could, but shuddered as they did so. Stark terror seemed to cling round the Gardners and all they touched, and the very presence of one in the house was a breath from regions unnamed and unnamable. Ammi accompanied Nahum home with the greatest reluctance, and did what he might to calm the hysterical sobbing of little Merwin. Zenas needed no calming. He had come of late to do nothing but stare into space and obey what his father told him; and Ammi thought that his fate was very merciful. Now and then Merwin's screams were answered faintly from the attic, and in response to an inquiring look Nahum said that his wife was getting very feeble. When night approached, Ammi managed to get away; for not even friendship could make him stay in that spot when the faint glow of the vegetation began and the trees may or may not have swayed without wind. It was really lucky for Ammi that he was not more imaginative. Even as things were, his mind was bent ever so slightly; but had he been able to connect and reflect upon all the portents around him he must inevitably have turned a total maniac. In the twilight he hastened home, the screams of the mad woman and the nervous child ringing horribly in his ears.

Three days later Nahum lurched into Ammi's kitchen in the early morning, and in the absence of his host stammered out a desperate tale once more, while Mrs. Pierce listened in a clutching fright. It was little Merwin this time. He was gone. He had gone out late at night with a lantern and pail for water, and

THE COLOUR OUT OF SPACE 239

had never come back. He'd been going to pieces for days, and hardly knew what he was about. Screamed at everything. There had been a frantic shriek from the yard then, but before the father could get to the door the boy was gone. There was no glow from the lantern he had taken, and of the child himself no trace. At the time Nahum thought the lantern and pail were gone too; but when dawn came, and the man had plodded back from his all-night search of the woods and fields, he had found some very curious things near the well. There was a crushed and apparently somewhat melted mass of iron which had certainly been the lantern; while a bent bail and twisted iron hoops beside it, both half-fused, seemed to hint at the remnants of the pail. That was all. Nahum was past imagining, Mrs. Pierce was blank, and Ammi, when he had reached home and heard the tale, could give no guess. Merwin was gone, and there would be no use in telling the people around, who shunned all Gardners now. No use, either, in telling the city people at Arkham who laughed at everything. Thad was gone, and now Merwin was gone. Something was creeping and creeping and waiting to be seen and felt and heard. Nahum would go soon, and he wanted Ammi to look after his wife and Zenas if they survived him. It must all be a judgment of some sort; though he could not fancy what for, since he had always walked uprightly in the Lord's ways so far as he knew.

For over two weeks Ammi saw nothing of Nahum; and then, worried about what might have happened, he overcame his fears and paid the Gardner place a visit. There was no smoke from the great chimney, and for a moment the visitor was apprehensive of the worst. The aspect of the whole farm was shocking—greyish withered grass and leaves on the ground, vines falling in brittle wreckage from archaic walls and gables, and great bare trees clawing up at the grey November sky with a studied malevolence which Ammi could not but feel had come from some subtle change in the tilt of the branches. But Nahum was alive, after all. He was weak, and lying on a couch in the low-ceiled kitchen, but perfectly conscious and able to give simple orders to Zenas. The room was deadly cold; and as Ammi visibly shivered, the host shouted huskily to Zenas for more wood. Wood, indeed, was sorely needed; since the cavernous fireplace was unlit and empty, with a cloud of soot blowing about in the chill wind that came down the chimney. Presently Nahum asked him if the extra wood had made him any more comfortable, and then Ammi saw what had happened. The stoutest cord had broken at last, and the hapless farmer's mind was proof against more sorrow.

Questioning tactfully, Ammi could get no clear data at all about the missing Zenas. "In the well—he lives in the well—" was all that the clouded father would say. Then there flashed across the visitor's mind a sudden thought of the mad wife, and he changed his line of inquiry. "Nabby? Why, here she is!" was the surprised response of poor Nahum, and Ammi soon saw that he must search for himself. Leaving the harmless babbler on the couch, he took the keys from their nail beside the door and climbed the creaking stairs to the attic. It was very close and noisome up there, and no sound could be heard from any direction. Of the four doors in sight, only one was locked, and on this he tried various keys on the ring he had taken. The third key proved the right one, and after some fumbling Ammi threw open the low white door.

It was quite dark inside, for the window was small and half-obscured by the crude wooden bars; and Ammi could see nothing at all on the wide-planked floor. The stench was beyond enduring, and before proceeding further he had to retreat to another room and return with his lungs filled with breathable air. When he did enter he saw something dark in the corner, and upon seeing it more clearly he screamed outright. While he

THE COLOUR OUT OF SPACE

screamed he thought a momentary cloud eclipsed the window, and a second later he felt himself brushed as if by some hateful current of vapour. Strange colours danced before his eyes; and had not a present horror numbed him he would have thought of the globule in the meteor that the geologist's hammer had shattered, and of the morbid vegetation that had sprouted in the spring. As it was he thought only of the blasphemous monstrosity which confronted him, and which all too clearly had shared the nameless fate of young Thaddeus and the livestock. But the terrible thing about this horror was that it very slowly and perceptibly moved as it continued to crumble.

Ammi would give me no added particulars to this scene, but the shape in the corner does not reappear in his tale as a moving object. There are things which cannot be mentioned, and what is done in common humanity is sometimes cruelly judged by the law. I gathered that no moving thing was left in that attic room, and that to leave anything capable of motion there would have been a deed so monstrous as to damn any accountable being to eternal torment. Anyone but a stolid farmer would have fainted or gone mad, but Ammi walked conscious through that low doorway and locked the accursed secret behind him. There would be Nahum to deal with now; he must be fed and tended, and removed to some place where he could be cared for.

Commencing his descent of the dark stairs, Ammi heard a thud below him. He even thought a scream had been suddenly choked off, and recalled nervously the clammy vapour which had brushed by him in that frightful room above. What presence had his cry and entry started up? Halted by some vague fear, he heard still further sounds below. Indubitably there was a sort of heavy dragging, and a most detestably sticky noise as of some fiendish and unclean species of suction. With an associative sense goaded to feverish heights, he thought unaccountably of what he had seen upstairs. Good

God! What eldritch dream-world was this into which he had blundered? He dared move neither backward nor forward, but stood there trembling at the black curve of the boxed-in staircase. Every trifle of the scene burned itself into his brain. The sounds, the sense of dread expectancy, the darkness, the steepness of the narrow steps—and merciful Heaven!—the faint but unmistakable luminosity of all the woodwork in sight; steps, sides, exposed laths, and beams alike!

Then there burst forth a frantic whinny from Ammi's horse outside, followed at once by a clatter which told of a frenzied runaway. In another moment horse and buggy had gone beyond earshot, leaving the frightened man on the dark stairs to guess what had sent them. But that was not all. There had been another sound out there. A sort of liquid splash—water—it must have been the well. He had left Hero untied near it, and a buggy wheel must have brushed the coping and knocked in a stone. And still the pale phosphorescence glowed in that detestably ancient woodwork. God! how old the house was! Most of it built before 1670, and the gambrel roof not later than 1730.

A feeble scratching on the floor downstairs now sounded distinctly, and Ammi's grip tightened on a heavy stick he had picked up in the attic for some purpose. Slowly nerving himself, he finished his descent and walked boldly toward the kitchen. But he did not complete the walk, because what he sought was no longer there. It had come to meet him, and it was still alive after a fashion. Whether it had crawled or whether it had been dragged by any external force, Ammi could not say; but the death had been at it. Everything had happened in the last half-hour, but collapse, greying, and disintegration were already far advanced. There was a horrible brittleness, and dry fragments were scaling off. Ammi could not touch it, but looked horrifiedly into the distorted parody that had been a face. "What was it, Nahum—what was it?" he whispered, and the cleft, bulging lips

THE COLOUR OUT OF SPACE

were just able to crackle out a final answer.

"Nothin' . . . nothin' . . . the colour . . . it burns . . . cold an' wet, but it burns . . . it lived in the well . . . I seen it . . . a kind of smoke . . . jest like the flowers last spring . . . the well shone at night . . . Thad an' Mernie an' Zenas . . . everything alive . . . suckin' the life out of everything . . . in that stone . . . it must a' come in that stone pizened the whole place . . . dun't know what it wants . . . that round thing them men from the college dug outen the stone . . . they smashed it . . . it was that same colour . . . jest the same, like the flowers an' plants . . . must a' ben more of 'em . . . seeds . . . seeds . . . they growed . . . I seen it the fust time this week . . . must a' got strong on Zenas . . . he was a big boy, full o' life . . . it beats down your mind an' then gits ye . . . burns ye up . . . in the well water . . . you was right about that . . . evil water . . . Zenas never come back from the well . . . can't git away . . . draws ye . . . ye know summ'at's comin' but tain't no use . . . I seen it time an' agin senct Zenas was took . . . whar's Nabby, Ammi? . . . my head's no good . . . dun't know how long since I fed her . . . it'll git her ef we ain't keerful . . . jest a colour . . . her face is gittin' to hev that colour sometimes towards night . . . an' it burns an' sucks . . . it come from some place whar things ain't as they is here . . . one o' them professors said so . . . he was right . . . look out, Ammi, it'll do suthin' more . . . sucks the life out. . . ."

But that was all. That which spoke could speak no more because it had completely caved in. Ammi laid a red checked tablecloth over what was left and reeled out the back door into the fields. He climbed the slope to the ten-acre pasture and stumbled home by the north road and the woods. He could not pass that well from which his horse had run away. He had looked at it through the window, and had seen that no stone was missing from the rim. Then the lurching buggy had not dislodged anything after all—the splash had been something else—something which went into the well after it had done with poor Nahum.

When Ammi reached his house the horse and buggy had arrived before him and thrown his wife into fits of anxiety. Reassuring her without explanations, he set out at once for Arkham and notified the authorities that the Gardner family was no more. He indulged in no details, but merely told of the deaths of Nahum and Nabby, that of Thaddeus being already known, and mentioned that the cause seemed to be the same strange ailment which had killed the livestock. He also stated that Merwin and Zenas had disappeared. There was considerable questioning at the police station, and in the end Ammi was compelled to take three officers to the Gardner farm, together with the coroner, the medical examiner, and the veterinary who had treated the diseased animals. He went much against his will, for the afternoon was advancing and he feared the fall of night over that accursed place, but it was some comfort to have so many people with him.

The six men drove out in a democrat-wagon, following Ammi's buggy, and arrived at the pest-ridden farmhouse about four o'clock. Used as the officers were to gruesome experiences, not one remained unmoved at what was found in the attic and under the red checked tablecloth on the floor below. The whole aspect of the farm with its grey desolation was terrible enough, but those two crumbling objects were beyond all bounds. No one could look long at them, and even the medical examiner admitted that there was very little to examine. Specimens could be analysed, of course, so he busied himself in obtaining them—and here it develops that a very puzzling aftermath occurred at the college laboratory where the two phials of dust were finally taken. Under the spectroscope both samples gave off an unknown spectrum, in which many of the baffling bands were precisely like those which the strange meteor had yielded

THE COLOUR OUT OF SPACE

in the previous year. The property of emitting this spectrum vanished in a month, the dust thereafter consisting mainly of alkaline phosphates and carbonates.

Ammi would not have told the men about the well if he had thought they meant to do anything then and there. It was getting toward sunset, and he was anxious to be away. But he could not help glancing nervously at the stony curb by the great sweep, and when a detective questioned him he admitted that Nahum had feared something down there—so much so that he had never even thought of searching it for Merwin or Zenas. After that nothing would do but that they empty and explore the well immediately, so Ammi had to wait trembling while pail after pail of rank water was hauled up and splashed on the soaking ground outside. The men sniffed in disgust at the fluid, and toward the last held their noses against the foetor they were uncovering. It was not so long a job as they had feared it would be, since the water was phenomenally low. There is no need to speak too exactly of what they found. Merwin and Zenas were both there, in part, though the vestiges were mainly skeletal. There were also a small deer and a large dog in about the same state, and a number of bones of smaller animals. The ooze and slime at the bottom seemed inexplicably porous and bubbling, and a man who descended on hand-holds with a long pole found that he could sink the wooden shaft to any depth in the mud of the floor without meeting any solid obstruction.

Twilight had now fallen, and lanterns were brought from the house. Then, when it was seen that nothing further could be gained from the well, everyone went indoors and conferred in the ancient sitting-room while the intermittent light of a spectral half-moon played wanly on the grey desolation outside. The men were frankly nonplussed by the entire case, and could find no convincing common element to link the strange vegetable conditions, the unknown disease of livestock and humans, and the unaccountable deaths of Merwin and Zenas in the tainted well. They had heard the common country talk, it is true; but could not believe that anything contrary to natural law had occurred. No doubt the meteor had poisoned the soil, but the illness of persons and animals who had eaten nothing grown in that soil was another matter. Was it the well water? Very possibly. It might be a good idea to analyze it. But what peculiar madness could have made both boys jump into the well? Their deeds were so similar—and the fragments shewed that they had both suffered from the grey brittle death. Why was everything so grey and brittle?

It was the coroner, seated near a window overlooking the yard, who first noticed the glow about the well. Night had fully set in, and all the abhorrent grounds seemed faintly luminous with more than the fitful moonbeams; but this new glow was something definite and distinct, and appeared to shoot up from the black pit like a softened ray from a searchlight, giving dull reflections in the little ground pools where the water had been emptied. It had a very queer colour, and as all the men clustered round the window Ammi gave a violent start. For this strange beam of ghastly miasma was to him of no unfamiliar hue. He had seen that colour before, and feared to think what it might mean. He had seen it in the nasty brittle globule in that aërolite two summers ago, had seen it in the crazy vegetation of the springtime, and had thought he had seen it for an instant that very morning against the small barred window of that terrible attic room where nameless things had happened. It had flashed there a second, and a clammy and hateful current of vapour had brushed past him—and then poor Nahum had been taken by something of that colour. He had said so at the last—said it was like the globule and the plants. After that had come the runaway in the yard and the splash in the well—and now that well was belching forth to the night a pale insidious beam of

THE COLOUR OUT OF SPACE

the same demoniac tint.

It does credit to the alertness of Ammi's mind that he puzzled even at that tense moment over a point which was essentially scientific. He could not but wonder at his gleaning of the same impression from a vapour glimpsed in the daytime, against a window opening on the morning sky, and from a nocturnal exhalation seen as a phosphorescent mist against the black and blasted landscape. It wasn't right—it was against Nature—and he thought of those terrible last words of his stricken friend, "It come from some place whar things ain't as they is here . . . one o' them professors said so. . ."

All three horses outside, tied to a pair of shrivelled saplings by the road, were now neighing and pawing frantically. The wagon driver started for the door to do something, but Ammi laid a shaky hand on his shoulder. "Dun't go out thar," he whispered. "They's more to this nor what we know. Nahum said somethin' lived in the well that sucks your life out. He said it must be some'at growed from a round ball like one we all seen in the meteor stone that fell a year ago June. Sucks an' burns, he said, an' is jest a cloud of colour like that light out thar now, that ye can hardly see an' can't tell what it is. Nahum thought it feeds on everything livin' an' gits stronger all the time. He said he seen it this last week. It must be somethin' from away off in the sky like the men from the college last year says the meteor stone was. The way it's made an' the way it works ain't like no way o' God's world. It's some'at from beyond."

So the men paused indecisively as the light from the well grew stronger and the hitched horses pawed and whinnied in increasing frenzy. It was truly an awful moment; with terror in that ancient and accursed house itself, four monstrous sets of fragments—two from the house and two from the well—in the woodshed behind, and that shaft of unknown and unholy iridescence from the slimy depths in front. Ammi had restrained the driver on impulse, forgetting how uninjured he himself was after the clammy brushing of that coloured vapour in the attic room, but perhaps it is just as well that he acted as he did. No one will ever know what was abroad that night; and though the blasphemy from beyond had not so far hurt any human of unweakened mind, there is no telling what it might not have done at that last moment, and with its seemingly increased strength and the special signs of purpose it was soon to display beneath the half-clouded moonlit sky.

All at once one of the detectives at the window gave a short, sharp gasp. The others looked at him, and then quickly followed his own gaze upward to the point at which its idle straying had been suddenly arrested. There was no need for words. What had been disputed in country gossip was disputable no longer, and it is because of the thing which every man of that party agreed in whispering later on, that the strange days are never talked about in Arkham. It is necessary to premise that there was no wind at that hour of the evening. One did arise not long afterward, but there was absolutely none then. Even the dry tips of the lingering hedge-mustard, grey and blighted, and the fringe on the roof of the standing democrat-wagon were unstirred. And yet amid that tense godless calm the high bare boughs of all the trees in the yard were moving. They were twitching morbidly and spasmodically, clawing in convulsive and epileptic madness at the moonlit clouds; scratching impotently in the noxious air as if jerked by some alien and bodiless line of linkage with subterrene horrors writhing and struggling below the black roots.

Not a man breathed for several seconds. Then a cloud of darker depth passed over the moon, and the silhouette of clutching branches faded out momentarily. At this there was a general cry; muffled with awe, but husky and almost identical from every throat. For the terror had not faded with the

THE COLOUR OUT OF SPACE 249

silhouette, and in a fearsome instant of deeper darkness the watchers saw wriggling at that treetop height a thousand tiny points of faint and unhallowed radiance, tipping each bough like the fire of St. Elmo or the flames that came down on the apostles' heads at Pentecost. It was a monstrous constellation of unnatural light, like a glutted swarm of corpse-fed fireflies dancing hellish sarabands over an accursed marsh; and its colour was that same nameless intrusion which Ammi had come to recognize and dread. All the while the shaft of phosphorescence from the well was getting brighter and brighter, bringing to the minds of the huddled men, a sense of doom and abnormality which far outraced any image their conscious minds could form. It was no longer shining out, it was pouring out; and as the shapeless stream of unplaceable colour left the well it seemed to flow directly into the sky.

The veterinary shivered, and walked to the front door to drop the heavy extra bar across it. Ammi shook no less, and had to tug and point for lack of a controllable voice when he wished to draw notice to the growing luminosity of the trees. The neighing and stamping of the horses had become utterly frightful, but not a soul of that group in the old house would have ventured forth for any earthly reward. With the moments the shining of the trees increased, while their restless branches seemed to strain more and more toward verticality. The wood of the well-sweep was shining now, and presently a policeman dumbly pointed to some wooden sheds and bee-hives near the stone wall on the west. They were commencing to shine, too, though the tethered vehicles of the visitors seemed so far unaffected. Then there was a wild commotion and clopping in the road, and as Ammi quenched the lamp for better seeing they realized that the span of frantic greys had broke their sapling and run off with the democrat-wagon.

The shock served to loosen several tongues, and embarrassed

whispers were exchanged. "It spreads on everything organic that's been around here," muttered the medical examiner. No one replied, but the man who had been in the well gave a hint that his long pole must have stirred up something intangible. "It was awful," he added. "There was no bottom at all. Just ooze and bubbles and the feeling of something lurking under there." Ammi's horse still pawed and screamed deafeningly in the road outside, and nearly drowned its owner's faint quaver as he mumbled his formless reflections. "It come from that stone . . . it growed down thar . . . it got everything livin' . . . it fed itself on 'em, mind and body . . . Thad an' Mernie, Zenas an' Nabby . . . Nahum was the last . . . they all drunk the water . . . it got strong on 'em . . . it come from beyond, whar things ain't like they be here . . . now it's goin' home. . ."

At this point, as the column of unknown colour flared suddenly stronger and began to weave itself into fantastic suggestions of shape which each spectator later described differently, there came from poor tethered Hero such a sound as no man before or since ever heard from a horse. Every person in that low-pitched sitting room stopped his ears, and Ammi turned away from the window in horror and nausea. Words could not convey it—when Ammi looked out again the hapless beast lay huddled inert on the moonlit ground between the splintered shafts of the buggy. That was the last of Hero till they buried him next day. But the present was no time to mourn, for almost at this instant a detective silently called attention to something terrible in the very room with them. In the absence of the lamplight it was clear that a faint phosphorescence had begun to pervade the entire apartment. It glowed on the broad-planked floor and the fragment of rag carpet, and shimmered over the sashes of the small-paned windows. It ran up and down the exposed corner-posts, coruscated about the shelf and mantel, and infected the very doors and furniture. Each minute

THE COLOUR OUT OF SPACE

saw it strengthen, and at last it was very plain that healthy living things must leave that house.

Ammi shewed them the back door and the path up through the fields to the ten-acre pasture. They walked and stumbled as in a dream, and did not dare look back till they were far away on the high ground. They were glad of the path, for they could not have gone the front way, by that well. It was bad enough passing the glowing barn and sheds, and those shining orchard trees with their gnarled, fiendish contours; but thank heaven the branches did their worst twisting high up. The moon went under some very black clouds as they crossed the rustic bridge over Chapman's Brook, and it was blind groping from there to the open meadows.

When they looked back toward the valley and the distant Gardner place at the bottom they saw a fearsome sight. All the farm was shining with the hideous unknown blend of colour; trees, buildings, and even such grass and herbage as had not been wholly changed to lethal grey brittleness. The boughs were all straining skyward, tipped with tongues of foul flame, and lambent tricklings of the same monstrous fire were creeping about the ridgepoles of the house, barn and sheds. It was a scene from a vision of Fuseli, and over all the rest reigned that riot of luminous amorphousness, that alien and undimensioned rainbow of cryptic poison from the well—seething, feeling, lapping, reaching, scintillating, straining, and malignly bubbling in its cosmic and unrecognizable chromaticism.

Then without warning the hideous thing shot vertically up toward the sky like a rocket or meteor, leaving behind no trail and disappearing through a round and curiously regular hole in the clouds before any man could gasp or cry out. No watcher can ever forget that sight, and Ammi stared blankly at the stars of Cygnus, Deneb twinkling above the others, where the unknown colour had melted into the Milky Way. But his gaze was the next moment called swiftly to earth by the crackling in the valley. It was just that. Only a wooden ripping and crackling, and not an explosion, as so many others of the party vowed. Yet the outcome was the same, for in one feverish kaleidoscopic instant there burst up from that doomed and accursed farm a gleamingly eruptive cataclysm of unnatural sparks and substance; blurring the glance of the few who saw it, and sending forth to the zenith a bombarding cloudburst of such coloured and fantastic fragments as our universe must needs disown. Through quickly re-closing vapours they followed the great morbidity that had vanished, and in another second they had vanished too. Behind and below was only a darkness to which the men dared not return, and all about was a mounting wind which seemed to sweep down in black, frore gusts from interstellar space. It shrieked and howled, and lashed the fields and distorted woods in a mad cosmic frenzy, till soon the trembling party realized it would be no use waiting for the moon to shew what was left down there at Nahum's.

Too awed even to hint theories, the seven shaking men trudged back toward Arkham by the north road. Ammi was worse than his fellows, and begged them to see him inside his own kitchen, instead of keeping straight on to town. He did not wish to cross the blighted, wind-whipped woods alone to his home on the main road. For he had had an added shock that the others were spared, and was crushed forever with a brooding fear he dared not even mention for many years to come. As the rest of the watchers on that tempestuous hill had stolidly set their faces toward the road, Ammi had looked back an instant at the shadowed valley of desolation so lately sheltering his ill-starred friend. And from that stricken, far-away spot he had seen something feebly rise, only to sink down again upon the place from which the great shapeless horror had shot into the sky. It was just a colour—but not any colour of our earth or

THE COLOUR OUT OF SPACE

heavens. And because Ammi recognized that colour, and knew that this last faint remnant must still lurk down there in the well, he has never been quite right since.

Ammi would never go near the place again. It is forty-four years now since the horror happened, but he has never been there, and will be glad when the new reservoir blots it out. I shall be glad, too, for I do not like the way the sunlight changed colour around the mouth of that abandoned well I passed. I hope the water will always be very deep—but even so, I shall never drink it. I do not think I shall visit the Arkham country hereafter. Three of the men who had been with Ammi returned the next morning to see the ruins by daylight, but there were not any real ruins. Only the bricks of the chimney, the stones of the cellar, some mineral and metallic litter here and there, and the rim of that nefandous well. Save for Ammi's dead horse, which they towed away and buried, and the buggy which they shortly returned to him, everything that had ever been living had gone. Five eldritch acres of dusty grey desert remained, nor has anything ever grown there since. To this day it sprawls open to the sky like a great spot eaten by acid in the woods and fields, and the few who have ever dared glimpse it in spite of the rural tales have named it "the blasted heath."

The rural tales are queer. They might be even queerer if city men and college chemists could be interested enough to analyze the water from that disused well, or the grey dust that no wind seems ever to disperse. Botanists, too, ought to study the stunted flora on the borders of that spot, for they might shed light on the country notion that the blight is spreading—little by little, perhaps an inch a year. People say the colour of the neighboring herbage is not quite right in the spring, and that wild things leave queer prints in the light winter snow. Snow never seems quite so heavy on the blasted heath as it is elsewhere. Horses—the few that are left in this motor age—

grow skittish in the silent valley; and hunters cannot depend on their dogs too near the splotch of greyish dust.

They say the mental influences are very bad, too; numbers went queer in the years after Nahum's taking, and always they lacked the power to get away. Then the stronger-minded folk all left the region, and only the foreigners tried to live in the crumbling old homesteads. They could not stay, though; and one sometimes wonders what insight beyond ours their wild, weird stories of whispered magic have given them. Their dreams at night, they protest, are very horrible in that grotesque country; and surely the very look of the dark realm is enough to stir a morbid fancy. No traveler has ever escaped a sense of strangeness in those deep ravines, and artists shiver as they paint thick woods whose mystery is as much of the spirit as of the eye. I myself am curious about the sensation I derived from my one lone walk before Ammi told me his tale. When twilight came I had vaguely wished some clouds would gather, for an odd timidity about the deep skyey voids above had crept into my soul.

Do not ask me for my opinion. I do not know—that is all. There was no one but Ammi to question; for Arkham people will not talk about the strange days, and all three professors who saw the aërolite and its coloured globule are dead. There were other globules—depend upon that. One must have fed itself and escaped, and probably there was another which was too late. No doubt it is still down the well—I know there was something wrong with the sunlight I saw above that miasmal brink. The rustics say the blight creeps an inch a year, so perhaps there is a kind of growth or nourishment even now. But whatever demon hatchling is there, it must be tethered to something or else it would quickly spread. Is it fastened to the roots of those trees that claw the air? One of the current Arkham tales is about fat oaks that shine and move as they ought not to do at night.

What it is, only God knows. In terms of matter I suppose the

THE COLOUR OUT OF SPACE

thing Ammi described would be called a gas, but this gas obeyed laws that are not of our cosmos. This was no fruit of such worlds and suns as shine on the telescopes and photographic plates of our observatories. This was no breath from the skies whose motions and dimensions our astronomers measure or deem too vast to measure. It was just a colour out of space—a frightful messenger from unformed realms of infinity beyond all Nature as we know it; from realms whose mere existence stuns the brain and numbs us with the black extra-cosmic gulfs it throws open before our frenzied eyes.

I doubt very much if Ammi consciously lied to me, and I do not think his tale was all a freak of madness as the townfolk had forewarned. Something terrible came to the hills and valleys on that meteor, and something terrible—though I know not in what proportion—still remains. I shall be glad to see the water come. Meanwhile I hope nothing will happen to Ammi. He saw so much of the thing—and its influence was so insidious. Why has he never been able to move away? How clearly he recalled those dying words of Nahum's—"Can't git away . . . draws ye . . . ye know summ'at's comin' but tain't no use. . . ." Ammi is such a good old man—when the reservoir gang gets to work I must write the chief engineer to keep a sharp watch on him. I would hate to think of him as the grey, twisted, brittle monstrosity which persists more and more in troubling my sleep.

The WORLD'S FIRST Science Fiction Magazine

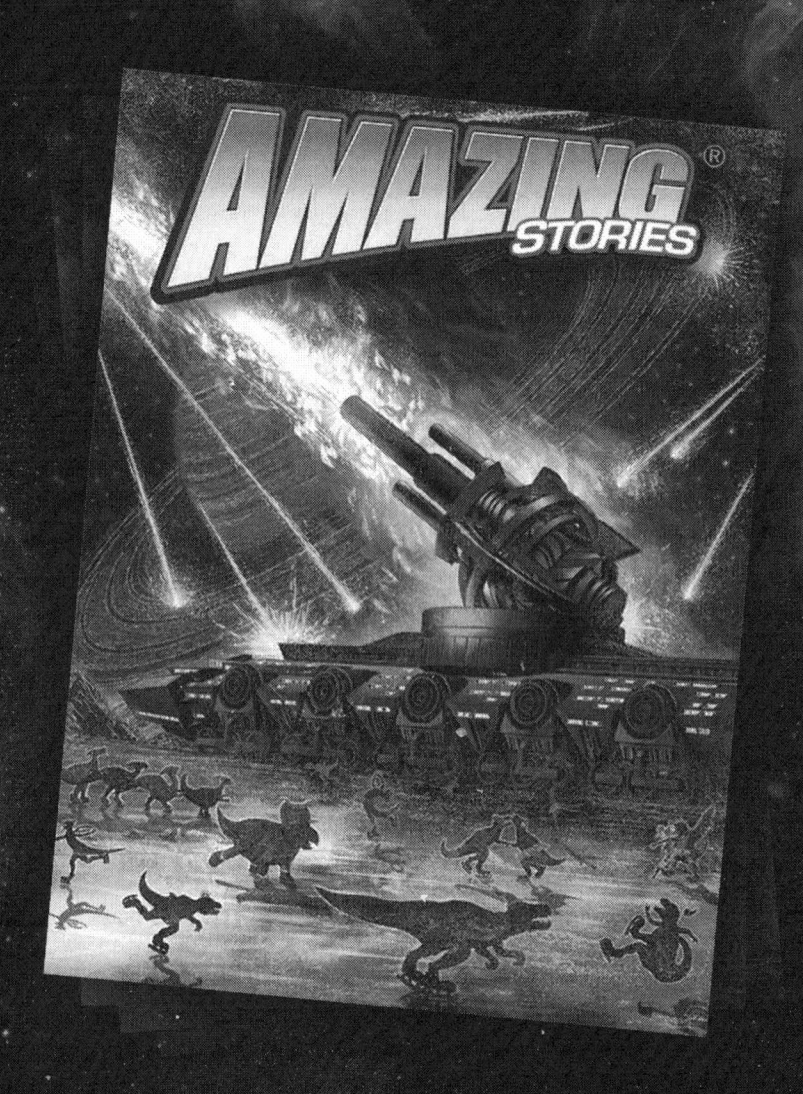

Now Available Free Online in an All-New Format!

Visit AMAZING STORIES at
amazingstoriesmag.com